No Shoes & Kitten Heels

A novel by
Sonja J Lawrence

ONE
SEMMY

Semmy Kyembo was 15 years old. She lived in a remote village of Eastern Uganda five miles from the town of Masindi. Semmy's mother had died six months earlier. Her father said the mosquitos killed her. They infected her with a parasite that stopped the blood getting to her brain. They buried her wrapped in bark cloth in the ground of their ancestors. Semmy felt like she wanted to be sucked into that black airless grave with her.

Semmy was left at home with her grief-stricken father Albert. As well as her oldest and more defiant sister, Lydia, who is seventeen.

On the day Semmy had buried her mother her father had handed her a blank notebook.

"You can write in this when you miss your mother. I know the way you'd talk." He said not looking at her. "You will need to start figuring things out for yourself now."

It provided little comfort for the chasm left by her mother's death. Semmy knew better than to complain. She took the notebook and placed it in her sleeping hut. It was the most her father could offer. He could never replace her mother and she respected the fact he'd never try to. It was hard though and Semmy missed her mother every day.

Her sister Lydia was like their father, she didn't talk much and was a closed book of emotions. Since their mother's death Lydia spent less time at home. Whenever

Semmy asked her where she went, she'd shrug her shoulders and tell her not to worry about it.

One Wednesday morning in early February Albert woke Semmy earlier than usual. She'd dressed into her school uniform being careful not to wake her sister who slept next to her. Her father told her she was to walk into the local town of Masindi to buy medicine for Lydia.

"Go and see Dr Aceng, he is expecting you." Albert said handing her 20,000 Uganda shillings note. "It's the only money we have so don't lose it." Semmy placed the money into the pocket of her cotton school dress.

"Is Lydia sick?" Semmy asked.

"She's with child." Albert spat the words at her angrily. "She told your aunt Grace she has missed her period for more than two months, that's all I know. Now, go and say nothing to anyone."

Semmy walked into town with fear and confusion suffocating every thought. She didn't trust Dr Aceng, he wasn't a real doctor. He sold his medicines without a prescription. They'd bought medicine from him when her mother had malaria. Semmy always wondered if they'd gone to the hospital and not to Dr Aceng would her mother still be alive?

It took several hours for Semmy to reach town on foot. At Dr Aceng's office she'd had to wait for him to arrive. She checked and double checked her pocket for the money. Semmy's family was poor, no mosquito net and no shoes poor. She couldn't afford to lose this money.

Dr Aceng arrived apologizing for his delay owing to an emergency. He was expecting her and took her money handing her a small bottle of medicine from his cabinet.

"Tell your sister it is normal to feel sick. She may experience very heavy bleeding with stomach cramps. The symptoms should pass in a day or two, but she must rest."

Semmy hurried back towards her homestead. Lost in thoughts about Lydia she'd wandered into the middle of the dirt track road. A helmetless rider was driving too fast and couldn't swerve to miss her in time. The motorbike hit her throwing her into the side of the road. Semmy blacked out. When she opened her eyes, she saw an old white man with blue eyes and a shiny bald head staring down at her.

"Can you hear me?" He said. "My name's Richard Greene. A motorbike knocked you unconscious. Are you okay?"

Semmy tried to sit up but the pain in her leg stung like she'd been stabbed.

"What's your name?"

"Semmy Kyembo." She said lifting her hand to her face where the trickle of blood was running down her cheek.

"Don't touch your face." Richard told her. "You have a deep cut on your eyebrow, and if you touch it, it may get infected. I'll take you to the hospital and they can fix you up."

"No, no hospital," Semmy said worried about how angry her father would be if she went home with a hospital bill that he couldn't pay.

Although fifteen years old, Semmy looked like she was twelve. Youthful genes, a calorie starved diet and a late launch into puberty kept her childlike. As she lay on the side of the road a crowd was beginning to form and with it the muffled sounds of chatter

"Do you know this Mzungu?" A woman asked Semmy while pointing to the old white man. The woman spoke in

Lugandan, a local dialect.

Semmy shook her head.

"He must have been the one to run her over." Another woman announced. "They always drive too fast, especially when there are children on the road."

More women crowded around Semmy pushing Richard away.

"I'll get my first aid kit." He said returning to his white jeep that was the only vehicle within sight. He returned with a large first aid kit packed with every kind of medical supply you could need. The crowd parted for him to begin attending to Semmy's wounds. He first took out an antiseptic wipe from a sealed packet. Then, he began cleaning the blood from Semmy's head as she flinched in pain. Next, he produced a sparkling white cotton bandage. He wrapped it around a thick piece of cotton wadding. It stopped the bleeding. He then bandaged up the cuts on her legs.

"Now at least let me call someone to come and fetch you?"

Semmy's father had no phone and no bike or car. She remembered Lydia's medicine that she must have dropped at the time of the accident. She began sifting through the rubbish that surrounded her at the edge of the road. There were old newspapers and discarded plastic water bottles. Women in the crowd began searching with her. A young woman with a baby strapped to her back announced she'd found it.

Semmy was so relieved she smiled.

"I'll take you home." Richard said helping her to stand. He carried her over to his jeep. The crowd dispersed back to their original plans. In the coolness and comfort of the jeep relief flooded over Semmy. She'd never travelled in a vehicle like this before, sitting up so high to watch the world race by.

At first, she didn't speak as she wasn't sure what an old white man would want to talk about. Then she asked.

"Are you here on holiday?"

"My wife and I own a house in Masindi, and we spend our time between here and the UK."

"Do you like it here?"

"Very much. Uganda is a beautiful country with beautiful people." He said smiling. "I expect your mother will be getting worried about you."

"My mother is not with us; it is only my sister and father now." Semmy said.

"And is someone else sick now, is that why you have the medicine?"

"The medicine is for my sister, she's with child."

"Why does she need medicine?"

Semmy shrugged her shoulders.

"Did your sister see a doctor?"

"My father arranged for her to have the medicine. I don't know why."

Richard nodded and they sat in silence until they reached the track that led to Semmy's village. She explained there was no road, and the path was only wide enough for motorbikes and push bikes. Richard parked the jeep and then carried her through the bush towards her homestead.

People from the village watched as they passed. The only white people that came to their village were from a Christian charity. They would visit to get children to go to school.

They reached Semmy's homestead. Lydia was sitting outside with her long legs stretched out in front of her. Taller and more striking looking than Semmy, she stood up showing no signs of her pregnancy. Her slim frame and face glowing with youth revealed nothing but vitality and health. When Lydia saw Semmy with Richard her face dropped.

"What happened to you and what's he doing here?" She said taking her sister from Richard's arms and looking at him with suspicion and anger.

"He helped me when a motorbike knocked me over as I was leaving Masindi. His name's Richard. He stopped to check that I was okay and brought me home."

Semmy's father walked from his hut. He wore a red and black checkered cotton shirt with black suit trousers that had holes in both knees.

"I'm Richard Greene." Richard extended his hand to Albert who did not take it. "Your daughter was in an accident. She can't walk on her leg and insisted I brought her home and not to a hospital."

Richard's eyes surveyed the homestead as he spoke. Three mud and wattle huts, two for sleeping and one for cooking. A small sitting area outside where there remained the ashes of an open fire and three large stones as seats. The only other building was a small stick made chicken coup. It held two scrawny and ill fed birds.

"Do you have the medicine I sent you to get?" Albert said.

"Yes," Semmy said.

"Why does your daughter need medicine if she is pregnant?" Richard asked. "She looks a picture of health to me?"

"What business is it of yours?"

"I've heard terrible stories. Pregnant women take these

medicines to make them sick. This sickness will cause them to abort their child. It can kill the mother too. There are other, safer ways to deal with unwanted pregnancies."

Lydia looked anxious.

"You could make her very sick."

"We'll manage." Albert looked angry.

"You won't." Richard said. "What about Semmy? She needs to see a doctor and get her head and leg properly dressed."

"I said we'll manage."

Semmy held out the medicine to give to her father. Before he could take it, Richard grabbed the bottle. He opened it and poured the liquid onto the dry red earth floor.

Albert began shouting at Richard calling him an ignorant, foolish white man.

"You should go before my father gets violent." Semmy told Richard.

"I'm not leaving you."

Albert kept shouting. He wanted the whole village to know about this stupid Mzungu had come to his house and destroyed his medicine.

"You must go. When my father drinks he does not know what he is doing. It isn't safe for you."

"Does your father drink every day?"

Semmy nodded.

"Is he violent when he drinks?"

"Sometimes."

Richard walked into the kitchen hut and reappeared holding a small bag of wheat flour.

"Is this all you have to eat?"

Semmy nodded.

"I cannot leave you and your sister here. You must come and stay with my wife and I until you are better. We can arrange for a doctor to come to the house and when you can walk again, I'll bring you home."

Semmy looked at Lydia who shook her head so slightly that it was barely visible. She looked at her father. He had changed so much. When they were little, he was one of the strongest men in the village. Other families would ask him for help to brand cattle and fell trees. But not anymore. The loss of his wife and the drink had made him angry and weak.

"Father, do you hear what Richard's saying? He can take me to a doctor. He says we can stay with him for a while, until I'm better."

"Then go," Albert shouted. "Lydia will bring only shame on us. What can I do, I've no money left." He walked back into his bedroom hut.

Lydia looked at Semmy pleading her with her eyes not to leave.

"We'll go with him only until I'm better." Semmy said.

"You know nothing of this white man and what he wants from us?"

"I know I can't stay and watch as father gets drunk and hits you again."

TWO
ANNA

I booked my thirtieth birthday off from work. I hated being thirty. It felt like a milestone I had reached without achieving very much. My high achieving and older sister Helen insisted we go out. She was treating me to lunch at the Ivy bistro in town.

Mark, my boyfriend of 10 years, had forgotten my birthday. I wasn't surprised. I've known for a while that there's something wrong between us. It's the kind of wrong, where you can no longer tell yourself everything will be alright.

Mark left for work early and I pretended to be asleep. I wasn't going to remind him it was my birthday. Petty, I know. Lunch with Helen was surprisingly pleasant. We ate duck salad followed by steak and chocolate bombes. I came home and spent the afternoon lying on the sofa watching Netflix.

Mark returned from work at five, he didn't notice I was never home from work this early. He went upstairs and I heard him having a shower. I started cooking dinner despite the fact I wasn't hungry. I put sausages in the oven and boiled potatoes for mash. He appeared clean shaven and smelling of aftershave. His short brown hair was sculptured with wax.

"Are we going out?" I asked. I thought for a second that he'd just pretended to forget my birthday.

"I'm having a few drinks with the lads, you don't mind, do you?" He said like I shouldn't.

"Of course not." I said my smile vanishing as I slapped down two piles of mashed potato on a plate.

"Can you make the gravy?" I said pushing the gravy granules towards him which he poured into a Bart Simpson mug.

"Can you not make it too thick?" I said.

"You say that every time."

"I hate it when it's like custard."

"I know." He snapped back.

He poured his custard thick gravy over his dinner. Then, he mumbled about a football game before disappearing into the living room. I ate at the kitchen table scrolling through Right Move. My escapism was searching for a dream home we'd never afford.

Thirty minutes later he was back in the kitchen dumping his empty plate in the sink and wiping gravy from his chin.

"I'll see you later." He said before leaving and slamming the front door behind him.

I looked at the sink of dirty dishes. It was too depressing to spend my birthday at home alone and washing up. I grabbed my keys and denim jacket and decided to follow Mark. What could he be doing that was so important it couldn't include me?

Out in the street I could see Mark's black jeep. I got into my old red fiat and as soon as he pulled out, I drove after him. It was a cold Wednesday night in late February. The roads were quiet. I turned on the radio to hear violin music reminiscent of movie death scenes. I changed channels as Abba serenaded me with the lyrics 'Waterloo, couldn't escape if I wanted to'. I turned the radio off.

Mark drove out of town towards the local industrial estate. We passed the ten screen Odeon cinema, Frankie and Bennies and the bowling alley. He pulled up and parked.

After checking his hair in his rear-view mirror, he went into a building I'd never noticed before. It had white stone brickwork and a black sign over the glass doors which read 'Genting Casino'.

I waited a few minutes before following him. Inside the glass front doors was a brightly lit reception area. A girl in her early twenties sat behind a shiny gold desk on her phone. Her eyes peered up at me under excessively long fake eye lashes. I had the sense that my no make-up, denim jacket, black joggers and Ugg boots were not meeting the dress code.

"Hi. It's my birthday and my boyfriend has forgotten and so I…"

"Down the stairs and turn left." She said cutting me off and turning her attention to her mobile phone.

"Thank you." I headed down the stairs past large prints of iconic Hollywood movie stars. Marilyn Monroe was kissing two red dice with her lips painted pillar box red. Jack Nicholson was tossing a stack of poker chips and grinning. Steve McQueen looked smolderingly cool watching a roulette wheel spin.

The casino itself, was as far from Hollywood chic as it was possible to get. It was a wide-open space with a bar in the middle a handful of card tables at one end and two rows of slot machines at the other. Mark was sitting at a far end table with a stack of poker chips in front of him. There was no sign of his mates.

It seemed a strange place to come on your own on a Wednesday night. He occasionally played poker online, but I'd never known him to play at a casino. I couldn't understand why he'd not told me this is where he was coming.

Two other men sat at his table. I didn't recognize either of them. A slim black guy who looked to be around Marks age who was wearing a black cap that obscured his eyes. The other man was older, early sixties at a guess. He wore a shirt and tie as though he'd come straight from the office.

I decided to get a drink and watch Mark for a while. It was possible he was meeting another woman, yet it seemed a strange place to come for an affair. I ordered a small glass of white wine and made a concerted effort not to fidget. I'm not comfortable sitting on my own at a bar. It's not that I'm hot and men hit on me. I'm slim but not curvy, I don't wear makeup or style my shoulder length brown hair. In fact, I'm very forgettable and average. I attribute my aversion to sitting at a bar alone to all the TV shows and movies of my youth. The only women who sat at bars alone were usually drunks or hookers.

I watched Mark as he won and lost a handful of chips. An hour dragged past; I was about to go and confront him when he pushed all his chips into the middle of the table. I had no idea how much they were worth. The black cap guy pushed his chips in, and the dealer flipped the last two cards.

I knew he'd lost. His face was a picture of anger and disappointment. He got up and walked away from the poker table. He was about to pass me when he glanced up and caught my eye. It wasn't a good surprise.

"What the fuck are you doing here Anna?" He said as if I was now responsible for him losing.

"I followed you."

"You did what?"

"I followed you. You'd forgotten it's my birthday and so I thought I'd surprise you."

"Well, you did that." He said grabbing my arm and steering me across the room and up the stairs, past Marilyn, and Jack.

"How much did you lose?" I asked as I was dragged past the fake eyelash receptionist and into the cold.

"You shouldn't have come." Mark said.

"Why, so I'd never find out that a night out with the lads is you coming to a casino and losing a shit load of money. So how much did tonight cost us?"

"Leave it Anna."

"Was it £50, £100?"

"Look, I'm sorry I forgot your birthday. I'll make it up to you. Now I'm asking you to please go home."

"Tell me what you lost?"

"I don't need to tell you anything Anna, please just fuck off and go home." He shouted, his tone nasty.

I walked away from him, got back into my car, and drove home. A sick gnawing feeling was swirling around in the pit of my stomach. I opened the front door and was greeted with the smell of congealed sausages and gravy. After pouring myself a large glass of wine I reached for my laptop. I needed to check that Mark hadn't completely fucked up and done the one thing I could never forgive him for.

I logged onto our current account and scrolled through to our savings account. I'd saved nearly £10,000 for a house deposit. I never ate out; I never bought new clothes and we'd not had a holiday in three years. The balance on our account was 50 pounds. He'd lost everything.

THREE
SEMMY

Semmy persuaded Lydia to go to Richard's house until she'd recovered from the accident. She'd told her sister she was going with or without her. Lydia was not able to let her sister stay in a strange man's house alone.

They arrived at Richard's house and were greeted with tall metal black gates that opened onto a long gravel driveway. An oversized red tile roof sat on top of the quaintest brick house. It wasn't large, but it looked like a palace compared to the huts in their village.

Richard pulled up in front of the house. His wife Rose and their housekeeper Edna were stood waiting. Rose was a short, slim woman, with light brown skin. She looked as old as the grandmothers in Semmy's village and wore pink from head to toe. She reminded Semmy of a graceful flamingo. Her long dark hair sat in a bun on top of her head. She had the warmest smile.

Edna was Ugandan and was in her early thirties. She wore a traditional style dress of a green patterned fabric with a matching head scarf. Edna had the round, cuddly figure of a woman that is a good cook and enjoys her own food.

Rose approached the jeep and opened the door on Semmy's side.

"I'm Rose; Richard's wife." She smiled with lips painted the same pink as her clothes.

"Are you in pain?" She asked Semmy.

"A little."

"We need to carry Semmy into the house." Richard said

getting out of the jeep. Lydia insisted she'd carry her siter and Richard did not fight her.

"This is Edna our housekeeper." Rose said. "She'll take good care of you both, feed you and ensure you are big and strong in no time."

The entrance of the house led into long hallway with a dark shiny wood floor. A small table covered with sandstone carved safari animals stood by a tall, wooden, coat stand. Framed family photos covered the walls.

"The house used to belong to my mother and father." Rose said. "My father built it in 1964 after he moved here from India. He owned a sugar cane business in Masindi, and this is the house where my sister and I grew up."

As Lydia carried Semmy down the hall Rose pointed to one of the photographs of her parents. An Indian man in a suit next to a short, white woman wearing a cotton tea dress.

At the end of the hall was the kitchen. It was bright and airy. It had cream-coloured cupboards, a wooden worktop, and a large wooden table. Semmy marvelled at all the modern appliances. A tall fridge, a ceramic sink and even a washing machine.

Lydia and Semmy sat down at the table with Rose while Richard went to call the doctor. Edna brought over a large bowl of warm soapy water so they could wash their hands. Followed by a plate of fresh pineapple and two glasses of homemade lemonade.

"You don't need to look so frightened." Edna whispered. "You'll be safe here; Rose is a good woman. I have worked for her my whole life, and she will take care of you."

Semmy and Lydia drank their lemonade and listened to

Richard speaking on the phone. He explained to the doctor about the accident and that he and Rose were taking care of the girls. Rose went into the hall and Semmy listened as Richard explained.

"I had to bring them back here, you can see that can't you?"

"Of course, my darling."

"Those girls need our help. You should have seen how they are living. They sleep in mud huts, with no beds, no food or water. They are skin and bones. As I told you on the phone their mother has passed and their father's a violent drunk. I couldn't live with myself if I'd driven away and left them."

"It's okay." Rose said. "You did the right thing."

"I realise we were supposed to have this time to be together."

"I love the fact that you care enough to bring them here. We have the rest of our lives to enjoy each other's company."

Rose and Richard came back into the kitchen and Richard took out his mobile phone and took a photo of the girls.

"What are you doing?" Rose asked.

"I'm taking a picture."

"I can see that. I'm not sure now's a good time for photos."

"You don't mind, do you?" He asked.

Semmy shook her head to be polite. Lydia said nothing.

The doctor arrived. A middle-aged man with a serious expression wearing a brown suit and tie. After examining Semmy he redressed her bandages. Telling her to take paracetamol for any headaches and get plenty of rest. When he'd gone Rose and Edna took the girls upstairs.

"This is where you'll sleep." Rose said. "It's the room where my sister and I slept when we were young." It was a honey-coloured bedroom with two single beds covered with mosquito nets. There were shutters on the window. Although closed, there was still a warm glow where daylight seeped in.

"Richard and I sleep in the room next door and the other room is the bathroom. I'll bring you clean towels and a couple of clean nightdresses for tonight. In the morning, I will drive to the market in town and pick you up anything else you will need."

"Thank you." Semmy said. Edna and Rose left the room and Semmy turned to her sister.

"Are you okay being here? How lovely is this house and have you ever slept on a bed as comfortable with sheets that smell so nice."

"No and I don't want to be here." Lydia said. "You mustn't get used to living here. We are very different from these people and no good will come of us leaving father to be with them. You may think this is a better life but there is no such thing. As soon as you are well enough, we are leaving."

Semmy nodded her head, but she couldn't see why Lydia was so against them staying there.

FOUR
ANNA

"I always knew he'd let you down." My sister Helen said when I told her about Mark gambling away our savings. I hated the fact my sister had to be right about everything.

Mark and I met when I was 20. I was in my second year at Reading university. I'd organised a pub quiz in the student union. Raising money so Bangladeshi women could start basket weaving businesses.

Mark was stood at the bar dressed in a tight-fitting pink polo shirt. He was not my type, but he was good looking.

"What do you get if you win the quiz?" He asked when I'd gone to the bar to get myself a drink.

"A bottle of wine."

"Per person?"

"Per team."

"How many in a team?"

"Six".

"It's going to be a wild night out." He said laughing.

"It's for charity."

"Even so."

A teasing smile flickered across his face.

"Could you stretch to two bottles of wine and make it worth our while."

I shook my head.

"What's your name?"

"Anna."

"Well Anna." He said. "As fun as a pub quiz looks, and,

it does look fun, I'd rather just give you the money."

"How much does it cost to -" He looked at the poster I'd stuck on the wall. It showed three smiling, toothless Bangladeshi women with bright headscarves and leather skin.

"A basket weaving business." I said.

"£125 to support five women to set up their own business." I said.

Mark pulled out a wad of notes from his pocket peeled off £150 and handing it to me.

I started the quiz and could see him watching me. When it finished, he came over to me.

"What happens now the intellectual bit is over?"

"Some of us are going to a house party."

"I don't get to go to many student house parties. If I get a few beers, can I join you."

"Are you a student here?"

"No, I came to visit a mate, but he bailed early. It's okay, I'm not some weirdo that hangs around at random pub quizzes trying to pick up the question master."

I laughed.

We walked to the party and my friends trailed behind us. It was like we were on a date.

"What do you do for a job?" I asked.

"I work for my dad; he's got his own building firm. It's not what I want to do, I'd like to join the police."

"Really?" He didn't strike me as police material.

"What about you."

"I'm doing a degree in International Development."

"What the fuck is International Development?"

"It's the study of the culture and politics of developing countries."

"Why would you study that?" He looked confused.

"Because you can try and improve people's lives."

"Hence the basket weavers." He said. "So, d'you have a boyfriend?"

"Yes, his name's Noel."

"So, where's Noel this evening?"

"Studying."

"He didn't even come out to support your pub quiz, he sounds like a jerk."

"He's studying law which is pretty intense."

"He sounds fun."

Mark was overconfident and arrogant, and at 20 this was attractive to me.

We arrived at the party and students had spilled out onto the pavement as trance music blared down the street. The narrow hallway was full of people and the living room was a fog of smoke.

We found space in the kitchen and after drinking Mark's beers he managed to locate a half bottle of tequila.

Drunk and feeling reckless I danced with Mark and let him flirt with me. A slim guy with short bleached blonde hair offered me a joint. I took two drags and my head started spinning. I pushed my way into the garden where some bloke with wandering hands pretended to help me. I was about to pass out and then Mark grabbed me. He bulldozed everyone out of the way. He sat me down and ordered people to get me water and find my friends.

The next day he called to see how I was feeling. A week later he arrived at my student house and invited me to Paris.

"You're not serious? Are you expecting me to go to Paris with you?"

"Why not?" He had not the tiniest flicker of self-doubt.

"I don't know you."

"You'll get to know me in Paris."

I broke up with Noel soon after Paris and Mark and I started dating. When my degree finished, I moved in with Mark. He stopped working for his dad and trained to join the police. I put my plans of working for an overseas charity on hold. They'd been on hold ever since. I was beginning to think now could be the time to change that.

FIVE
SEMMY

Four weeks after the accident Semmy's wounds had healed. During this time the girls had not had any contact their father. Richard reassured them that Albert would be okay. He'd understand they were being looked after. They should view their extended stay as a holiday.

Semmy was enjoying the comforts of their new home. A large screen TV, new clothes, warm baths, Edna's delicious cooking and sleeping in a bed. Richard had hinted to her that if they stayed, they could enroll her at the local school. She could pass her exams, go to university, and even get a job. She could have a future that was greater than marrying for a dowry and having children before she was 20.

Lydia was not like Semmy. She didn't daydream about her future, and she was far more cynical about life. Her mind remained fixed on leaving.

"We don't need an old white couple's help. I've heard stories of do-gooders coming to villages like ours and promising a better life. It's all a lie. The sooner we return home, the better."

One day after lunch they were sat out on the veranda. The temperature was above 30 degrees. Even sat in the shade, Richard had to wipe beads of sweat from his forehead.

"We wanted to talk to you about what you want to do now." Rose said, her voice gentle and kind.

"It's time we went home to our father. He will worry about us. You've been good to let us stay but Semmy is better." Lydia said looking across the table at her sister encouraging her to speak.

"We don't wish to outstay our welcome." Semmy said although she didn't sound convincing.

Richard smiled picking up his wine.

"No one is outstaying anything. You're welcome to stay with us as long as you wish, we love having you here."

Rose looked across the table at Lydia. Her pregnancy had started to show. Rose had never had children. She had tried with both of previous husbands, but it wasn't to be. When her sister died of cancer, Rose had adopted her 16-year-old nephew Kip. He had become like a son.

"D'you think your father will be okay about your pregnancy if you return home?" Rose asked.

"He takes time to get used to things that's all."

"Why not stay until you've had the baby." Richard said and Rose looked surprised at his suggestion.

"It would enable your baby to have the best start in life." He continued. "You'd have a good diet and access to the best healthcare. Semmy could complete primary school. We could even pay for a tutor, to give her the best chance of passing her exams."

"You don't have to decide now." Rose said smiling.

"I don't see why it's a difficult decision." Richard said. "We have the room, and we can afford for the girls to stay."

"When you told Albert you'd bring his daughters here, he imagined it would be a temporary thing. I don't expect he thought they were leaving home."

"They're not leaving home. It would be a few more months."

"We want to leave." Lydia said.

Richard grinned. "What if I go and speak to your father this afternoon. I can find out if his thoughts about you having a baby are different."

"I'm coming with you." Lydia stared defiantly at Richard. He wiped his forehead with his handkerchief.

"That wouldn't be a good idea. Your father struck me as a very proud man. This will need to be approached in a calm and logical way without pride or unnecessary emotion."

"We know our father." Lydia said her voice raised.

"Why don't you let Richard go and talk to him." Semmy pleaded. "If we can stay for a few more months, it could be the best thing for both of us."

Lydia shot her sister a look to be quiet. Richard got up from the table and left before she had a chance to say another word. Rose looked uncomfortable. She helped Edna clear the table and Semmy overheard her talking in the kitchen.

"I married Richard because he was kind and impulsive. Trying to find a man over 65 that isn't stuck in their ways is like trying to find good wine in the local supermarket. But, taking on the responsibility of two teenage girls, and one pregnant. It's too much, don't you think?"

"I wouldn't worry." Edna said. "Albert will have told him to bring his daughters home and that will be the end of it."

Semmy went and sat under the fan in the living room whilst she waited for Richard to come back. Lydia had gone up to their room. He was smiling when he returned.

"Your father is fine." He looked at Semmy. "We had a long talk, and he agrees it's in everyone's interests for you to stay. A baby out of wedlock will be difficult. You will stay with us until Lydia has had the baby."

Rose glanced over at Edna but said nothing.

SIX
ANNA

When I broke up with Mark, his response was that I was overreacting. I didn't argue. I packed as much stuff as I could fit into my car and left. I moved out of our small, rented house in the cheaper part of Tunbridge Wells, to move into my sister's spare room.

My sister Helen lives in the expensive part of Royal Tunbridge Wells. The part near the Pantiles, a Georgian colonnade. A place where, in days gone by, the gentry could enjoy the revitalizing waters of a natural spring. I have to say, I don't feel more gentrified since moving in with my sister.

Tunbridge Wells is not a great place to live when you're broke. The DFL's (Down from Londoners) have relocated to Tunbridge Wells from the leafy suburbs of Greenwich and Dulwich. They live mortgage free whilst tutoring their kids into grammar schools. They've increased liberal thinking to a town which was previously unbearable Conservative. Yet, the Tories still get voted in.

Moving in with Helen was an act of desperation. We're close but different. I inherited dad's laid-back approach to life. Helen got Mums uptight gene which means everything she does is intense.

At 33 Helen has her own estate agent business. Our surname is Sellers. As Helen loves to remind everyone, 'she was born to sell.' She's married to a solicitor named Tim. They have two boys, my adorable nephews, Ben, who is four, and Lewis, who is six. They're the epitome of an upwardly mobile family.

"I'm worried about you." Helen told me the first morning I was living there. Her voice a mix of concern and judgement. "You need a purpose in your life. Your thirty, single and homeless."

The morning pep talk continued whilst she stacked the dishwasher. Every chore she undertakes a fraction quicker than is necessary, it's unnerving. I've offered to help but I know I don't meet her exacting standards.

"I'm going to look for a new job."

"Really. That's fantastic news. God only knows why you've spent so long at that software place with that dreadful boss Ferguson."

My boss Ferguson was lazy with rancid breath that he tries, and fails, to cover up with polo mints. I'd been his office manager, financial assistant, and dog's body for years. He tried and often failed to fix people's computer's and sells them software they don't need. Helen threw a dishwasher tablet it into the door of the machine and turned it on.

"What kind of job are you looking for?"

"I'm going to look for work at an international development charity and try and use my degree for once. I doubt if I'll even get an interview, but I thought I'd try."

"They'd be lucky to have you."

"Really? I'm over thirty with no relevant experience. I'll be competing with 21-year-olds that have spent a year volunteering in an orphanage in Timbuktu, have one million followers on their social media accounts and produce YouTube videos for fun."

Helen looked at her watch.

"Remember positive things happen to positive people."

I couldn't believe she just said that. I put on my best fake smile.

"I'll swing past the job centre today and see if there's anything in there." Helen said hurrying out of the door.

SEVEN
SEMMY

Semmy had gone up to their room to tell Lydia the news, that they were to stay at the Masindi house until after she'd had the baby.

"Are we prisoners?" Lydia said annoyed.

"Of course not." Semmy laughed to try and lighten the mood. "Father thought it would be better with you being unmarried and pregnant."

"What's going to happen when I have a baby, how will he explain that. Or does father not intend for me to ever return home?"

"I don't know."

"This is your fault Semmy. Yours and that ridiculous white man. I knew he'd manipulate things, so we had to stay."

"He only wants to help."

"Don't be so stupid and naïve." Lydia screamed. "Why would he want to help two girls he'd never met before? Think about it."

Semmy had never seen Lydia so angry and the more she pressed her on why they shouldn't stay the angrier Lydia got. She never did explain it. Semmy had confided in Edna and asked her what she thought her sister had meant.

"I wouldn't worry." Edna had told her. "Lydia is going through a huge change both mentally and physically. She'll settle down and relax you need to give her time."

Lydia sulked for the rest of the week. Semmy began to

worry that her bad mood would make them unwelcome. Rose then announced.

"Richard and I need to return to the UK."

"Why?" Semmy asked.

"We only planned to be in Uganda for a holiday. Our home is in the UK, and we need to go back for a while. Don't worry, you'll be well looked after when we're not here. You'll have Edna to take care of you and we are employing a friend of Richard, a lady called Margaret Brown."

"Have we done something wrong?" Semmy asked.

Rose smiled.

"Of course not. Meeting you girls has been great for us and has given us a new outlook. If we are to take care of you, we must do this properly. When we are in the UK we can register as a charity which would mean that there is a legal framework we'd follow. We wouldn't just be two old people taking you in."

A week later Rose and Richard flew back to the UK and Margaret Brown moved in.

The only similarities between Margaret and Rose were their age, gender and race. Everything else was different. Margaret was taller, had broader shoulders and was stern looking. She never wore make up and her clothes were functional and bland. The day she arrived at the house she shook Semmy and Lydia's hands.

"My name is Margaret Brown." Her voice was deep and loud. "I am very pleased to meet you both and to have the opportunity to get to know you."

She sounded well educated with each word clear and precise. When she smiled, she reminded Semmy of the local MP that would visit their village looking for votes. There was none of the warmth or kindness of Rose.

"I'd like to move some of my personal things into my room." Margaret said. "Please come and have tea on the veranda with me in thirty minutes so we can get to know one another."

"Yes, thank you." Semmy said feeling like she was at school. Lydia said nothing.

"Bring me up some water please Edna." Margaret said before disappearing up the stairs.

Semmy watched her leave. She'd only been in the house for minutes and already the atmosphere was changing.

EIGHT
ANNA

I applied for a job that was being advertised for a charity based in Tunbridge Wells called WOMAID. It was supporting vulnerable girls in Uganda. The role was for an office administrator. I sent in a covering letter and my CV and was surprised and delighted when a week later I was invited to attend an interview.

The WOMAID office was close to the town centre. It was in a street of large Victorian houses where half of the buildings had been converted into offices. Allen's Architects was on the top floor, and the Wells dentist surgery was on floor two. There was a handwritten sign for WOMAID on the ground floor. I pushed the buzzer, reapplied my lip gloss and waited. I felt sick. Job interviews, public speaking and going to the hairdresser all made me feel sick.

The door opened and I was greeted by a tall man that was older than my father. His bald head shone like a polished conker in the spring sun.

"Hello, I'm Richard Greene the charities founder."

He reminded me of a scout leader. He wore a khaki waistcoat, a white short sleeved shirt, and beige shorts. His worst fashion crime was white socks. They were pulled up tight beneath brown open toe leather sandals.

"Come through. My wife Rose will be joining us shortly."

The first room we enter would have been the old front room when this was a house. It was now WOMAID's reception area. It reminded me of an African tour company. There was a large bamboo coffee table stacked high with glossy photo books. A chaise longue covered in a bright orange fabric and in the corner of the room a six-foot wooden giraffe.

"We call him Jessie." Richard said catching my eye.

I smile.

"Can I get you a drink? Tea, coffee?"

"A water please."

We go through to a small kitchenette.

"It's all very new we only moved in a week ago." Richard's towering figure hovered over me with an awkwardness magnified by his size.

I followed him down a narrow hall and into the main office. It smelt of fresh paint and the walls were all painted magnolia. There were a handful of framed photos hanging from the walls. The photos showed women in colourful traditional African dress. Children with wide smiles in front of mud huts and some scenic shots of waterfall and sunsets.

In the middle of the office were two ordinary desks a lamp and laptop on each. Two large white bookshelves stood empty except for a handful of books. On the floor were several brown cardboard storage boxes. Off the main office was a smaller room partitioned with a glass wall.

"We'll hold the interview in here." Richard said entering the smaller room. He sat down on his high-backed leather chair and motioned for me to sit opposite him.

It was hot in his office. Sunlight beamed in through the large sash windows. It felt as if the radiator was pumping out a rain forest worth of heat. I'd worn a tight black pencil skirt; a silk white blouse and tailored suit jacket. It was the only smart outfit I possessed. I was starting to sweat.

Richard leant forward and retrieved my CV from his black plastic in-tray. He patted down the pockets of his utility waist coat and retrieved a pair of thick black framed glasses.

"Now, what was it about this job that made you want to apply?" He had a creepy looking smile.

"I want to do something meaningful and rewarding with my life."

He laughed. "I like your honesty. Don't get me wrong Anna. It's admirable and who doesn't want that. I was in the army which, in many ways, is like charity work. They're both rewarding in part but also thankless in many ways. Society sees the army and charities as needed. But it treats them with such cynicism, don't you think?"

I nodded.

"I don't want to put you off. It's important you understand you need a little grit about you that's all. You're trying to fix a part of society that isn't working. The parts that government lack the means or motivation to sort out and big corporates can't monetize."

He picked up a silver fountain pen from his desk and twiddled it between his thumb and forefinger.

"At times it will feel the opposite of rewarding. You'll be completely dependent on the goodwill of the public for your salary. As their bills go up, charity donations go down. It doesn't help that every time you turn on the TV there's another telethon. They make it look like raising a few million pounds is easy. It's a lie. Getting people to donate to charity is hard . Are you prepared for that?"

"Yes."

Richard removed his glasses and sat back in his chair.

"Do you know where Uganda is?"

"It's in East Africa, between Kenya and Tanzania."

"Good. My wife, Rose and I own a place there. To be more accurate it's my wife's place but as we're married, it's now my place too. You may think I'm long in the tooth to be a newlywed."

I shook my head.

"Great things come to him who waits." His weird smile again.

"We were in Uganda recently and I saw a 15-year-old girl called Semmy in a motorbike accident. Her leg and head were all cut up. She looked so tiny and frail lying by the side of the road. She reminded me of a small bird that had fallen from its mothers' nest. I stopped to help her. She was unconscious and was unable to walk. When I drove her home to her village, I saw how she lived.

At her homestead there was no food or water and they slept in a mud hut. Semmy's father, I discovered was a violent alcoholic and her mother had recently died. Her 17-year-old sister Lydia is pregnant, and their father had tried to get rid of her unborn child. I took Semmy and Lydia away from their abusive father and their life of poverty. My wife and I gave them a new home in our house in Masindi. It was at that moment WOMAID was born."

He looked as if was expecting me to clap or something. I smiled which seemed to please him.

"It's amazing how your life can change in a matter of moments. A few weeks ago, we returned to the UK to register as a charity and to start fundraising. Our ambition is to help other girls and young women in Uganda."

Listening to Richard I wondered if he was a truly

amazingly altruistic person or whether he was a bit mad. I couldn't decide. The door to the main office opened. I turned around to see a short woman with her hair piled up high dressed in a silk, leopard print, two-piece trouser suit. She looked a little older than Richard. Her small frame, sharp cheek bones and small nose gave her a look of aged beauty that her husband lacked.

"Darling, you must be Anna." She said as she ran over to meet me. "I'm Rose, Richard's wife. My apologies for being so late."

"What have I missed?" She smiled at Richard.

"I was telling Anna about the girls and how the charity came to be."

"Yes, it's all very new." Rose said. "Your job would be to help run the office and support our fundraising efforts. We'd like to raise enough money to build a refuge."

"I see from your CV that you have been the office manager at a computer software shop for the past nine years." Richard said his tone more serious than Rose. "Have you done any fundraising?"

"At university I raised £1,000 to enable 50 Bangladeshi women to set up a basket weaving business."

"You have a degree in International Development though."

"Yes."

"Do you have any practical experience of working overseas?"

"No."

"I see."

"Have you ever worked for a charity?"

"No."

Richard looked down at my CV, he didn't look impressed. I stared at the top of his bald head where he had a large brown sunspot.

"I'd like to hear more about you." Rose said. "I want to hear about the Anna that is not on your CV. We can see from your resume that you have the experience to run the office. You wouldn't have been at the computer company for so long if you hadn't. What I need to know is whether you have the passion for what we're trying to achieve."

I looked at Rose not knowing what to say.

"There are no right or wrong answers Anna. I want you to speak from the heart."

Rose was sweet. Sweetness poured out of every sparkling, perfume scented orifice. She wanted me to dazzle her and sell myself. The problem was I couldn't sell myself.

What could I say? I'd only stayed at my current job for too long because I was too much of a coward to leave. I split up with my boyfriend of 10 years because he gambled away our life savings. I live in my sister's spare room and if I don't do something interesting with my life, I'm going to have a mental breakdown.

"Anna, you have to tell us something about yourself or how will we know whether this is the job for you." Rose said.

We sat there for what felt like an uncomfortably long time.

"I get annoyed how people spend money on handbags and cars whilst half the world lives in poverty," I said, "I hate food waste. We throw food away whilst kids in Africa cry themselves to sleep because of hunger. Since working at the computer company, I've enabled my boss and his sun-obsessed wife to buy a time share in Tenerife. There is nothing else to show for my time there. I want the chance to do something that can improve people's lives. I'm hard working, diligent and honest. I promise you, if you give me this job, I won't let you down."

Rose smiled. "You know what Anna; my husband thinks he's going to be the next Bill Gates. I, however, don't have such grand ambitions. I'm lucky. I have some money and I have wealthy friends. If we can help Semmy, Lydia and girls like them to have a better future then I'm happy to do what I can. I don't want to recruit someone who has years of experience at Oxfam and speaks to me like I know nothing. We need someone organised, who can keep us on track and who believes in what we're doing. Do you believe in fate Anna?"

"I guess so." I said, although I wasn't sure I did.

"My mother's maiden name was Seller's. As soon as I saw your application letter and your name was Anna Sellers, I knew you were perfect for this job."

NINE
SEMMY

"Edna the meat needs to go on the bottom shelf of the fridge." Margaret said as they were sat at the kitchen table having breakfast. Margaret had been living with Semmy and Lydia for a week. Semmy noticed how her favourite pastime was instructing Edna on how to do things. Semmy suspected it made her feel important. A step above Edna in the ranking of paid employees.

"Put the meat below the cheese and butter please Edna." Margaret said again. She spoke with such certainty. Listening to Margaret, you'd think that God sanctioned the organization of the fridge.

Semmy had asked Edna if she minded the way she told her what to do.

"I have friends that work in houses with women like Margaret. Women, often white women, with too much time on their hands."

Today it was Lydia that Margaret seemed most interested in.

"Where's your sister?" She asked as soon as Semmy had started eating her morning porridge.

"She's upstairs in our room."

Margaret shook her head with disapproval.

"When you've eaten come outside and sit with me. We need to talk."

Semmy finished her breakfast. Outside Margaret was sat on one of the white wicker chairs. Her beige hat sat limply above her small beady blue eyes. Her thin skin was so pale it was like she was allergic to the sun. Her clothes were cream and shapeless.

"It's hot again." Margaret said fanning herself with a battery-operated fan. It made a low buzzing noise that reminded Semmy of the sound of mosquitoes.

"The rains have still not come; it will only get hotter until they do." Margaret continued, it's quite exhausting."

Margaret stared at Joseph, the gardener, as she spoke. He was pulling weeds from one of the flower beds. Semmy expected Margaret to begin telling him how to garden. Instead, she shook her head and continued sipping her tea.

"When I lived in Kenya, I never found the heat quite like this. I was much younger then. Everything is easier when you're younger. Make the most of your youth Semmy."

"When did you live in Kenya?"

Margaret raised her eyes to the sky as she calculated.

"48 years ago, I was twenty-three and recently married. My husband Andrew was an officer in the British army. Richard was training under him which is where we met."

"You and Richard have known each other for a long time."

"Almost a lifetime."

"Is your husband still alive?"

Margaret smiled. "He's my ex-husband and no, he's not."

"I'm sorry."

"Don't be, I'm not. It was the death of my husband that prompted me to come and live in Uganda and buy my hotel. Richard came to Masindi to help me with my renovations and that's how he met Rose."

"Where is your hotel?"

"Not far from here. I am renovating it and hope to have it open within six months."

"When will Rose and Richard come back?"

"I've no idea. Richard said they are to stay in the UK as they are fundraising to build a refuge in Uganda."

"What for?"

"Their new charity. They have big plans. You two girls are just the start of things."

"Rose said we can go back to our father whenever we want. We plan to go home as soon as the baby comes."

Margaret turned off her fan and stared at Semmy.

"You and your sister are young. You've had a very primitive upbringing. I don't mean to sound harsh but what good would come of you girls going home? Trust me, you have opportunities that other girls, in your situation, could only ever dream of . Staying here is best for you."

Semmy didn't like Margarets ignorant assumptions about what was best for her.

"How long will you stay here?" Semmy asked.

"For as long as I'm needed. Richard is a good friend of mine and I'm happy to help him out. You know there are plenty of men at his age that would turn a blind eye to your circumstances. I hope you appreciate how lucky you are to have his help."

Margaret called to Edna to bring them a plate of fresh mango.

"I'll fetch it." Semmy said.

"Nonsense, Edna wouldn't want to see you doing something she's paid to do. She might worry about becoming redundant. Besides, I asked you here so we can talk. How's your sister doing? She hasn't said more than two words to me since I arrived."

"She's okay, she's quiet that's all."

"There's quiet and there's rude. I'm starting to think she doesn't like me. What do you do in your room all the time?"

"We talk."

"Well, if you and your sister spend every minute talking up in your room things are going to be very boring for me. What about the baby, d'you know who the father is?"

Semmy shrugged her shoulders.

"She hasn't told you?"

"No."

"Has she told anyone?"

"No."

"Richard tells me your father tried to get rid of the baby?"

"Yes."

"But she wants to keep it?"

Semmy shrugged her shoulders.

"Well, she'll need to start to make some decisions soon. She got herself into this state and now she needs to be grown up about it. For one, she'll need to see a midwife."

They sat in silence watching Joseph continuing to dig.

"Do you have any children?" Semmy asked.

"We decided against having a family. We moved a lot with my husband's work. First Kenya, and then in the middle east. If you can't provide a stable upbringing, I think having children is rather selfish."

"What's Kenya like?"

"It's not so very different from Uganda. Lush green

countryside, exotic wildlife and busy towns or remote villages."

"I'd like to go to Kenya one day."

"Maybe you will. Who knows what your life will be like now you're living here. I doubt you ever thought you'd be living in a house like this."

Margaret looked at her watch.

"I have errands to run in town. Don't forget you have your first day at Masindi Primary School tomorrow. A good education will be essential, especially for a girl like you."

TEN
ANNA

I woke at 7am with my parent's calling me from their home in France. They wanted to wish me good luck for my first day of my new job. Dad thinks I'm the next Angelina Jolie. I've been happy to let him think it's as impressive as working for the UN. Mum can't understand why I'd leave a secure and well-paid job at a software company. to work for a charity.

I thanked them for their call and hung up promising I'd visit soon. I arrived frazzled for my first day at WOMAID. Rose greeted me wearing a long, flowery pink dress and a big smile. It was so big it made the makeup around her mouth and eyes wrinkle.

"Welcome to WOMAID" she said beckoning me inside. On my desk she had placed a box of handmade chocolates with a red bow.

"They're a little first day welcome gift."

Richard waved to me from his office and the comfort of his over-sized director's chair.

"Now settle yourself in. The first thing I want you to do is the charity website. It seems no one can do anything these days without looking you up on-line first. We thought you'd have a better idea of what we need. Working at a software company must have given you some idea."

"I'll try." I told her smiling.

Richard emerged from his office wearing his scout leader

shorts.

"I was telling Anna that we need a website." Rose said.

Richard removed his glasses.

"It needs to make the charity look well established and professional. Also, will you avoid this incessant trend where charity websites make beneficiaries so bloody cheerful. I don't want to help happy, smiling people. The point of a charity is to help those who are suffering, or am I missing the point?"

He looked across at Rose who smiled to placate him.

"I took the liberty of getting a few photos of Semmy and Lydia when they first arrived at our Masindi house." Richard took out his phone.

My first thought was how young Semmy looked. I'd never have thought she was 15. Her eyes revealed how scared, hurt, and vulnerable she felt. She had a white bandage wrapped around her head, and dried blood was across her face. She looked sweet, kind, and honest.

Lydia looked as old as her 17 years, older if anything. She was as thin as Semmy, but her sharp cheek bones and long eyelashes gave her a striking appearance. Her eyes showed less fear and vulnerability. They revealed an anger and defiance instead. I suspected Lydia hated Richard and his insensitivity to point a camera at them on arrival. It was an intrusion and an affront to her privacy, and her eyes showed it.

"Are the girls happy for these photos to go on the website?" I asked.

"Why wouldn't they be?"

"It's just they look -" I searched for the right word thinking exploited could be a little too honest. "They look exposed."

"They look like shit and that's the point. The worse they look the more people will donate."

I considered advocating for their rights to have some say in how they were portrayed. I sensed Richard wouldn't appreciate this on my first day.

"If it makes you feel any better, we'll post new photos in six months. The girls in their new clothes and smiling. For now, the message has to be that if people don't support WOMAID these girls will suffer."

"Like a before and after makeover at the hands of the charity?" I said not hiding the sarcasm from my voice.

"We have a job to do Anna and that job is to raise money. Raising money will have a greater impact than following some left-wing liberalist mumbo jumbo."

"The two aren't mutually exclusive."

"Trust me Anna I know what I'm doing. Let me give you some advice. If you insist on applying everything you learnt on some degree course, you'll make it harder on yourself and the rest of us. You must see Semmy and Lydia as products and our job is to sell them."

I was horrified and Rose looked embarrassed.

"What Richard is trying to say is that to do our best for these girls we have to raise the money. Unfortunately, the more desperate the girls look the more people will support them."

"Now, is there anything else?" Richard asked his voice impatient.

"How much do you need to raise?"

"£200,000 and I was thinking we should get some merchandise to sell on the website, a few mugs, tote bags and t-shirts. Look into that after you've done the website will you Anna?"

I smiled, although inside I wanted to scream. Richard returned to his office.

"He means well." Rose said. "Tomorrow we'll go and visit a good friend of mine called Robert Cunningham. He's one of our trustees. He's a banker, philanthropist, and an insanely well-connected man. Any charity would give their right teeth to have him as a trustee. If anyone is going to be able to raise the money to build this refuge, it's Robert. I tell you something, his friends are not going to be interested in mugs, tote bags and t-shirts. Although we might have to order a few to keep Richard happy."

ELEVEN
SEMMY

The sound of Margaret's car horn carried up to Semmy and Lydia's bedroom.

"You better hurry up or you'll be late for your first day. Margaret won't be happy." Lydia said from the comfort of her bed.

"Are you sure you're going to be okay here, you will leave this room, won't you?"

"Go." Lydia shouted. "I'll be fine don't worry about me."

Semmy ran down the stairs and out to the jeep. Margaret was sat impatiently tapping the steering wheel. It was Semmy's first day at the new school. She wore her new school uniform. A white short-sleeved shirt, maroon pleated skirt, a maroon tie, white socks, and black buckle up shoes. Semmy got into the passenger seat and started biting her lip and fiddling with her skirt.

"What's the matter, you look jumpy?" Margaret asked.

"I'm nervous, that's all."

"Why, whatever do you have to be nervous about?"

"I don't know anyone and everyone else will have their own group of friends."

"I never had friends at school. You don't go to school to make friends you go to school to get an education."

"What if I'm not as smart as the other kids and I can't do any of the work?"

"You do your best it's of no concern to anyone else what you can or can't do."

Semmy started to chew her bottom lip again until Margeret told her to stop. For the next fifteen minutes they drove in silence. There was one main road through Masindi. It was the long red earth road that was the main artery for the town. The same road where Richard had found her.

Semmy stared out of the window. School children in neat uniforms with smiling faces lined the road. The sight of them made her miss her own school friends. She missed how she'd walk with her best friend Mercy to their village school.

They pulled up outside Masindi Primary School. There was a large expanse of red earth for parking but no other cars. A handful of bikes were lent against a large mango tree.

Margaret instructed Semmy to stand in front of the school sign so she could take a photograph. Her cheeks burnt with embarrassment as the other children walked past staring at her. Margaret appeared oblivious to how she felt.

Masindi school was very different from Semmy's village school. There were eight concrete classrooms that ran in a line. They were painted turquoise blue along the bottom and white along the top. Large metal grates sat over each of the windows and there were metal doors. Semmy's old village school didn't have a single concrete classroom let alone one for each year group.

A tall thin man who looked forty approached them. He wore a neatly pressed beige shirt, a brown tie, and brown chord trousers. He was smiling.

"You are very welcome." He said shaking Margaret's hand. "My name is Mister Okelo. We met when you came to enroll Semmy. I'm the head teacher."

"Yes, of course." Margaret said taking his hand. "This is Semmy."

"Hello, Semmy, we are pleased to have you joining us. You will be in P7 the last year of primary. You'll be a few years older than the other children in your class. Your guardian tells me you have not sat your end of primary exams."

Semmy shook her head.

"You have to pass these before you can go to secondary school. We understand that it is hard at a village school. There are never enough teachers and those you do have may not be well trained. Did you have any proper classrooms?"

"A few temporary structures made from mud and wattle. Most of the time we sat under trees."

"It is hard to learn like this. When the rain comes, you're sent home."

"Yes."

"I understand." Mr. Okelo nodded. "Do your best, it will be up to you to catch up and we will do all we can to help you."

He looked at Margaret. "You may return to pick her up at 3."

Semmy followed Mr. Okelo into the school. They walked past the classrooms which sat empty as the children were still out playing in the field. Inside Semmy's classroom the four large windows flooded the room with light. There were rows of wooden desks. A blackboard covered the front wall with the date handwritten along the top in chalk. Posters, maps and health messages were stuck onto the walls.

"This is Miss Lambao." The head teacher said. "She teaches P7 here and will be your teacher."

Semmy noticed how young, pretty, and neat Miss Lamboa was. Her hair was braided in thin straight lines. She had immaculately painted red fingernails. Her white blouse was tucked into her long navy-blue skirt.

"It's nice to meet you Semmy. You can sit here at the front of the class." Miss Lamboa said handing her a blue lined exercise book. Semmy sat down and a few minutes later the bell rang. Semmy took a deep breath. The classroom was soon filled with the sound of laughter and excited chatter. She'd missed the sound of other kids and yet she was too anxious to turn around. The laughing voices reduced to hushed whispered tones as one by one the children noticed her.

"Children we have a new student that will be with us until the end of the year." Miss Lamboa announced. "Semmy please stand up and introduce yourself."

"My name is Kyembo Semmy," she said biting her bottom lip. "I am pleased to be here, and I hope to get to meet you all soon."

She sat back down; her stomach was in knots. The hardest part was behind her.

TWELVE
ANNA

We took the train to London, to meet Robert, one of the charities trustees. He was also Rose's wealthy, and well-connected friend. He lived in a grand, three-story townhouse. It sat around a private square garden in Kensington. His house, like all the houses in his street, had three white marble steps from the street to his door. The houses had identical black pillars and polished black front doors. The monochrome unity to the street epitomized good taste and wealth.

Rose rang the doorbell. A petite girl with iron straight brown hair and the wholesome air of an exchange student greeted us. She took our coats and escorted us upstairs to the drawing room. We sat on a plump antique sofa with cushions embroidered with fox hunting.

Above the fireplace was a large oil painted canvas of a middle-aged man. He was sat in a brown leather Chesterfield armchair. He was holding a cigar in one hand and a glass of whisky in the other. The painting's subject was Robert. When he arrived, I was glad to see he looked much friendlier than the artist had conveyed.

"Rose how are you my dear?" He kissed her on both cheeks. "You must be Anna." He said shaking my hand.

Robert was a little younger than Rose. He had a thinning head of hair and the facial lines of middle age, yet he looked distinguished. His clothes were simple but expensive. He wore a tailored white shirt with the collar open. High waist tailored navy trousers and navy-blue suede loafers. He sat down across from us. He adjusted his tortoise rimmed glasses and straightening the cuffs of his shirt.

"So, Rose, tell me what your plans are for the charity."

"It's called WOMAID. It is now registered with the charity commission. You and my nephew Kip are our two trustees. Richard and I are the two named Directors."

"Very good."

"Anna will take care of all administrative and office management tasks. She is also getting us a website built and will help support the fundraising. We have employed a friend of Richard's called Margaret Brown who is looking after Semmy and Lydia in Uganda. I know from the time you spent in Africa that you'll appreciate how little support is available. Girls, like Semmy and Lydia rely on the goodwill of neighbours or the extended family for support. We are starting WOMAID so vulnerable young women without a safety net, can find help."

The exchange student girl came in with a tray of tea for us.

"So how many girls do you plan to support?" Robert asked.

"We want to build a refuge that will house up to 20 girls and women. A few years ago, I bought a plot of land with money I inherited from my parents. I always intended to do something with it. I had thought about building a new house but have never wanted to leave the house where I grew up. I will use this land to build the refuge."

"What is it you need from me?"

"Your contacts, we need to raise £200,000."

Robert nodded his head. He looked at me.
"Anna, do you live in Tunbridge Wells?"
"Yes."
"And your parents, what do they do?"
"They live in France. My father's a writer and my mother's an administrator for a wine exporter."

Robert put down his cup.
"What school did you go to?"
"Sevenoaks school"
"I've heard of that, it's a very good school."

Robert had heard of the private school where rich families send their children. I went to the comprehensive school with the same name at the other end of town, but I didn't correct him.

Robert is posh. I've not met many posh people before. Aunt Judith, on my mum's side decided she wanted to be posh when she was fourteen. According to mum she started speaking like Lady Di and wearing a pearl necklace and hunter boots. My mother and her parents thought it was a phase she'd grow out of. Judith ended up marrying a public-school accountant called Alistair and had two children my cousins Romney and Hugo.

Robert stood up, straightened the cuffs of his shirt again and walked to a bureau in the corner of the room. He returned with a printed out copy of his outlook calendar. It had various engagements highlighted.

"You know Rose, it's not the easiest climate for fundraising I'm afraid. Tax hikes, foreign wars and the cost of living are all making people, and the markets nervous. Everyone is being cautious with their money."

"I see." Rose said her smile dropping.

"On paper, people look like they earn good salaries. After you take out school fees and higher mortgages, and the cost of running a household, there's not much left. That said, this is a very good little charity we'll make sure that we get the right people behind you."

Robert began to flip through his printed outlook calendar.

"We should have a Fundraising dinner with an auction. I know an incredible events company I can put you in touch with. Between the two of us I'm sure we can put together quite the guest list. This should give you a good head start."

"That would be wonderful," Rose said, "Didn't I tell you Robert is exactly the person we need."

THIRTEEN
SEMMY

Semmy was conscious that she was the new girl at school. She was also a couple of years older than most of the children at the primary school. She hadn't started school until she was eight and had repeated a year. Playground gossip would have amplified the news of her arrival. It would also have been known that she was from a local village now living with a white woman. Semmy assumed that these were all the reason that no one was keen to befriend her.

Each lunchtime, she ate the packed lunch Edna provided sitting alone. She chose a place to sit on the far edge of the playground in the shade of the trees. Her packed lunch was her main source of daily delight. Two freshly baked chapatti, a hard-boiled egg, an apple, a slice of watermelon and a carton of juice.

From her viewpoint under the trees, she could watch the children from her own school playing. She could also see the field of the neighbouring secondary school in the distance. At 15 these children were her age. If she'd started school earlier or she'd learnt more at school, she'd be attending secondary school instead.

At the end of her first week, she was sitting enjoying her lunch. Three older girls from the secondary school walked across the field and stood over her.

"Hey, you girl, you are the Mzungu girl, aren't you?"

Semmy knew that calling her a Mzungu was an insult. It

was the Swahili word used to label white people. She also knew that these girls may not be poor like her family, but their thick rubber shoes showed that their parents couldn't afford new ones. The tallest of the three girls had her tie wrapped around her forehead. It gave her an air of defiance.

"What are you doing at this school why don't you go to a white girl school if that is what you are now?"

"I'm Ugandan like you are." Semmy said her words quiet and mumbled.

"What's that food you eat?" Headband girl said leaning over to get a better look in Semmy's lunch box.

"You eat white girl food?"

"No, our housekeeper is Ugandan."

"Ooh," the girl said mimicking Semmy "Our housekeeper is Ugandan. Give me that carton of juice." She shoved her hand into Semmy's lunchbox and extracted the juice.

"What is it you want?" A boy, that Semmy had never seen before, shouted as he marched over to them. He had dark brown skin, sparkling brown eyes and big white teeth.

"Can you find nothing better to do?" He said staring at the girls.

Headband girl dropped the carton of drink at Semmy's feet and strutted off.

"They don't mean anything by it. I know those girls; they're bored that's all."

"Thank you for rescuing me."

"No problem, I'm Sydney."

"Semmy."

Sydney put the pile of books he was holding down onto the floor and sat down next to her.

"So, are you new here, I haven't seen you around?"

"I've just starting at the primary school. I'm 15 but I must catch up on my studies, before I can start secondary school. Do you go to the secondary school?"

"Yes, it's a good school; I get to take drama which I like. I want to be an actor one day."

"An actor?" Semmy laughed. "I've never met anyone who wanted to be an actor before."

"It will take some time. My father does not approve, he works for the police. He tells me I need to get a proper job working for the council or for a charity as these are the jobs that pay."

Semmy wondered if Sydney knew she lived at a charity. The bell rang, and he stood up.

"It was good to meet you." He said smiling.

For the first time Semmy started to think that perhaps her new school would be okay.

FOURTEEN
ANNA

By April I'd been at WOMAID for five weeks. It was evident that Richard liked the kudos, power, and status of charity founder. He did, however, seem to be allergic to anything resembling work. Every Monday he'd deliver a blustering speech about his ambition for WOMAID.

Rose and I focused on planning the fundraising dinner. It was to be held on Thursday 18th October at a new venue in Mayfair, London. Tickets cost £250 per person or £2,000 for a table of ten. There would be a silent auction for which I had been tasked to secure prizes. A live auction, that Richard had insisted he would run would also take place.

The new website was complete. I contracted a local company to build the site and I had uploaded most of the content. I was responsible for adding weekly updates about the charity. The WOMAID mugs, t-shirts, and tote bags arrived. I'd photographed and uploaded them onto the website. My last job was to write biographies on each of us for the 'Who we are' page.

Rose said my biography should sell my attributes. It should bestow confidence in donors to give. Everything I wrote sounded too cheesy and I hated writing about myself in the third person.

'Anna Sellers has extensive experience in office management and accounts. She's organized, trustworthy, and passionate about the cause. If you choose WOMAID and donate through Anna, you're sure not to be disappointed.'

It sounded like a dating app bio and was so toe-curlingly bad that I pressed delete. Richard approached my desk. His tall bulk of awkwardness hovering uncomfortably close to me.

"Could you let me know what I should write in your biography?" I asked knowing he'd have no aversion talking about himself.

Richard clicked out each of his knuckles and then ran his hand over his bald head. He did this a lot. I wondered if it was his way of stimulating his brain to start working.

"You can write the following. Richard Greene trained for the British army in Kenya. He had several postings around the world. When he retired from the army he focused on his philanthropic interests. This includes the development of a water filtration machine. The machine prevents sickness and death from water-borne diseases. It has helped men, women, and children in poor countries and disaster zones."

"I didn't know that." I said interrupting Richard's flow and curious that he'd not mentioned this previously.

"There's a lot you don't know about me Anna." He said. "You should then add in a few lines regarding WOMAID. Something along the lines of Richard is a co-founder and Director."

"Okay Anna," Rose said getting up from her desk and gliding across to mine. She perched on the corner of my desk.

"I'd like my biography to show my roots with Uganda. How I grew up there with my Indian father, English mother, and sister Nadine until I was 15. Growing up in Uganda has instilled in me a deep and lasting affection for the country and its people. Through WOMAID my hope is that I can help vulnerable girls. Girls who are the same age that Nadine and I were when we first left for England."

"Why did you have to leave?" I asked.

"Idi Amin came to power in 1972 and forced all people of Indian heritage out of the country. He claimed Indian people were an economic threat and they took work away from Ugandan's. The man was a ruthless, mad racist. As my father was Indian and my sister and I were half Indian, it wasn't safe for us. We moved to the UK to be close to my mother's family. My parents kept our Ugandan home so we could return one day."

"Did they ever go back?"

"No. By the time they could return we had built our lives in the UK. Nadine and I were at school. My mother's parents were older and needed us close by. We went out as often as we could to visit. I thought one day I'd move back there myself."

"Maybe we will." Richard said smiling. "Once we get the charity established and the fundraising started."

FIFTEEN
SEMMY

Margaret collected Semmy from school, as usual. When she saw the white jeep pulling into the school car park her heart sank. Margaret had plastered the name WOMAID on the sides of the jeep, on the back and bonnet. Semmy got into the jeep keeping her head low so she would not see the other children staring at her.

"I'd prefer to walk to and from school." Semmy said feeling humiliated.

"Nonsense, it's too far to walk and what if something were to happen to you."

"I always walked to town and back from my village at home."

"Things are different now, besides Rose and Richard are paying me to take care of you. I'd be neglecting my duties if I let you wander off on your own."

"I'm not wandering off. I'd go straight to school and home again."

"I don't care. You're my responsibility, and I'll not have you walking."

Semmy stared out of the window. She thought about the charities that came to her village school with branded vehicles. They'd visit the school to photograph the sponsored children. They were always the youngest children, Lydia said it was because they were cute.

The photos of the children were sent to supporters, so

they'd continue to donate. At Christmas, the 'sponsored' children would get a shoebox. It had pens and stickers inside. In return for their sponsorship, children had to send letters to their sponsor. Most of the time the teachers wrote the letters as the children were too young and couldn't write.

"What homework d'you have tonight?" Margaret asked interrupting Semmy's thoughts.

"Science. I must look up and label the different parts of the eye."

"I always enjoyed biology at school." Margaret looked across at Semmy. "Have you made any friends yet?"

"I've met a boy called Sydney who attends the secondary school and wants to be an actor."

"An actor!" Margaret laughed. "I hope he doesn't go filling your head with silly ideas. I can't see there is much work for budding actors in Masindi. You need to make friends with children in your own class?"

"They're young and they don't speak to me."

"You must be careful. You're getting older. Sometimes, boys may act friendly but want something different."

"Sydney's not like that." Semmy said annoyed.

Back at the house Semmy ran upstairs to see Lydia. Her sister stayed in her room to avoid Margaret. Semmy opened the door to their bedroom. Lydia was lying on her bed, her hand across her stomach and a confused expression on her face.

"What is it?" Semmy asked.

"The baby moved." She pressed Semmy's hand against her tummy.

"What am I supposed to feel?"

"The baby stupid, it's the baby moving."

Lydia glided Semmy's hand across her stomach in even motions. Semmy thought her tummy felt bigger, but she felt no movement.

"I've felt it twice today. Ever since we left the village, I've had nightmares that the baby is dead. Aunt Grace told me once of a woman that had a dead baby inside of her. I think that's what will happen to me. God would punish me by letting the baby die."

"Why would God punish you?"

"Because I'm not married; I was stupid and made myself vulnerable and having a baby like this isn't right."

Margaret opened the bedroom door.

"Whatever's the matter?" She asked.

"Lydia felt the baby move."

"That's impossible. You cannot feel a baby move until the final few weeks; you must be mistaken, it's probably indigestion. Now, Semmy, this doesn't mean you can take time off from your studies, homework please."

Semmy went downstairs to the living room and turned-on Rose's old desktop computer. Rose had said she could use it and had asked Margaret to show her how.

"The internet's an amazing thing," Margaret had told Semmy when she first set her up on the computer. "Anything you could ever want to know can be found on the internet. All you do is click onto Google and then type in a question. For example, if you want to know tomorrow's weather, you just type in 'weather forecast for Masindi, Uganda'. There see it's going to be sunny."

Semmy couldn't see what was impressive about a forecast telling them it was sunny.

It was always sunny during the dry season.

"Let's ask what the capital of Uganda is?" Margaret said typing her question into Google.

"See the capital of Uganda is Kampala."

Since this first lesson Semmy had preferred to use the computer on her own. The more she typed into Google the more she realized it was amazing. She'd looked up Ugandan Independence for her history assignment. She'd researched deforestation for geography.

For her biology homework she looked up a diagram of the human eye. There were so many to choose from. She selected one and copied it into her exercise book. Having this knowledge at her fingertips was a revelation.

Semmy had never looked to see if there was a website for WOMAID. She typed the charity name into Google. The website appeared with a large photo of her and Lydia.

It was the photo Richard took on their first night at the house. Semmy dressed in her old and torn school uniform. Her hair was dirty, her face swollen and bruised from the accident. Beneath the photo were the words, 'Please help these girls to have a better life today.'

Margaret walked into the living room as Semmy was fighting back tears.

"Why would Rose and Richard put this picture up of us? We don't want people to see us like this."

Semmy continued to read. 'Richard Greene, the founder of WOMAID, found Semmy Kyembo, 15, lying unconscious on the roadside in the Masindi district of Uganda. Semmy, and her 17-year-old, unmarried, pregnant sister Lydia, lost their mother to malaria. Their father is a violent alcoholic. They live in poverty. They have simple mud huts that let the rain in and are chronically malnourished. Richard and Rose

Greene have taken these two sisters into their home to give them a better future. With your help they want to build a refuge to house and support vulnerable girls like this. Please give what you can today."

"Do they think we have no shame?" Semmy asked.

"Richard and Rose must raise money to build the refuge that's all. You mustn't take it too personally."

Tears began streaming down Semmy's face. How could she not take it personally.

"What if the children at my school see this?"

"The children that you go to school with won't look at this website, why would they?"

Semmy thought about the jeep with WOMAID stuck all over it. Many of her classmates had parents that could afford smart phones.

"You have to take that photo of Lydia and I off the website."

"Now don't be ridiculous." Margaret said. "Besides, you know perfectly well I have no say in this. I will speak to Richard, but I'm sure he has only done what is best for the charity."

"Without us you don't have a charity."

Margaret walked over to her.

"Unfortunately, you know as well as I do that there are plenty more girls like you in Uganda. I could drive to your village tomorrow and find another two girls living like you. They would be happy for the chances you now have. Now, turn the computer off and forget all about it."

SIXTEEN
ANNA

My brother in law's alarm woke me at 6.15am every day. My nephews would then get up screaming as they ran around the house. I'd rise at 7.00 by which time Helen looked frazzled. She made breakfast whilst answering emails and applying make-up. My nephews unloaded an endless stream of consciousness. It was usually about their latest video game, favourite TV show or birthdays.

Helen left with the kids at eight, giving me fifteen minutes of peace and quiet before leaving for work. Richard and Rose were always in the office when I arrived. Rose a picture of rested glamour with her bright painted lips and styled hair. She'd always be sat at her desk answering emails. Richard would be in his office, always wearing shorts and reading the paper.

On this particular day Margaret had already been on the phone from Uganda. Her call had left Richard pacing, red-faced around the office. Rose was trying to calm him down.

"What's happened?" I asked.

"Lydia and Semmy have demanded we take down the photo of them on the website or they'll go home." Rose said her voice calm.

"Those girls have no right to demand anything of us after all we've done for them?" Richard shouted.

"Darling, there's no point in upsetting yourself. It must have been a shock to them seeing themselves. Anna did try and tell us at the time."

Richard waved his hand to dismiss this.

"Is it so bad that we take the photo down?" Rose asked.

"I'm not having those girls telling us what photos we can and can't show of them."

"We can get new photos."

"Who's going to give us money when they see two well-dressed, clean living and happy girls. I'm not changing it."

"You'd rather the girls leave?"

"They're bluffing. Why would they leave. Besides, it's not my problem if they do." Richard was still pacing as he spoke. "It's you that will have the embarrassment of going back to your friends. What will you say. Thanks for supporting us but it seems Semmy and Lydia would prefer to be at home. Life with their drunk father is preferable to our charity."

"I won't force them to stay to save my embarrassment at telling friends we made a mistake?"

"We didn't make a mistake." Richard shouted. "Going home to their father would be a disaster."

It was the first time I'd heard Richard raise his voice to Rose. I could see by her face that she wasn't happy. She turned away from him and sat at her desk. He strutted off towards his office like a child having finished a tantrum.

"Shall I take the photo down?" I asked Rose.

"I don't know. Richard's right, we can't let the girls dictate how we run the charity. However, I don't wish to use a photograph that upsets them. My biggest problem right now is Richard. He may think he's the one running WOMAID. What he fails to remember is it's my house those girls are living in. It is my name on the lease of this office and it's my friends who are giving us money. For this reason, I'll make the decisions and I'll not be shouted at to do what he wants."

SEVENTEEN
SEMMY

Lydia had wanted to return home since they'd arrived. The photo of them on the charity website had been the final straw. She told Semmy she would not stay and be humiliated further.

They waited until Margaret had gone to bed, before leaving. They crept down the stairs careful not to wake her. Semmy ran through to the kitchen and took three chapatti that were left over from dinner. She knew they'd be hungry once home. In the hall Lydia had her shoes on and was sliding the latch open on the front door. They stepped outside, closing the door behind them.

Semmy shivered. It felt wrong sneaking out in the night. Lydia had insisted it was for the best. Neither girl looked back at the house as they wandered down the drive and through the side gate. A left turn led towards their village. With no streetlights and the earth road so covered in potholes their pace was slow.

It felt strange being out so late. The normal bustle of bikes and people was absent. The only sign of life was a handful of fires burning outside huts in the distance.

"I'll miss Edna" Semmy said, "She's been so kind to us."

"Yes, although I won't miss Margaret. I can't stand another day of her questioning, the woman's a gossip."

By the time the girls had reached the path that led from the main road to their village, Lydia's back and legs ached.

"Let's lie down here until it is light. It's better we arrive in the morning then wake father now."

Semmy stretched out next to Lydia on the grass bank. Using their bag of clothes for pillows they stared up at the stars.

"It's nice to be back." Lydia said with her hand rested on her bump. "I need to get fit as I am so tired."

Semmy looked across at her sister with tears in her eyes.

"I miss mum more when I'm here. I hate the fact that when we return tomorrow, she won't be there."

Lydia took Semmy's hand and squeezed it.

"I know, but being away will not bring her back. Get some sleep."

They slept so deeply that the first light did not wake them. What woke them was the sound of Margaret's voice.

"Wake up Semmy".

It took Semmy a minute to wake. She opened her eyes to see Margaret in front of her and the morning sun already bright in the sky.

"It's Lydia; we have to get her to a midwife."

Semmy sat up and looked at her sister who was waking up next to her. Her skirt had a large dark brown patch on it and a patch of dried blood on the ground beneath her.

"What's happened?"

"I don't know. I have called Edna who is phoning for a midwife. We have to take her home."

"Home to father?" Semmy said.

"No. Home to Richard's house. We need to get her help and make sure the baby's going to be okay."

EIGHTEEN
ANNA

There remained a tension between Rose and Richard throughout the day and into the next. Rose wanted to take the photo of the girls down. Richard demanded it stay up. I suspected it was their first dispute as a married couple and it didn't bode well.

At twelve I escaped the office to get lunch. It was wet and cold. I had my head down avoiding puddles and disgruntled office workers. I got to the sandwich shop and that's when I saw Mark.

His black hair was waxed into place despite the rain. He was wearing his green Barbour raincoat, a white t-shirt and jeans. He looked both shocked and pleased to see me.

"Anna, you look great." He said.

"Really, I feel like a drowned rat." I touched my hair feeling self-conscious. It was cut into a short bob. Mark always liked it long, my new hair felt like an act of betrayal.

"How have you been?"

"Fine."

"Did you get the flowers I sent?"

"Yes, thank you."

"You never called."

"I've been busy with work; I've got a job at a local charity raising money for girls in Uganda."

Mark smiled, "Finally you get to do it. It only took what 10 years to get a job working for a charity? How did Ferg take the news you were leaving. He thought you were going to be at that software company for life."

"He wasn't happy, but things change, people change." I could hear the edge of bitterness to my words which, I hadn't intended.

"Are you working today?" He asked.

"I'm on my lunchbreak."

"Can I buy you lunch?"

I hesitated for too long to come up with a reason for him not to. We went to Wagamamas. My suggestion as the food is fast and there are no romantic corners. Our waitress sat us besides a couple who look barely old enough to have finished school. They were in love. Their touching and wide-eyed enthusiasm made our situation even more pitiful.

The waitress took our order, and we sat in awkward silence for a few minutes.

"How's the gambling?" I asked.

"I've stopped."

"Have you?"

"Scouts honor." Mark said holding up two fingers.

I laughed, "You were never a scout."

"How do you know?"

"I know everything about you. So, you're still gambling?"

"I'm trying not to."

The waitress returned with a pint of beer for Mark and a glass of white wine for me.

"You don't need to lie to me anymore Mark."

"I've been to the casino a couple of times since you moved out, that's all, I promise."

He looked tired, like he'd not slept in days.

"You're coming back, aren't you?"

There was an uncertainty in his eyes that I'd never seen before. Mark was always so self-assured and confident. Maybe it was my new job, my hair, or the fact we hadn't spoken in weeks. I hoped he'd started to realise that this time I wasn't staying with Helen to teach him a lesson.

"You gambled away our savings Mark and you lied to me."

"I know and I'm sorry. I need you."

"You should have told me you had a problem."

"I didn't, I don't."

"Mark, you lost £10,000 in a casino; I think that constitutes a problem?"

We ate in silence as the teenagers giggled next to us.

"How's work?"

"Fine, I'm on nights."

"That explains the dark circles."

"It pays more and I'm taking overtime."

I wondered if I'd be kinder, more forgiving if he was struggling with an addiction that hadn't cost us our savings.

"Do you ever ask yourself why you gamble?"

"I probably got it from my dad. The only two conversations we ever had, were about the football scores or the horses. Maybe gambling reminds me of my old man."

"I'm not coming home." I said. "I need time on my own. We've been together my entire adult life and I need to be myself, figure out what I want, what I need."

Our waitress brought over a steaming plate of noodles for Mark and salt and pepper squid for me.

"All couples go through bad patches. I'm putting in loads of extra shifts, I'll get the money back soon and then we'll get our own place like we always planned."

"I don't want to go back to how things were. It's over."

It was weird and frightening to say this. I'd thought it a hundred times in the last few months, but voicing it out loud, made it real. I got back to the office feeling dreadful. Rose was the only one there. She told me to remove the photo of Semmy and Lydia and she'd deal with Richard.

NINETEEN
SEMMY

Lydia was in pain and was starting to panic about why she was bleeding. Margaret pulled into the drive and Edna ran over to the jeep. She helped Lydia telling her over and over that she'll be okay, she needed rest that was all.

Upstairs Lydia removed her blood soiled skirt and Edna ran her a warm bath. Margaret made no comment about them leaving. Semmy realised the seriousness of Lydia's condition was the reason. This did nothing to reassure her that Lydia would be okay.

After her bath Lydia got into bed and Edna brought extra pillows. Her pain grew worse. Her face, that normally revealed so little of her thoughts or feelings, was a picture of fear.

"What's happening? Is the baby coming?"

"It's possible," Edna said. "Women can go into labour this early. It may be nothing. Try not to worry."

Semmy took Lydia's hand expecting her to pull it away, but she didn't. Lydia lifted the bed sheet and looked down and Semmy followed her gaze. There was blood in the bed, lots of blood.

The midwife arrived. A short stern-faced woman of Margaret's age. She wore a navy blue short sleeved dress with a white collar. Her manner was formal and professional.

"My name is Luwanga Beatrice. You must be Lydia." She put the black case she was holding on the bedside table.

"May I examine you?"

Lydia nodded. Beatrice retrieved a pair of blue latex gloves and a small wooden funnel from her bag. She placed one end of the funnel against Lydia's stomach and the other end to her ear.

"How pregnant are you?"

"Six months."

"The baby is ready to come out." Beatrice announced. "It may not be time, but we cannot control these things. The baby's heartbeat shows it is in some distress. We don't have time to get you to the hospital. You must push, do you understand?"

Lydia looked at Semmy her eyes searching her sister for some comfort or reassurance. Semmy could offer nothing.

"This is no place for a girl of your age." Beatrice said. "We will do all we can, and it is in God we must trust." Edna nodded confirming she should leave.

Semmy sat outside the room with her head in her hands. Lydia must be trying to push the baby out. Her screams were louder, more filled with distress. Semmy thought about the river and the rope swing that they played on when they were younger. Her mother would watch them and smile as she washed their clothes. Edna walked out of the bedroom and smiled at Semmy.

"It will be okay." She said.

She went into the bathroom and returned with a bowl of water and towels that smelled of lemons. Semmy legs ached where she'd sat on them for so long. She refused to leave until the baby was delivered. She wanted to be the first to see her sister and the baby.

Silence eventually came. It was like the silence when the

rains stop at the end of a storm. All very sudden. Semmy pushed her whole body closer to the door to listen for a noise. She waited - there was nothing - only silence - and then a whimper. The anguished screams of Lydia were replaced by the shallow and fragile cry of the baby.

Edna would fetch her soon. She was going to see her new baby niece and she'd call her sister mum. This would make her laugh. Semmy could always make Lydia laugh. Minutes passed. Semmy wondered why they didn't come out to get her.

Margaret appeared first from the room. She didn't look at Semmy. She was in a rush, always rushing. The midwife came out next. She set her eyes on Semmy and with them a thousand sorrows. She had the baby in her arms.

"Can I see Lydia now?" Semmy said trying to see past the midwife and into the room.

"I'm sorry Semmy; your sister didn't make it. She lost too much blood; we did everything we could to save her but there was nothing any of us could do. She is with our most heavenly Lord now and she will rest in peace."

"No" Semmy screamed pushing past Beatrice and into the room.

Lydia was lying on the bed, her eyes closed as if she were sleeping. A clean sheet had been placed on top of her and Semmy took her limp, lifeless hand and held it to her face. She couldn't lose her sister; her sister was everything she had. She begged to God to bring her back; why must he take her; First their baby brother Issac, then her mother and now Lydia.

Semmy's body shuddered as she fought to breathe. Two strong hands gripped her. It was Edna. "You have to come away now Semmy, Lydia's with your mother now."

Semmy fell onto her knees.

"You have to leave her." Edna said lifting Semmy to her feet. All Semmy could think about was Lydia's words, 'no good would come of them moving to this white man's house'. She was right.

TWENTY
ANNA

It was 8pm in the evening when I got the call from Rose.

"Lydia has died in childbirth." She said. "Her baby survived; a premature daughter weighing five pounds and two ounces. Margaret and the midwife have taken Lydia's baby to Masindi hospital. She is in an incubator until her lungs are big enough for her to breathe on her own. There was nothing anyone could do."

"How's Semmy?"

"Distraught, of course. The poor girl had to be dragged from her sister's bedside. Edna is taking care of her. Richard has booked himself on the first flight to Uganda in the morning. If you would rather take tomorrow off that's fine."

"Thank you, I'd rather come in."

The following morning, I walked to work on what was the first sunny day in weeks. It was far too nice a day given the news of Lydia's death. When I die, I want it to be cold, wet, and stormy, the kind of day that makes dogs howl and kids scream.

Rose had discarded her usual exotic wardrobe for a black trouser suit. Her bright lipstick was absent, and her red tired eyes revealed how little sleep she'd had.

"Thank you for coming in."

"I'll make us tea." I said dumping my bag behind my desk. Rose followed me through into the kitchen.

"Has Richard left already?"

"Yes, and I'm pleased to not have to listen to him right now. According to Richard maternal deaths are still commonplace in Uganda. I should try not to take it to heart. He also said we should be pleased because Semmy and Lydia's baby will stay with the charity now. Can you imagine what kind of person says this kind of thing?"

She took a packet of cigarettes from the pocket of her cardigan. Rose never smoked in the office.

"Tell me Anna, how am I not to take it to heart?" She waved her hand over the smoke imagining this will make the toxicity disappear.

"He also said we should put something up on the website announcing Lydia's death. Who would even think about updating the website at this time?"

"What did he want us to write?"

"He didn't say exactly. He stressed that we must be careful. Her death must not reflect badly on WOMAID."

"No one will see it as a failure of the charity?"

"Won't they?" Rose said staring at me. "Well, they should." Her words were bitter and angry. "Lydia was in our care, and we took her from her home to give her a better life, to keep her safe and now, she's dead."

"You can't think like that." I said handing Rose her tea.

"Honestly, I don't know what to think. It never occurred to me that something as awful as this would happen. I wanted to go to Uganda with Richard to enjoy our first holiday there together. The next thing we'd taken in the girls and started a charity. God knows what Richard thinks he is going to do when he gets to Uganda, but I feel so bloody useless staying here."

This was the first time I'd sensed any doubt in Rose.

"Richard said we should try to turn this bad situation into something good. Do you think there is something wrong with a man that says this when a woman in our care has died?"

"I don't know."

"I blame his time in the army. That place would desensitize anyone. I'll tell you one thing, there's no way I'm calling my friends to tell them what's happened and then asking for money."

Rose ran the stub of her cigarette under the kitchen tap and threw the butt into the bin. The front door buzzer rang. I expected to see the postman. Instead, I found myself face to face with a man about my age. He had a thick brown beard, tanned skin, and red Ray-Ban sunglasses. I thought he was attractive in a 'I've just spent three days at a festival' kind of way.

"Hi, I'm Kip." He said. "You must be Anna."

I'd seen photos of Rose's nephew Kip. He and Robert were the two WOMAID trustees. Kip owned a bar in the French Alps and spent his time skiing in the winter or climbing in the summer. He was wearing long grey denim shorts, a faded light blue t-shirt and green trainers.

"Is the old girl around?" He asked.

"I should warn you we've had some bad news."

"Yes, I heard." Kip said, "That's the reason I came. Rose called me last night; she sounded pretty shaken up. I gather Richard has flown out to be the hero of the moment?"

"He wanted to help."

"What's he going to do, bring the poor girl back to life?"

"I thought I heard your voice." Rose said appearing

behind me and moving towards Kip to give him a hug. "What on earth are you doing here?"

"I wanted to come and see if you were okay."

"You know me. It's such a shock that's all. The poor girl should have her whole life in front of her. Now she's gone, and her child will have to grow up without a mother or a father."

Kip removed his sunglasses to reveal the same dark brown eyes as Rose. His eyebrows had streaks of blonde in them from where he'd spent months in the sun.

"I am going to cheer you up. I'm taking you to lunch and we'll stop your brain whirling around and making you crazy."

We went to Rose's favourite Italian bistro a few streets away from the office. There were four tables covered in red and white cotton cloths. Small plastic flower arrangements sat on each. The menu was a blackboard with a handful of dishes scrawled across it in white chalk. Four of the dishes were homemade pasta by Rene.

Rene and his wife Marianne had owned the restaurant for 45 years. Rene was Rose's age and had the body of a man who lived on a diet of pasta, cheese, and wine. He flattered Rose with how beautiful she looked and commented on how handsome her nephew was. He recommended we order mushroom ravioli with white truffle shavings and a bottle of Chianti.

Once we'd ordered Rose turned her attention to Kip.

"Are you looking after yourself? You don't look like you're eating enough."

"I've just finished the winter season; I've been working all hours and I've hardly had time to take a piss let alone eat."

"I don't need that much detail thank you." Rose smiled

in mock annoyance. "Kip is like a son to me." She looked at him with pride. "His mother, my sister Nadine died when he was sixteen, I've looked after him ever since. Believe it or not, at 16 he was very shy."

"Do we need to bring up stories of when I was sixteen?"

"What do you want to talk about?"

"The charity and what's going to happen to Semmy and the baby now?"

"I don't know, I'm guessing they'll stay at my house for a while. You're still not convinced that we can make this charity work, are you?"

"I don't know. I want you to make sure you know what you're doing."

Kip looked at me. "I realise it's your job Anna, but Aunt Rose is in her 70's. She doesn't need to be dealing with 17-year-old girls dying during childbirth in her spare room."

"I want to do this."

"You want to, or Richard does?"

The slick haired bistro owner came over with our plates of ravioli and topped up our wine.

"We both want to. We may seem ancient to you, but I feel the same as I did thirty years ago. I don't want to retire and sit around getting old".

"Don't you think it's all moving too fast. Within a year you meet Richard, marry him and now you've got a charity together."

"Kip was awful to Richard at the wedding." Rose said.

"I was very drunk."

"Being drunk would have been okay. Being obnoxious and rude wasn't. Kip turned up hung-over with some girl he'd known for a week. He proceeded to drink all the champagne.

He accused Richard of being a gold digger and then left without even saying goodbye."

"Are you married?" Kip asked ignoring Rose.

"No."

I said picking up my wine.

"You look the marrying type." He said which annoyed me.

"Kip's a terminal bachelor." Rose said.

"You make it sound like an illness."

"I think settling down would do you good." Kip raised his eyebrows.

"Darling, you will try and get along with Richard, won't you? It would mean a lot to me, and you could have a little faith in what we are doing."

"Too many charities are set up by people with good intentions. They don't have a clue what they're doing. I don't want you to be one of them."

"I won't, I promise." Rose said, but Kip didn't seem convinced.

TWENTY-ONE
SEMMY

Less than 48 hours after Lydia's death, Richard flew into Entebbe airport. Semmy received news of his arrival with dread and irritation. Responsibility for Lydia's death didn't rest with him, but Semmy wanted to blame him. If he'd never found her at the roadside that day and if he'd never brought them home to his house, would Lydia be alive?

He arrived and drank tea with Margaret. Edna came to Semmy's bedroom telling her she was wanted downstairs.

"Oh, there you are." Margaret said when Semmy appeared. Her small eyes staring up from beneath her beige canvas hat.

"How are you feeling?"

Richard stood up and walked across to Semmy.

"I'm so sorry for your loss." He said putting his thick sweaty arms around her.

She pulled away.

"You assured us that you would take care of us. You brought us here so Lydia would be okay."

"We did what we could. No one could have prevented this." Margaret said.

"Going home was what she had wanted from the first day we arrived." Semmy said wiping her eyes with the back of her hand.

"We need to tell our father. We need to take Lydia home. How we bury our loved ones is important. She must be laid to rest in the soil of our ancestors, or her spirit will never find peace."

"Tomorrow Richard will go and see Lydia's baby at the hospital. We've arranged for him to collect Lydia from the morgue. He will take her home to your father and break the news."

"I want to come. I need to be there to tell father what's happened."

"If you think you'll be okay, you're welcome to come." Richard said. "Have you given any thought to a name for the baby?"

"I want to call her Hope."

Richard and Margaret glanced at each other.

"Lydia would like that name."

"Hope it is." Richard said leaning forward to retrieve something from his black travel case. He held up two teddies, one white and one brown with red Harrods labels on their feet.

"I bought one for you and one for Hope." He was smiling as he held them out to Semmy. At fifteen years old the last thing she wanted was a teddy. She took her gift and returned to her room and didn't reappear until the next morning.

Richard was already at the house waiting for her when she came into the kitchen for breakfast. He'd stayed at Margaret's hotel and kept telling her how much he liked her improvements.

Richard was full of energy and eager to get to the hospital. They arrived and went to the neonatal unit to see Hope. Richard bent over the plastic incubator staring down at Semmy's little niece. His expression was so tender. For a moment any hatred she had towards him subsided. He put his fat fingered hand through the hole in the incubator to stroke Hope.

"She's beautiful." He said. "So tiny, precious and perfect."

"Lydia would have loved her so much." Semmy said with tears in her eyes.

"It is up to us to ensure she wants for nothing." Richard said sitting down on a chair. Time passed, the nurses came in and out checking on Hope. They always reassured Semmy she was doing well. Richard continued to sit there staring at her.

It was the middle of the afternoon before they left. Richard collected Lydia's body from the morgue. He paid four men from the town to help carry the coffin and transport it in their van. Soon they were stood in the road at the path that led to her father's village. Lydia encased in a coffin in the back of a rusty blue truck. Semmy walked slowly keeping her head bent and her eyes to the floor. The men carried Lydia behind her. They passed people she'd known her whole life, she couldn't bear to meet their eyes.

The children from the village, followed them. Their bare feet, dirty tufts of hair and torn clothes made her realise how different she looked. She'd eaten well for weeks. Her hair was neatly braided, her clothes were modern and clean. So much had changed, yet she'd have given anything to time travel and have Lydia back.

Two tall trees framed the entrance to their homestead. Semmy saw her father Albert sat on a stone next to the fire. He wore the same red and black checked shirt and torn black trousers he always wore. He had a penknife in one hand and log of wood in the other to make kindling. He looked at Richard first, then the coffin and the strangers who carried it. Lastly, his eyes bore down on Semmy revealing a toxic mix of confusion, anger, and pain.

Semmy ran to him. She buried her face into his chest so the only noise she heard was his heart. His smell, the familiar smell of bonfires and home smothered her. Albert held her for second before pushing her away to demand answers.

"What happened?" Albert said his voice catching in his throat.

"Lydia went into labour too soon. We were coming back home to you. We'd walked to the road outside the village. Lydia felt tired and wanted to rest. When we woke up, she'd started bleeding. Margaret drove us back to the Masindi house. A midwife came but Lydia had lost too much blood." Semmy sobbed. "She had a little baby though."

"I'm sorry this must come as a terrible shock." Richard said. "We've brought Lydia's body home, so she can be buried here. Her baby is doing well. You have a granddaughter. She was premature and is being looked after at Masindi hospital."

Richard pulled out his wallet and began paying the coffin carriers so they could be on their way home. Albert's head started to sway from side to side before he let out a deep groaning noise which sounded inhuman.

"I have nothing." He screamed. "I have nothing, first my beautiful son, then my wife and now my most precious daughter.... all taken from me." He buried his face in his hands, and he continued to shake his head. "I've not been so bad to deserve this have I?"

The homestead was a mess. Maize shells littered the

floor, along with empty plastic bottles from the home brew. There was also debris from the surrounding forest and animal faeces. Albert looked older and weaker to Semmy. Every day of their absence had eaten away at him.

Albert's sister Grace appeared through the trees. She took one look at the coffin and let out a scream. She ran over to her brother, put her arm around him and guided him away from the coffin into his sleeping hut. Semmy moved to accompany him, but Grace shook her head. She returned a few minutes later alone.

"Tell me everything that has happened since you left."

Semmy explained about their life in Masindi. She told her about her new school. How Lydia felt the baby move. Their walk back to the village and Lydia going into labour.

Richard explained that he and Rose had registered their house as a charity. They had employed Margaret, who was acting as their guardian and took Semmy to and from school.

Grace nodded her head as she listened.

"What about the baby? Where is she now?"

"She's in the hospital." Richard said. He took out his mobile phone and brought up a picture of Hope.

Grace gasped. "She's so very tiny. What will happen when she's ready to go home?"

"We wanted to see how Albert took the news of Lydia's death and if he'd want Hope here."

Grace turned her head to look at the hut that Albert had gone to lie down in.

"He's a broken man. He cannot look after a newborn baby. He needs time." She stared at Semmy. "You know your father loves you, but he's not in a good place. The drink still robs him of his senses. I'd worry about you and the baby if you return too early; do you understand?"

Semmy nodded.

"I'm sorry." Richard said full of remorse. "We need to agree on what's best for Hope and Semmy. This is not the outcome that any of us wanted."

Grace nodded and looked at Semmy, "Your father will come for you when he is ready and Richard, I'll need your address. Albert said he had no way to reach you. If he knows where to find you, he can come for you when he feels better."

Richard took out his wallet and handed Grace a small white card. 'WOMAID' was printed at the top. It had his address in Masindi and one in the UK. Semmy wondered if her father had lost the details before or if Richard had never given them to him.

Richard took the money left in his wallet and gave it to Grace.

"For Lydia's funeral. Please make sure Albert gets this."

"Thank you, you are most kind and generous." Grace said. She turned to Semmy.

"You must go with Richard now."

"Can't I stay until after the funeral?"

"Go now; you've said your goodbyes."

Semmy knelt by Lydia's coffin and said one last prayer. Walking away, she felt a loneliness and pain she'd never experienced. The same pain and loneliness driving her father to drink. She couldn't let her grief consume her, she had to be strong for Hope.

TWENTY-TWO
ANNA

Kip's presence at the office was annoying, he wouldn't stop harping on about what a terrible idea the charity was. He failed to concede that Lydia could have died with or without WOMAID. His dislike and disapproval of Richard didn't help.

Kip thought Rose should have remained single and three failed marriages was enough. She should spend her time having lunch with friends. Or, doing anything fitting for a seventy-two-year-old woman. Rose reassured him that her new husband made her happy and without the charity she'd be bored.

I got up to make a cup of tea. Kip followed me into the kitchen his jeans hung low enough to reveal the yellow elastic of his boxer shorts.

"I'm guessing that Rose is not going to give up on this charity anytime soon." He said.

"I guess not."

"As one of only two trustees, I'm thinking perhaps I need to get on board, pull my weight."

He smiled.

"Can I take you out tomorrow night?"

"What?"

"Tomorrow night, are you free? They're showing the director's cut of Apocalypse Now at the local Trinity theatre in town. I thought we could meet there at 7, grab a drink at the bar and then watch the film together. It would be good to get to know you a little better."

I was about to make my excuses when I remembered Helen had organized a dinner party the following night. It was going to be awful. A night with Tim's solicitor friends who were all very intelligent, loud, and rich.

"Tomorrow would be perfect." I said.

"Great," Kip said picking up his tea.

After work I accompanied Helen to Waitrose as she had last minute shopping for the dinner party. One of Tim's lawyer friend's messaged that he's now Vegan.

"What is it with people being Vegan?" Helen said as we slipped into the comfortable leather seats of her BMW. Lewis and Ben were strapped into their car seats at the back.

"I mean I get it on every level, it's just really inconvenient when you're hosting a dinner party."

She turned around to scold the kids for throwing raisins which were sticking in her blow-dried curls.

"Can't you serve falafels or something?" I suggested. Helen breathed deeply like she was meditating.

"Falafels are what people have for lunch. I'm going to need to cook something like a chickpea terrine."

"It sounds disgusting."

"I'll make sure you get seconds then. You're still coming, aren't you?"

"Mm, I was going to talk to you about that. I've made other arrangements."

"What arrangements?" She thought I was lying.

"I've said I'll go to the cinema with Rose's nephew Kip."

"Kip?" She said like it's the most ridiculous name she'd ever heard. "So, what's this Kip like?"

"Arrogant, opinionated and scruffy."

Helen laughed.

"I can't believe you're calling someone scruffy. You only ever wear jeans and sweatshirts. I thought you preferred people that didn't care what they looked like?"

"That's the whole point. He's trying to make out like he doesn't care when clearly, he does. I genuinely don't care what I look like or what people think of me. His t-shirt looks twenty years old, but I bet he bought it a few weeks ago from one of those retro shops. I'm don't like people that try to be something they're not."

"How do you know he's not what he says he is?"

"I can just tell. You know he said he thought I looked like the marrying type. What does that mean? D'you, think it means I look boring?"

"Does it matter?"

"No, I don't give a fuck what he thinks." Helen threw me a scolding look for saying the F word in front of the kids.

We got out the car and were thrust into the serenity of Waitrose. Nice wide aisles and smiling shareholder staff.

"So why are you going to the cinema with him if you hate him so much?"

"He's a trustee of the charity, I can't say no."

Helen raised her eyebrows at me as she threw a concoction of chickpeas, quinoa, and seeds into the trolley.

"It's nice to see you pissed off with someone other than Mark."

"Well, I'm due on." We steer past the hygiene aisle, and I threw a packet of Tampax into the trolley.

"I'll give you some money for the shopping."

"No, you won't especially as you're not even coming

now."

"You don't mind, do you? And about me staying, I know it's not ideal still being in your spare room."

"You're welcome to stay for as long as you want. We love having you."

"Are you sure?"

"Of course. Tomorrow night, if the cinema ends early, you must come with Kip and have at least one drink with us. I want to meet him."

The following evening, I arrived at the cinema and Kip was waiting outside.

"Sorry, we should have booked. It's sold out. It seems I misjudged the film watching demographic of Tunbridge Wells."

Opposite the cinema was a wine bar. It was early, and aside from a few post-work drinkers, the place was deserted. It's the kind of place Mark would come. I scanned the place to make sure there were no signs of him.

"Tell me, what's Rose like to work for?" Kip asked.

"Slightly mad, as you'd expect and very passionate about what she's doing."

"And Richard?"

"He's okay. He has some strange ideas."

"Like what?" Kip asked sipping his beer.

"He likes to fundraise as if it's the 1980's. He also thinks he's a third world savior."

"I imagine that's exactly what he thinks of himself."

"What about you? How comes you own a bar in the Alps?"

"Rose bought it for me. I know it sounds crazy that my aunt bought me a bar but, she's more like a mum to me.

When I left university, I went to the French ski resort of Alpe D'huez with my mate Alex to do a ski season. This bar came up for sale. It needed a lot of work. Alex had inheritance money to put into it and I had nothing. I asked Rose if she could help me raise the money and she offered to pay for half of it. She's very generous, sometimes too generous for her own good. That's why I worry about her."

Kip went to the bar returning with two beers and two shots of tequila.

"Salute, we always drink shots in France." He said smiling.

I gulped down the tequila and started to cough with my eyes watering.

"You're not much of a drinker I take it?"

"No and I can't drink shots."

"Well don't worry about what you do or say in front of me. As far as I'm concerned, we're a couple of people on a night out and you're not my aunt's employee."

"Okay, then tell me why you're so against the idea of this charity?"

"I don't trust Richard that's all. There's something about him I don't like. You can't have a conversation with him. He talks at you. Always another story about his life in the army, his work inventing a water filter or his travels in Africa. What has he got to show for it? He has no house, no friends or family. When he met Rose, he was helping to renovate a friend's hotel in Uganda in exchange for board and lodgings. My aunt believes this is because he's a nice person who wanted to help an old friend. I think it's because no one will employ him and he's looking for his next meal ticket."

"He makes Rose happy."

"Maybe, but for how long. What happens when he gets bored. Worst still, what if he takes all her money and then leaves."

"You think he's after her money?"

Kip shrugged his shoulders. My aunt is an incredible woman, I don't get the impression he sees this.

I went to the bar to buy the next round of drinks. The post work crowd were being replaced by a younger clientele dressed for a Friday night. I looked at my watch and it was close to ten.

"I need to have these drinks and then shoot off. I told my sister I'd go back for the end of her dinner party. You're invited although I don't advise you to come. My sister can be a bit much."

"I like a bit much." Kip said.

We finished our drinks and walked back to Helen's. She threw her arms around me as Tim poured us two glasses of his special reserve Bordeaux.

"You must be Kip." Helen screamed like I'd spent all my time talking about him. "You guys can help us settle an argument. Would a Glastonbury revolution be more or less likely to succeed than a Harvard one?"

"Really, that's what you're talking about?" I said looking apologetically at Kip.

"Forget it." Helen said. "Impress us with your juggling skills."

She threw me three foil covered truffles which I threw up in the air. I was too drunk to juggle and lost my balance knocking over two glasses of the expensive Bordeaux. As I turned to sit down, I fell into Kip's lap. He laughed. Maybe he wasn't as arrogant as I first thought.

TWENTY-THREE
SEMMY

Richard visited Hope every day that he was in Uganda. Semmy resented his constant presence at her niece's bedside. She'd heard Margaret telling him it wasn't necessary.

"Drop Semmy off and she can sit there with Hope. It doesn't need two of you to be there especially as all the baby does is sleep."

Richard was insistent that he stay. Semmy begun to take her schoolbooks in so that when Hope slept, she didn't have to speak to him.

It was four weeks until Hope was able to leave the hospital. It was only then that Richard returned to the UK. Margaret waved him off promising weekly photo updates.

Hope lay in Semmy's arms on her first day out of the hospital. Her dark brown eyes blinking up at her from her still tiny and fragile body. It was a miracle she'd survived and all Semmy could think was how she was her responsibility now.

"Hope's father must have been a white man." Margaret announced as she stared down at Hope.

"I thought her skin looked light in the hospital. I'd assumed the heat lamps made her skin look fair. I see how much darker your skin is, as you hold her. Are you sure your sister didn't say anything to you about who the father was?"

"No."

"What did she say exactly?"

"Lydia had said something once about making herself vulnerable, that was all."

"Vulnerable? Maybe she went looking for money in exchange for sex. Plenty of young girls do over here. They get so desperate; it will make them do things that otherwise they wouldn't. That could be why she never wanted to speak to me about the father."

"SHUT UP, SHUT UP!" Semmy screamed. "Lydia would not have sex with a white man for money." Her shouting made Hope flinch and she began to cry. Margaret took Hope from Semmy and tried to comfort her, but she would not be soothed and so she passed the baby to Edna.

"Now Semmy, there is no need to get upset." Margaret was unaware or unconcerned that she'd been the sole cause of upset. "I doubt we'll ever know who Hope's father was, but the good news is she is WOMAID's little girl now and we will take care of her."

"She is not WOMAID's girl, she is Kyembo Hope, daughter of Lydia, granddaughter of Albert and my niece."

"Yes, yes, yes." Margaret said dismissing Semmy's outburst like she was an emotional teenager. "She'll always be your family, but she has an extended family now."

Semmy stormed out of the living room to join Edna in the kitchen where she was feeding Hope a bottle of milk. Her emotions were still too raw to get into an argument with Margaret.

"That woman."

"She means nothing by it." Edna said passing Hope to Semmy.

"You need to know how to take care of her." Edna smiled.

"Do you think her skin is light?" Semmy asked.

"Maybe. All babies are different. It is best not to worry yourself over the things Margaret says. You know what she can be like."

Hope drank the bottle of milk. Her eyes were closing, and her face had that happy, almost drunk look of fulfilment.

"You are very good with her." Edna said as Hope slept in Semmy's arms. Her tiny body took shallow breaths under her small cotton vest. For the first time, Semmy was sure she could see traces of her sister in her face.

TWENTY-FOUR
ANNA

It was June, the office was hot and airless despite having each of the large sash windows open onto the street. Richard returned from Uganda looking like he'd been on vacation in the Costa del Sol. His bald head was peeling, and he had panda eyes where he'd been wearing his sunglasses.

"I've found a contractor." He announced smiling. "To be more precise it was a recommendation from one of Margaret's contractors. I spoke to them on the phone. They're finishing a job outside of Masindi. They will be available to start work on the refuge in a few weeks."

"Good grief." Rose said. "This is all very sudden. I mean we haven't raised the money yet and what if we can't get anyone to donate?"

"You said that your friend Mary donated twenty thousand pounds. This is a fantastic start. We'll send that across as a down payment. There's at least another ten thousand pounds in the charity account. We'll raise the rest at the fundraising dinner. The contractors are very understanding of our situation, they want to help."

"Waiting until we'd raised all the money would make me more comfortable," Rose said. "What if we only get half the amount we need, we'll have a half-built house."

"We need to have some faith in what we're trying to achieve here."

"I worry we're rushing things."

"Is this Kip putting ideas into your head? Think about the new baby and Semmy; they are both very much alive and in need of our help and a place to live in the future."

Richard began to pat his glistening, sweaty forehead with a blue cotton handkerchief.

"If it makes you feel any better, we'll wait." Richard said with as much martyrdom as he could muster.

"I don't mean to be negative. It's great you've found some builders. I need time to catch up with everything, that's all."

"Take all the time you need." Richard kissed Rose's forehead.

The contractors were not mentioned for the next week. Instead, Richard focused all his energies on fundraising. Every week he'd wave new photos of Hope in front of me and tell me to update the website. He badgered Rose to call all her friends and meet as many as possible to let them know of the charity's plans. His trip to Uganda and the arrival of Hope appeared to have invigorated him and prompted a new zeal for the cause.

A week later Rose had lunch with a good friend and returned with a cheque for ten thousand pounds.

"Let's transfer the down payment for the refuge now." Rose smiled at me. "I guess there's no going back now."

TWENTY-FIVE
SEMMY

Margaret insisted that Semmy returned to school once Hope was home and settled.

"It's one thing needing time to grieve for the death of your sister, but you have your own future to consider." Margaret said. "It's time for you to get back to normal life."

Semmy wanted to scream. Margaret seemed to understand nothing of how un-normal her life was now.

The day before her first day back Margaret drove Semmy to the local hairdressers. School rules meant that girls must wear their hair short. Semmy's had grown longer in the last few weeks. Edna had taken her before, but Margaret wanted to get her own hair done.

They drove into town and took the short walk to the salon. Semmy had got use to people staring at her when she was with Margaret. She wondered if they'd guessed she was a charity girl. Or did they think Margaret had adopted her like Madonna?

The saloon was lime green. It had black plastic chairs and shiny black sinks with flecks of silver. A slim man in his early thirties was the salon owner. He wore a pale blue shirt with white flowers on it, a blue apron, and blue latex gloves.

"You are most welcome." He said.

"Thank you" Margaret replied, "Now, I need a haircut and Semmy needs to have her head shaved for school. Can you do that?"

"Of course, madam, have a seat."

Margaret and Semmy sat down next to a woman who was waiting for her red hair dye to take.

"I wasn't expecting to see a man running a female salon in a town such as this?" Margaret commented.

"You know us women. We want to do things our way. You tell a woman what you want, and she thinks she knows better, and she does your hair like she thinks is best. But men, when you tell them something that you want that's what they do for you."

"Good, that's exactly the way I like it."

In a short while a younger girl took Semmy to get her hair shaved. The salon owner dealt with Margaret.

"I've not seen you in here before?"

"I'm not one to bother with my hair but as I had to bring Semmy I thought I could do with a tidy up. I'm renovating a hotel in Masindi and I'm managing a new charity here called WOMAID."

"This is very good of you. Thank you for coming all this way to help us. What does WOMAID do?"

"We give vulnerable girls and women a safe place to stay."

"That is good. I am a salon owner by day and a music artist at night. I'm known as Humble Todd as I am humble to man, and I am humble in the kingdom of God. I have done a charity night before where we raise money, I can do one for you."

"That is most kind of you." Margaret said opening her handbag and handing Humble Todd one of her business cards.

"Director of African Affairs." He said reading the card.

"You must be very important."

"Running a charity is a big responsibility." Margaret replied.

At school the following day the children stared at Semmy all over again. Her absent was no doubt a source of wonder, thankfully no one enquired why. Her teacher knew.

"I'll provide you with a list of everything we've covered so you don't fall behind." She patted Semmy gently on the shoulder.

At lunchtime, Semmy found her usual spot overlooking the secondary school playing field. It was vacant and secluded enough to sit alone. Away from her peers, the tears she'd fought to contain all morning flooded out of her. It was then that she heard Sydney.

"Are you okay?" He asked. "What's happened? I've been coming here every day and searching for you. I'd begun to think you'd returned to your village."

"My sister Lydia passed. She died in childbirth after having a baby girl; we've called her Hope."

"I'm so sorry." Sydney said sitting down next to her. "I don't know what to tell you other than it is God's way. You must think it was meant to happen and there's a higher purpose to it. Or else it makes no sense, and it will drive you mad."

"Is God's way always to take the people you love?"

"I don't know." Sydney said shrugging his shoulders. "To be honest with you I don't understand it. There are things we've always been told to believe by our parents, our teachers, or our priest. Things that made sense to me when I was younger but now – I'm not so sure about."

They sat in silence for a few minutes. Semmy wiped her

tears away with the back of her hand.

"If I was a gentleman, I'd offer you my handkerchief, but I don't have one."

"It's okay, it's good to see you."

"Would it help to talk about your sister?"

Semmy shook her head. "It's too sad and I don't want to be this sad all the time, it's exhausting, and I've cried so much my eyes have no more liquid in them."

"Shall I tell you, my news? I'm going to enter a talent contest." Sydney's smile was so wide his teeth shone. "It was announced this morning on the radio. It's to be held at Masindi town hall in two weeks' time and the winner gets the chance to travel to Kampala, attend a theatre workshop and see a play."

"That's great."

"You should apply Semmy, what's your talent?"

"I don't have one."

"You must have, everyone has a talent. You've just not found yours yet."

"I always wished I could learn to play a musical instrument, or I could sing."

"What if you helped me." Sydney said becoming more animated. "I'm going to re-create and act out a scene from the Shakespeare play Romeo and Juliet. Do you know this play?"

Semmy shook her head.

"It's a beautiful love story. It's about two young people that fall in love. But, because of their warring families, they cannot be together. I'm going to write a couple of scenes with an African twist. Juliet can't marry Romeo. Her family can't afford the bride price. This is why Romeo's family are against the union. It is not warring families but hard economics that will keep the star struck lovers apart. I have one small problem."

"Which is?"

"I need to find someone that can play Juliet." He stared at Semmy. "What about if you play Juliet? I can teach you; it will be fun I promise, and you'll have a new talent."

Semmy smiled. It sounded ridiculous. But, as she sat looking at the sun falling through the tree behind Sydney, she realized something. For the first time since Lydia died, she felt almost normal.

TWENTY-SIX
ANNA

It was pouring with rain as Richard, and I went to catch the train to London. We were going to see a friend of Robert's, a potential new major donor for the charity. Rose was supposed to go, but she woke up with a migraine, so Richard called me at first thing. He suggested I wear a skirt as this would help to make the meeting a bit less formal. His exact words were 'if you dress up a bit you can help to put the fun into fundraising'. I almost vomited into my porridge.

As testament to my inability to defend my feminist beliefs I found myself tottering along Charing Cross Road. I wore blister producing kitten heels and a tight black skirt. I also had my best fake smile lip glossed across my face.

"Martin's a hedge fund manager." Richard informed me.

"What's that?"

"Someone who's very rich." Richard replied, "and nothing to do with gardening".

The restaurant where we'd arranged to have lunch was trendy and dimly lit. Two huge glass chandeliers hung from the ceiling. They were as effective as my solar camping torch.

Richard scouted the room before approaching a table in the corner of the restaurant. A short, dark-haired businessman sat alone. He was peering down at his mobile phone with his glasses on his forehead. He looked like a cave man discovering technology.

"Martin?" Richard said.

"Richard." Martin lifted his head and smiled. His thin lips were so pressed tightly together he looked desperate to conceal his teeth. His tie had his initials embroidered across. His little finger had a gold signet ring squeezed onto it.

"This is Anna." Richard announced. "She's our administrator, fundraiser and PA."

I smiled obligingly and lent across to shake Martin's fat hand. He stood up and kissed me. His shirt rose up under the weight of his belly and shattered any illusion of him being a smart businessman.

"Sorry Rose couldn't join us but she's not feeling too good." Richard said as the waitress brought over three menus.

"Why don't you start by telling me a little about this charity you've set up. Forgive me, but I've forgotten its name."

"WOMAID". Richard replied.

"Ah yes."

"We're building a refuge in Masindi, Uganda. It will help young women that are victims of domestic violence."

Martin nodded and his predatory eyes surveyed each young waitress that walked by.

"Have you spent any time in Africa?" Richard asked.

"Enough time to understand a little of what life is like over there and it's damn hard."

"Yes quite." Richard said.

I zoned out as Richard and Martin shared stories of their worldliness. I glanced at the menu. It was in French. The waitress came over. She looked harassed, as if she couldn't decide who she hated more: her boss or the customers.

"Would you like me to take your order now?" She asked

a pained smile on her face and a French accent.

"I can order for you, if you like?" Martin asked looking at me and trying to appear chivalrous.

I studied him from across the table. I wondered, who would want a disgustingly unhealthy-looking man giving their food order?

"It's fine, thank you." I said pointing at something called Matelote which was the first thing on the menu. I had no idea what it was, it could have been goat's penis for all I knew.

Lunch arrived, and I was delighted there was not a penis in sight except for the two men I was sat at the table with.

Richard managed to bring the conversation back to the charity. Martin looked bored and started talking about his home in Antibes. I was annoyed at watching two grown men get drunk and stuff their faces with foie gras. It didn't seem right when the money that was being spent on lunch could have paid Semmy's school fees for a month. When coffee was served, I decided to take matters into my own hands.

"So, Martin," I asked nervously "Do you think you'd be able to help us to build the refuge?"

Martin looked at Richard as if to say, 'I think this girl has just stepped over her pay grade'.

The whole restaurant seemed to go quiet. Then he said.

"You know what, Anna, I would."

I sighed with relief and felt victorious. I'd asked, and he'd said yes.

"This is a great cause and I'd like to help. I have your details and so I'll be in touch."

"IN TOUCH!" I wanted to scream. 'Just write us a fucking cheque.'

I bit my tongue and didn't trust myself to speak.

"That would be wonderful." Richard said.

On the train ride home, I had to listen to Richard telling me what I did wrong. This included not ever asking someone for money as I was far too junior. As far as Richard was concerned the main reason Martin didn't give was because I'd asked. I also had to be more enthusiastic and to make men like Martin feel important. It felt like the rules of a stupid game and one that I didn't have any interest in playing.

TWENTY-SEVEN
SEMMY

"I've given you six lines." Sydney told Semmy a week later as he handed her two pages of his handwritten notes. "I can give you more if you want but I know you're a little nervous about being on stage."

"Thank you." Semmy said feeling a giggly excitement as she cast her eyes across his large and curvy writing. This simple act of sharing lines of a play brought with it an intimacy she hadn't expected.

"The words will sound funny at first. They're old English. You just say them with your own voice and soon they'll sound natural. We can practice every day at lunchtime, so you won't be as nervous on the day. I promise it will be good for you and keep your mind away from sadder things."

"It sounds great." Semmy said putting the notes into her school bag as if they were precious.

After school, Semmy finished her homework. Then, she sat outside on the veranda to read the script. She took Hope with her to lay in her Moses basket at her feet. She had grown so much. Her fragile, premature look was gone. Replaced with the normal features of a well-fed and contented baby.

Semmy focused on the script. She read through it three times. It took that long for her to understand the meaning. Through conversations she'd assumed Sydney was clever. The latest revelation of him as a budding playwright confirmed it. She smiled to herself. What a strange and unexpected new friendship this was. At that moment the back door swung open, and Margaret ran out as though the house was on fire.

"Semmy take Hope and go up to my room." Margaret shouted.

"I'm practicing my lines for the play."

"I don't care what you're doing." Margaret picked up Hope from her basket and shoved her towards Semmy.

"EDNA." Margaret shouted.

Edna appeared at the back door looking as confused and concerned as Semmy.

"You left the front gate open, and we have a visitor." Margaret said her voice high pitched and flustered. "Go upstairs to my bedroom with Semmy and Hope and lock the door behind you, do you understand? She must not come out of that room."

"What's happening?" Semmy asked Edna as they climbed the stairs.

"I've no idea."

They reached Margaret's room and Edna locked the door and sat down with Hope on the small chair in the corner of the room. There was a double bed covered with a silk bedspread embroidered with a golden elephant. In the corner of the room stood a large, dark wooden wardrobe. Next to this was a matching dressing table. On the table was a hairbrush and a pot of face cream.

Semmy heard the front door open and Margaret's voice as stern as she could muster asked.

"How can I help you?"

"I'm Kyembo Albert, daughter of Kyembo Semmy. I would like to see her and my granddaughter and bring them home."

"It's my father." Semmy said turning to Edna. "He must have come to see us at last. I can't believe it. Edna, open the door please."

"Margaret will come for you when it is safe for you." Edna said bouncing Hope on her lap.

"Safe for me? It's my father."

From downstairs, Semmy could hear Margaret. She was telling her father that he couldn't just show up and expect to see them.

"She's, my daughter." Albert said. "That man who took her away said I could come when I was ready, and I'm ready now and I want her home."

"Have you been drinking?" Margaret asked.

"What business is it of yours? I am not here to beg of you. I tell you that I need her home and I will have her home, or you must provide for me."

"Your daughter and granddaughter are who we provide for not you. I'm very sorry Albert, but you are in no fit state to see your daughter and I won't allow it. I suggest you return home and stop drinking. Then, clean yourself up. After that, you will be welcome. Do you understand?"

The front door closed, and Margaret came up to the room to announce Semmy was free to come out.

"I wanted to see him."

"It will do you no good. Your father still suffers under the curse of the drink, he was only here to get money for more."

"You don't know that." Semmy said tears rolling down her face.

"If your father deems to visit when he is sober, you can

see him, but until that time he will not step into this house."

TWENTY-EIGHT
ANNA

The unusually wet summer months passed uneventfully. Richard seemed to work less than usual. He received a message from the contractors saying work had begun on the refuge. This pleased everyone.

Rose and I had got the invitations to the dinner, designed, printed and sent out. We had also booked the entertainment. Robert had secured a couple of luxury holiday homes for live auction prizes. It was my job to secure items for the silent auction.

Spending a week begging companies to donate was tiring and disheartening. I had a list of luxury prize ideas. This included spa's, Michelin star restaurants, sporting venues and luxury goods retailers. Some rejections were polite and apologetic. Others were downright rude and obnoxious. A Saville Row tailor informed me I must understand the difference between a bespoke suit and a made to measure one, before calling. Like I gave a shit.

Rose took pity on me and invited me to accompany her to sample the delights of a recommended caterer. The caterers were in an unremarkable building on an industrial estate in Putney, South London. A makeshift dining room was set up to create the illusion of a restaurant. A waitress, dressed in black and white, appeared with a tray of mouthwatering and unusual canapés. Then, five delicious starters and five exquisite main courses came.

"The menu tasting is definitely a perk of the job." Rose said. "I used to be on the committee for all manner of charity events with my last husband. I'd be invited to taster events as a thank you for hosting tables or providing prizes. It's great to try new dishes. You can give feedback to the chef to get them just as you want."

"How long were you married for?"

"10 years with my first husband and 15 with the second."

"So is Richard husband number three?"

"Yes, you know what they say, third time lucky."

"How did you and Richard meet?"

"Through Margaret. Her husband Andrew was high up in the army and Richard served under him as a recruit. This was way back in the 1980's but Margaret and Richard remained in contact. A year ago, Andrew dropped dead from a heart attack. Margaret packed her things and arrived in Masindi, Uganda. She came while I was there on holiday. I met Margaret and she introduced me to Richard."

"Was she grief stricken?"

"She was furious. She'd discovered her beloved husband had spent their married life having an affair. They even had two children together."

"That's terrible."

"It was for someone like Margaret. She prides herself on succeeding where lesser women have failed. To discover that her marriage was a scam was humiliating."

"So why did she relocate to Uganda?"

She'd visited it once on her way to Murchinson Falls. It was far enough from the UK to make a fresh start. She took the money she had, bought an old hotel. The ex-pat community is small and dreadfully nosey. So, she quickly made friends."

"What was Richard doing in Masindi?"

"He'd been living in the UK and was Facebook friends with Margaret. She'd posted photos of her hotel and the work that was needed, and Richard volunteered his services. According to Margaret he was her very own knight in shining armor. After Richard and I decided to get married and start the charity, he insisted we employ Margaret. It was to tide her over."

"I see."

"All marriages come with a little compromise."

"And Margaret is yours."

"I guess she is." Rose smiled. The waitress brought over a colourful selection of desserts. A deconstructed raspberry trifle, a candy floss strawberry explosion and a fig and walnut chocolate tart. They were delicious and soon I was in sugar heaven.

TWENTY-NINE
SEMMY

Semmy had begun to experience a new kind of nervousness. It wasn't the sickening feeling she'd had when her mother was ill. Neither was it the fearful anxiety she felt when her father returned home drunk. Romantics would blame her jitteriness on the first flurries of love. Yet, Semmy had no experience of such things. She put it down to her debut as an actor.

Sydney had brought her a dress. He hadn't previously mentioned she'd need to wear anything special.

"I thought you'd like to have this as your costume." He'd said casually as he handed her a brown paper bag. "I thought it could help you get into character. Only wear it if you want too though."

The dress was emerald, green. It was a traditional Ugandan style dress with puff shoulders and a wide gold sash. There was decorative gold embroidery around the neckline. It extended down the arms and it sparkled in the sun. She didn't know what to say, it was so luxurious and expensive looking.

"It belonged to my sister." Sydney said. "She's outgrown it. It would make the perfect Juliet dress, don't you think?"

Semmy had tried it on when she'd first returned home but hadn't let Margaret or Edna see her in it. On the day of the play, she'd stood in front of the mirror and looked at her own reflection. She wondered what Sydney would think of her in this dress. Edna walked in her eyes widening with pride.

"You look like such a beautiful young lady."

"I've never worn anything like this before."

"You'll have to be careful, or it will be Sydney's parents asking Margaret for a dowry."

Semmy and Edna were laughing when Margaret walked in.

"Who is asking me for what?" She said.

"Sydney's parents asking for a dowry."

"As Syndey's father's a police officer and his mother's a civil servant I'm quite sure they won't be asking us for anything." Margaret said.

People talking about how pretty she looked scared Semmy. The idea of Sydney wanting to marry her and the fact that she was a young woman, not a little girl, scared her. She'd never held hands with a boy before let alone kissed one. At the end of their scene Sydney had told her he would kiss her. Her first response was to giggle until she'd realised, he was serious.

"It's an acting kiss." He said reassuringly. "I must end the scene in this way to show how in love Romeo is with Juliet. Will you be okay if I kiss you?"

Semmy had nodded but now the thought of the kiss was terrifying. She started to panic and felt so hot and uncomfortable like she'd faint.

"I need to get out of this dress." She said to Edna desperately trying to unzip the dress and take it off.

"I don't know what I was thinking but I can't go through with this. I will be the laughingstock and I can't breathe."

"It's just nerves." Edna said taking Semmy's hands away from the zip and doing the dress back up. "Count to ten and you'll be fine."

"Now pull yourself together." Margaret scolded taking Semmy's arm. "We don't have time for this nonsense, or we'll be late." And with that she marched her downstairs to the jeep.

The talent competition was being held in the church hall in the centre of town. It was a large concrete building with a wooden beamed roof. Inside there were four large windows on each of the walls. These baked the hall in natural light. Rows of wooden benches, already full of people covered the floor. Three generations of families all chattering excitedly. At the far end, was the stage. Sydney waved to Semmy from the side of the stage. He wore a dark brown suit and smart white shirt; all she could think was how handsome he looked.

A boy from Sydney's class took to the stage and sang a popular Ugandan song called Common Boy. When he'd finished everyone clapped. There were two more singing acts and then Sydney and Semmy. As they walked onto the stage all Semmy could see was a hall of faces staring back at her.

"I'd like to present an adaptation of Shakespeare's play Romeo and Juliet." Sydney announced.

They took up their positions as rehearsed. Sydney delivered his speech as a frustrated and desperate Romeo. He dropped down on one knee and took hold of Semmy's hand and some of the children in the audience laughed. Semmy felt confused. It wasn't a comedy. It was a love story. Sydney declared his love with such sincerity and passion. She couldn't understand why people would laugh.

It was her turn to speak but the words stuck in her throat. Her mind raced in a million-different directions. Semmy tried not to think about why people were laughing.

Her hand was sweaty under Sydney's grasp. The sea of faces staring back at her was overwhelming. Where was Edna and her comforting smile. Why could she not have a mother, father, or sister in the crowd?

Semmy took a deep breath and then began speaking, her voice choked with emotion. As she faltered and stuttered through her lines every insecurity and fear that had plagued her, echoed through her words. And then, something wonderful happened. As the room of strangers stared up at her, Semmy felt a sense of peace. It was this odd feeling that the audience were on her side.

Semmy sat on a blanket in the middle of the stage. Picking up the glass medicine bottle that Sydney had provided, she pretended to drink the poison. Laying down afterwards as if unconscious. Sydney ran across the stage; let out a scream, bent his head over her and then kissed her.

It was Semmy's first kiss from a boy and she need not have worried. It was soft and gentle; a kiss that she would revisit a thousand times over with the same thrill as that moment.

"You see I knew you'd be fine." Sydney said when she opened her eyes.

The audience started to clap; they'd enjoyed it despite the laughter. Sydney took Semmy's hand and walked her to the front of the stage for their bow. Semmy was so relieved and excited that she burst out laughing.

How strange that her first kiss should be on stage in front of a room full of strangers. She knew her father would not approve. Lydia would say 'she mustn't let it all start getting to her head.' But, in that moment she did.

They walked off stage. Some of the performers came

over to congratulate them. They said they were brave to do something so unusual. There were more singing and dance acts. There was a magician and even a comedian. Then, the judges were ready to announce the winner.

"We're blessed to have so many great performances today." The head judge, a short man with a bald head and a black suit, said into his microphone.

"Who would know such talent lies among us? Unfortunately, there's only one spot for the acting workshop in Kampala. So, we can choose only one winner. We feel Lutaya Sydney gave the most original performance and is worthy of the prize."

"You won." Semmy said looking at Sydney.

"We won."

They stepped forward and shook the hand of the chief judge.

"Thank you for your help Semmy." Sydney said as they walked off the stage. "I could never have done this without you."

"You don't need to thank me." She said following Sydney to where his mother was.

"So, you are Semmy." Sydney's mother said, her tone polite but not friendly. "I have heard a lot about you." She looked at her son but didn't smile.

"We must go, say goodbye to your friend Sydney."

"I'll see you around." He said and followed his mother out of the hall. Semmy quickly lost sight of him among the crowd of people all trying to leave. As she stood there, she couldn't help but think Sydney's mother disapproved of her.

THIRTY
ANNA

It was late afternoon on the day of the fundraising dinner event. Rose and I were in the office.

"Darling, I wanted to get you something special to wear tonight." Rose said holding out an expensive looking bag with Fenwicks written across it.

"I already have a dress for tonight." I said. It was a knee length black dress which I'd had for years, it was my standard little black dress for all smart occasions.

"I want you to shine like the star that you are."

I'd seen what Rose was wearing, a shimmering floor length silver gown with a sequined shawl. Rose could pull this off, I couldn't.

"I'm very good at knowing what suits people and I won't take no for an answer. You have excelled at getting us organized and professional. We could not have done this without you. This is a small token of our appreciation."

"Thank you." I took the dress.

"Go now, try it on."

I retreated to the bathroom and pulled out of the bag a midnight blue tutu skirt style dress with a fine lace top. It was very pretty albeit more feminine than anything I'd normally wear. There were shoes too. They were four-inch silver stilettos. I pushed my feet into them and walked out of the bathroom. It felt as precarious as exploring rock pools on stilts.

"You look wonderful." Rose said as Kip walked in. He'd flown back from France to help with the dinner. He looked remarkably polished. His beard was neatly trimmed, his shoulder length hair was waxed. His black tuxedo fitted his athletic frame to perfection. My cheeks flushed red with embarrassment.

"Rose bought it for me." I said in a tone that made it clear the dress was not of my choosing.

"You look very nice." He was smiling.

Richard was the last to arrive at the office at just past five. His eyes were blood shot red and his cheeks were blotchy.

"Someone's started a bit early?" Kip said under his breath.

"Be kind, he's not terribly comfortable at these events."

Rose walked over to Richard. She brushed a few bits of dirt flakes from his suit with her well-manicured fingers.

"I've only had one," Richard barked irritably.

"Yes darling, you'll just need to slow down a little that's all."

We took a taxi to London. Rose insisted we arrive fresh and un-frazzled. This was not possible with British Rail.

Richard sat in the front with the driver while Rose sat between Kip and I in the back.

"Now Kip, I take it you've seen the guest list?" Rose said. "There are some very influential people coming tonight. I'll introduce you to as many as possible so you can charm them?"

"I'll do my best."

"What do you want me to do?" Richard asked from the front seat his voice laced with sarcasm.

"Well, you can do what you like. I thought Kip would be a little more used to networking."

"It's just bloody talking to people Rose and even I can do that". Rose lent forward and placed a reassuring hand on Richard's right shoulder.

"I know you can." She said her smile strained.

Rose kept the conversation flowing for the one-hour journey to London. This was remarkable given nerves had struck me mute and Richard and Kip were not talking.

"This is it," Rose announced as we pulled up outside One Mayfair. "Tonight, we present WOMAID to the rest of the world. Remember the most important thing is that everyone has a good time."

"The most important thing is we raise some bloody money." Richard said his mood not improving.

The venue, One Mayfair, was a converted church. It was one street away from the hustle and bustle of Mayfair high street.

A thick necked security guard with a black coat, short army hair and an earpiece stared at us.

"We're with the charity." Rose informed him pointing at the two artist easels erected behind him. One easel had WOMAID written on it and the other held a large black and white print of Semmy and Hope.

"This is very impressive." Kip whispered in my ear.

"Now the guests will be here soon." Rose said. "Kip and Richard, you go and wait upstairs; Anna can you stay by the door while I find Candice?" Rose pushed a clip board into my hands and scurried off.

Candice was from the events company that Robert recommended. They had helped to pull the whole thing together. She was supposed to be on the door and checking all the guests in. The first couple arrived before we'd found her and so it fell to me. They were early and I was nervous.

"Hello," I said smiling self-consciously.

"Good evening."

"Thank you for coming, can I take your names please?"

"John and Caroline Fairweather." John said, every vowel well rounded. I ticked them off, smiled awkwardly again and pointed them upstairs.

Robert was the next guest arriving with his wife Elizabeth and immediately putting me at ease.

"This is wonderful, you've done a fabulous job Anna; the evening will be a huge success."

He kissed me and then darted off in search of Rose.

"Mr. Jacques Bouduin" said a French man in a sharp blue suit and a tie covered in penguins. He helped me to locate his name on the clip board and informed me what a pleasure it was to be invited.

Every time I looked up, there was another expensively styled guest. They'd spent a lot of money to iron out and hide as many imperfections of aging as possible.

Rose appeared with Candice. Candice was tall and slim. She wore a short gold sequined dress that showed off her Olympic swimmer physique.

"Candice will see to everyone from now on Anna." Rose said. "I need you to accompany me upstairs to schmooze and mingle. Your job is to sell the charity and get people donating."

I followed Rose upstairs. I was dreading the mingling bit. What was I supposed to say, 'Hello my name's Anna can I talk to you?'

Rose thrust a glass of champagne into my hand and steered me across the room to a white haired, grey faced man.

"Hello, I'm Rose" she said, "I'm the founder of WOMAID and this is Anna. Her job in the next five minutes is to wow you with what an amazing charity this is and to persuade you to support us." She smiled once more before disappearing.

"So how do you know Rose?" I asked.

"I don't, it's Robert I know." The grey faced man replied.

"Ah." I nodded and gulped down my champagne. "Have you heard of WOMAID before?"

"No."

"Would you like me to tell you a little about it?"

"I already give a lot to conservation charities in Zimbabwe and Tanzania. I know you work with women in Uganda is there anything else I need to know?"

A waitress came over with a tray of quail egg canapes. He dug into them like a truffle hunting pig. He then held out his glass for a refill.

"So, what do you do?" I asked.

"I'm a risk assessment officer for a large multi-national."

"Oh, that sounds interesting." I said not bothering to lie convincingly. A tall, slim black man with full pink lips and grey flecks along his hair line introduced himself.

"My name's Otim." He said holding out his hand, "And you are?"

"Anna, I work for WOMAID."

"Oh, wonderful." He said, "It looks like I've found exactly the right person to speak to." Mr. Boring excused himself. Otim then said something which I didn't hear over the growing cacophony of social chatter.

"I'm sorry what did you say?"

"I said you have a nice dress and asked you how old you are?'"

"I'm 30."

"Well, I guess everyday must feel like Christmas."

I stood staring at him.

"Don't look so worried, I'm teasing you. I'm a good friend of Robert's and you're very lucky to have him support your cause."

He handed me a cheque for five thousand pounds.

"Spend it wisely," he said looking me directly in the eye.

"Thank you, we will."

He continued staring at me and then asked.

"Have you ever been on an African game hunt?"

I nearly spat my drink out.

"Are you joking, surely no one still travels to Africa to hunt the wildlife?"

"It's big business. Elephants do huge amounts of damage to farmer's crops and kill about 500 people a year. Their unpredictable and very protective of their young. Hunting is a way to cull them, although the success rate is low."

"There must be other ways to keep down numbers?" I asked.

Otim was about to answer when a woman, I assumed to be Otim's wife, called him over to her.

I was stood on my own with the horrible feeling I'd have to launch myself on someone else. I scanned the room. Rose had a dozen people surrounding her and hanging on her every word. Kip was talking to the French guy with the penguin tie. Richard was even redder and talking to a woman of Rose's age. She looked like she was keen to escape. I considered going to rescue her. But, the unhealthy looking Mr. Wilby, approached me. He, once again, managed to hide his teeth when he smiled.

"I hope my little contribution helped in some way, I'm sorry it took a while to get it to you."

"Your contribution?" I said trying to conceal my surprise.

"I transferred £10,000 towards the refuge to the bank details that Richard sent across."

"£10,000, that's very generous of you, thank you."

"Don't mention it; great event by the way."

The gentle sound of metal tapping glass filled the room. Rose asked me to start moving the guest's downstairs.

Dinner was in the main part of the church. The congregation pews had been replaced by tastefully decorated white tables with orange and green floral centre pieces. Kip and I chose not to sit with the guests so we could help collect donations during dinner.

The starter was smoked trout and edible flowers. It was served while a mime artist entertained everyone from the stage. A close-up magician accompanied the main course of mint lamb. He wandered around each table wowing guests with card tricks. Once the main course was cleared, Robert stood on the stage. A hush fell across the room.

"Lords, ladies and gentlemen." Robert announced and a muffled laugh floated across the room. Friends, thank you for coming to our event. This evening, you will hear about a wonderful new charity called WOMAID. My dear friend, Rose Greene, started it."

Robert paused for dramatic effect.

"I know we get many requests to support worthy causes.

This charity is special. WOMAID will supports girls and women in Uganda. They are dealing with crippling poverty as well as suffering abuse. At 15, Semmy has already lost her mother to malaria. Her sister died in childbirth. Her father suffers with an addiction to alcohol that can make him violent. With your help WOMAID will give this poor girl the chance for a better future. With your help tonight we can raise enough money to build a refuge. We will give her a new home. She can live free from fear and harm. With your help, she will get an education. It will give her the power to change her life today and in the future. Please do support this charity tonight. Together, we will make something wonderful happen."

Rose was next on stage. There was a spontaneous round of applause. She looked emotional. She thanked everyone for coming and for the generous gifts the charity had received. The main part of her speech was about her early life in Uganda and her ambition for the charity.

"Lastly," she said. "I want to tell you about Hope. Hope is an orphan. As Robert said we are a charity set up to help women that have been victims of abuse, but we also help their children. If you go on to our website, you can read and see photos of both Semmy and Hope. Supporters of the refuge will get updates and photos. They will also get letters from Semmy. These will show how her life changed thanks to you. Giving to WOMAID is personal. Our priority will be connecting you to the women and children you support."

"Are photos and letters from Semmy really what people want?" Kip asked me.

"It's Richard's idea. He thinks it makes people feel like they're getting something for their money."

"People need to be looking at the real difference their money could make. A photo of a baby and a letter from a 15-year-old girl won't tell them that. It's just a vanity project."

I looked back to Rose on the stage.

"Now, I'd like to hand over to my husband Richard who will be running our auction tonight."

Richard pushed himself up from his table. He moved slowly and deliberately, like a man desperate to seem sober.

"Good evening" he shouted into the microphone.

"Is everyone having a good time?"

He sounded like a wedding DJ. It was embarrassing. In a world where everyone knew exactly the right things to say and how to say them, Richard was out of his depth.

"As Rose mentioned we're delighted to have an auction tonight so if you can just bear with me." Kip and I exchanged a nervous glance. Richard fumbled in his pockets and got out a folded-up piece of paper and his thick black glasses. The wait was painful, Rose grabbed back the microphone. The first prize for tonight's auction is a script from the very first episode of Casualty. It has been signed by all the cast."

Richard took back the microphone.

"Will anyone start the bidding at £50?" For a second, I panicked that no one would bid. I searched the room for anyone who would save the day and then Robert's hand went up.

"Can anyone give me £100?" Another hand up and so on and so forth until the script reached a respectable £500.

The bidding continued and I felt myself holding my breath for every lot. A week in Antigua for 12 people with a pool sold for £15,000. The six-bedroom property in Tuscany with a wine tour sold for £12,000. The final auction prize was a week in Uganda. It included a trip to see the gorillas, three nights in Masindi, and the chance to meet Semmy and Hope at the new refuge. This prize sold for £15,000 and it was so popular they auctioned it twice making £30,000.

"Thank you for bidding so generously," Rose said. "You've truly helped us to make a remarkable difference to the women WOMAID will support. There are plenty of wonderful prizes to bid for in the silent auction. We have also placed gold envelopes on the tables if you wished to donate to the refuge further. The delightful Anna and my nephew Kip will come around to collect these. Please enjoy the rest of your evening and thank you once again."

Rose walked off stage. Richard should have followed her but instead he picked up the microphone.

"Before I go, I hope you won't mind indulging me for a minute more." He had his hand across his chest like he was pledging allegiance.

"Like Rose, I hope you enjoy the rest of the night. Enjoy another drink and eat another homemade chocolate. Then ask yourself, 'have you given all you can?' If you have, then thank you. But -" He paused.

"If you haven't then dig deeper. Please give us the money you're going to waste on all those fancy lunches you have planned. What about the money for your London flat refurbishments. Maybe you could give us a small fraction of that cost. Perhaps even forego one day of Après Ski next time you pop across to Verbier."

Rose clambered back on stage and ripped the microphone from Richard's hand.

"Thank you once again." She said her smile smothering

136

how mortified she was. She dragged her drunk and embarrassing husband from the stage.

It was past midnight when we got in the taxi to drive home. Rose sat in the front leaving Richard in the back between Kip and me.

"How could you embarrass me by asking our friends for money like that?"

"Oh, am I not good enough for your friends, is that it?"

"My friends have donated over £100,000 in auction prizes and donations. When you tell them to give us more money. Money they'd spend on lunch, it's incredibly embarrassing."

"Well perhaps next time you should do these events without me. I'm sure your darling nephew would be only too happy to step in." Richard said, his words slurred.

"Maybe I should, it would save me from having to spend the end of the evening apologizing for you."

A horrible silence filled the taxi the entire journey back to Tunbridge Wells. At Helen's I got out and Kip jumped out with me.

"I'm going to walk from here." He said to Rose.

"Really, whatever for?"

"I could do with some fresh air."

Kip closed the car door, and we watched as the taxi disappeared out of sight.

"Well, that was a head fuck of a car journey home."

"Do you want to come in for a drink?"

"Thanks, but I'd better start walking back; I've got an early flight in the morning."

"You're flying back so soon?"

"I've got a lot to do for the start of the season. You

should come out for a holiday, I'll put you up and you can have all your food and drink at the bar. All you'd need is money for your flight and lift pass."

I laughed.

"I'm serious Anna."

"I don't ski."

"Then I'll teach you."

Kip leant forward and kissed me on my cheek. With his tired eyes all bleary from champagne and his waxed hair now ruffled and messy he looked cute.

"I'll see you in the Alps." He said as if it was as simple as going to the corner shop to get milk.

THIRTY-ONE
SEMMY

Semmy came down for breakfast. Margaret was already at the kitchen table reading the paper and drinking earl grey tea.

"Richard called to say that the fundraising dinner was a success. It sounds like they've raised enough money to complete the refuge."

"That's good." Semmy said.

"I was thinking," Margaret continued, "we should ask Sydney and his parents over for dinner next week."

"Sydney and his parents?"

"Yes, don't you think it would be nice. Besides, I'd like to get to know them. It always pays to extend your network in a small town where you have a new business. My new hotel will rely on local recommendations. Who better than Sydney's parents? A member of the local constabulary and a civil servant."

The following day, when Margaret dropped Semmy at school, she reminded her of the dinner invite. At lunchtime Semmy waited for Sydney in the usual spot underneath the tree by the playing fields. She wondered if things would be different between them now. In her mind, something had changed between them, but she had no idea if he felt the same way. He appeared, his smile as wide and welcoming as ever.

"I had fun at the play," Semmy said. "I'm glad you won."

Sydney smiled. "We both won". He said. "I was thinking about the prize. You could take it if you would like to go."

Semmy shook her head. "I don't want to be an actor, not like you. Besides, you wrote the play and did most of the acting, I did very little."

They ate their lunch while watching boys kicking a football into two goals marked by stones.

"Margaret wanted me to ask if you and your family would like to come to dinner."

"Dinner?"

"If you wanted."

"Why?" Sydney looked serious.

"I don't know, she thought it would be nice. She's still quite new to Masindi and I think it would be a good way for her to meet more people."

"Please thank Margaret for the invitation, I'm afraid my family and I wouldn't be able to come."

"But you don't know when it will be?"

"It doesn't matter. My father is always too busy with work, and my mother is not that keen on socializing without him."

"You could come," Semmy said.

"I have my studies and my mother is already annoyed that the play has distracted me. She won't be okay with me coming to yours."

"Because you are with me or you're not studying?" Semmy asked.

"I'm sorry."

It was the way Sydney said he was sorry that made Semmy feel sad. On the way home she told Margaret what he'd said.

"Are we beneath them?"

"I think they're just busy."

"We're all busy," Margaret said, looking harassed. "Now that Richard and Rose have raised all that money, they'll be lots to do in overseeing the building of the new refuge. On top of that I have you and Hope to run round after, and I have my own hotel to keep on top of. I really can't see that Sydney's parents are so busy they can't come for dinner."

"Shall I ask him again?" Semmy said, hoping to appease Margaret.

"No, don't. You have exams in a few weeks, and they're all you should be thinking about. If Sydney and his family don't wish to socialise with us, then it's their loss."

Semmy didn't feel the same. For her, it felt like a big loss, as Sydney was the only friend she had.

THIRTY-TWO
ANNA

Through the cold and dark mornings of December, my mind wandered to Kip's offer of a week's holiday in the Alps. He had messaged me a few times to ask how things were going at the charity. He always added a line asking if I'd booked my flight. I had used excuses about work.

The truth was I was scared I'd embarrass myself. I thought Kip and his friends would be way cooler than me. I wasn't a naturally sporting person and was sure skiing would be impossible. Besides, I hardly new him, what would we talk about for a whole week?

I had started flat hunting. I'd concluded that living without Helen would boost my self-esteem. The issue was that doing anything on one salary was a nightmare. I couldn't face renting a room with a house full of strangers.

"I spoke to Mum last night." Helen said as we drank coffee in her white kitchen.

"How is she?"

"Fine; you know what she's like. She says you never call. It wouldn't hurt to check in with them, would it? Anyway, they're coming over for Christmas and wanted to check if you'll be here?"

"Of course, where else will I be?"

"I didn't want to assume that's all." Helen had that sympathetic smile again. "We'll have a good time."

"No, we won't. It will be the same as it is every year.

Dad will drink himself to sleep in the armchair while Mum hogs the TV and insists on our annual game of scrabble. There will be the annual argument. It will be between you and Mum over something as small as when to start cooking the turkey. By Boxing Day, we'll all feel like killing each other."

Helen picked up her phone and started sending a text message. I watched my nephews open their Pokemon chocolate advent calendars.

"I know this year's been tough." Helen said. "We all want you to be happy, that's all. Since the breakup with Mark, you don't do anything. You go to work, come home again, watch TV and go to bed. You need to start going out and seeing your friends."

Helen looked over at Ben and Lewis. They had opened half the doors on their calendars, and their faces were covered in chocolate.

"BOYS; why have you done that?" Helen shouted. "Off you go and clean your faces and wash your hands. I'll need to buy another advent calendar for you both now."

When my nephews had disappeared to the bathroom Helen turned her attention back on me.

"I worry about you."

"I'm fine."

"Then why do you seem so sad? Don't you want to see your friends?"

"Most of them are planning weddings or having kids. I don't find those things interesting. So, I'd rather stay out of wedding dress or cloth nappy conversations."

Helen looked at me like she was going to cry.

"I'm going skiing," I announced to demonstrate I wasn't

completely useless.

"What?"

"Kip invited me to France. I need to save the money for my flight, and lift pass and then I'm off."

"But you've never skied?"

"So, I'll learn."

"Are you serious?"

"Yes, why?"

"It's so unlike you to go skiing."

"You said I need to get out."

"Let Tim and me pay for your flight; it can be your Christmas present from us."

"Thanks, but that's not why I mentioned it."

"I know, but we'd like to and if Kip's kind enough to look after you."

I left the house and arrived at the office irritated. Rose was at her desk, wrapped in her pale pink pashmina. Even though she was wearing her reading glasses, her face was inches from the computer screen. Richard was in his office.

"Whatever is the matter?" She asked.

"Nothing, I'm fine," I said, turning my attention to my computer screen. My emails consisted of a graduate looking for work experience. Three cold-calling emails and a woman in Cardiff, who had 12 boxes of books she wanted to donate. I wrote back that the cost of postage to us and then out to Uganda could be better spent on buying books in country.

"You don't look fine?" Rose said.

"It's my sister. I told her I was thinking of going to see Kip for a ski holiday."

"That's exciting," Rose looked suddenly more animated.

"Well, I only said I would go to stop her worrying about

me. If you need me here, I can stay."

"Nonsense, a holiday will do you good."

Richard strolled in. "Who's having a holiday?"

"Anna's going to see Kip."

"Is she?" He said as though there must be more to me going to see Kip than a free ski holiday. "You need to watch him," Richard said, winking at me as if we were friends. I ignored him and turned my attention to sending my email to the Cardiff woman.

"Margaret's been on the phone again this morning," Rose said, changing the subject. "Albert has been to the house asking for money. They've started locking the side gate, and if Margaret sees him, she runs out, threatening to call the police. The poor man has lost his wife and daughter; he's got no money, and moreover, he has Margaret chasing him down the street."

"I'll give her a call," Richard said, "Check everything is okay."

"Will you ask her what's going on with the building of the refuge? We sent the first batch of money to the contractors months ago. Now they've had the full amount. I want to make sure she's watching them for us. I haven't heard a single word about what's going on, and every time I ask her, she tells me I need to be patient. If you ask me, she's too caught up with her own hotel to oversee the refuge."

"I've told you I'd be more than happy to go out there and see what's happening?"

"Now, you're overreacting. You don't need to go over there; just speak to Margaret. Ask her to send us some photos and a few updates, that's all we need."

"I want to go. Margaret shouldn't have to deal with

Albert on her own; I can go and see him and find out if there's anything we can do to help. While I'm there, I'll visit the contractors and see what's happening with the refuge."

"Why don't we both go?" Rose said smiling. "It could be like a second honeymoon."

"I'm not sure we should all go away at the same time," Richard said. "Besides, I was thinking of this as a quick trip. You and I could go for a longer stay in January as a holiday."

Rose smiled. "Okay. One week only, though. I want you home by Christmas."

"Of course," Richard said, smiling. "I wouldn't want to be anywhere else."

THIRTY-THREE
SEMMY

Richard's return to Uganda was not welcome by everyone. He arrived with beads of sweat lining his bald head, red-faced and dressed in shorts. Margaret ran down the stairs to greet him.

"You should have called." She shrieked embracing him.

"I'm quite capable of getting a hire car and driving myself." He said, taking out his handkerchief to mop his forehead. "Besides, it's too hot to have you running around after me."

"It's only going to get hotter." Margaret's said playfully touching Richard's cheek. "Don't you remember it was this time of year when we were clearing the weeds from the grounds of my hotel. You'd not long arrived, and you kept getting me to soak you with the hose to cool you down."

Richard laughed. "That seems a long time ago."

"They say time flies when you're having fun."

"And are you?" Richard asked.

"I wouldn't exactly call it fun spending time with a teenage girl, a newborn baby, and the housekeeper. I feel like I'm going mad half the time. I'm pleased you're here."

"You're doing a great job."

"Am I? That's not what Rose thinks."

"Nonsense."

"She called me yesterday to tell me that you were coming

out to check on the building of the refuge. I could tell by the tone of her voice she's worried I'm not keeping on top of things. To be honest, I hardly have time to watch my own hotel. I'm busy taking Semmy to school, managing Edna, and helping with the baby. When we agreed, I'd come and stay, looking after a newborn was never part of the deal."

"I know Margaret, and we're very grateful for all you are doing. You know what Rose can be like."

"Neurotic, precious, and demanding."

"She's anxious, that's all."

"How's married life suiting you? Is it all you had thought it would be? You look tired. Didn't you sleep on the plane?"

"I had the misfortune of sitting next to an eight-foot Ghanaian man. He kept telling me that the only way to get Africans to adopt new technology was to make it cool. By the end of the flight, if he'd said "cool" one more time, I would have throttled him."

Richard raised his eyes to the top of the stairs, where Semmy was standing.

"Are you hiding from me?" He joked. "Why aren't you at school?"

"I'm in the middle of my exams."

"Exams, I see. Well, are you going to come down and say hello to me?"

Semmy walked down the stairs and Richard pulled her towards him for a hug. She hated the feel of his hot and clammy arms against her skin. Extracting herself she turned her attention to Margaret.

"You haven't forgotten that you're driving me to school for my exam today, have you?" Semmy said.

"Give me a moment, Semmy. I want to catch up with

Richard."

"How long are you staying?"

"A week, maybe longer."

"Are you staying at my place again?"

"That would be very nice, thank you." He smiled. "Where's Hope?" Richard asked, heading to the kitchen. Edna was sat at the table with a sleeping Hope on her shoulder.

"Wow, she's grown," he said, taking her from Edna.

"You never struck me as the paternal type," Margaret said.

"Just because I never had children, it didn't mean I didn't want them."

"Can we go?" Semmy pleaded as the time disappeared.

"YES," Margaret snapped. She picked up the keys from the kitchen table and marched out to the jeep. For the entire journey Margaret talked about Richard.

"Don't you think he looks tired?" She asked Semmy who shrugged her shoulders. "It's Rose, she expects too much of him. That is the problem with marrying a woman like her. She doesn't care about what Richard wants as long as she's happy. I suspect their marriage isn't happy. He probably volunteered to come and see us to get a week of peace and quiet."

Semmy arrived at school relieved to leave Margaret's talk of Richard. Inside her class all the other children were seated whilst exam papers were being placed in front of them.

"You're late." Semmy's teacher scolded her.

"Sorry, I had to wait for my guardian to bring me."

For the next hour, Semmy tried to think of nothing but the questions in front of her. Margaret returned to collect her with Richard in the passenger seat with Hope on his lap.

"Why does Edna not have Hope?" Semmy asked.

"We gave her the rest of the day off. Anyway, never mind that, how was the exam?"

"Fine."

"Only fine," Richard said, turning to look at Semmy. "We are expecting a lot from you in these exams."

Semmy sat in the back, watching Richard play with Hope, and she had the weirdest thought. Did Lydia have a reason to hate Richard as much as she did? What if Lydia knew something about him that she had never told her?

THIRTY-FOUR
ANNA

Kip had booked me a seat on a minibus from Chambéry airport to the French mountain resort of Alpe d'Huez. It was 7 pm on a Saturday evening. As we began the climb up the mountain our young driver hurtled around each corkscrew corner. He drove as if we were in the Michael Caine film, "The Italian Job". The possibility that we could skid off the road to our death at any second scared and exhilarated me. The piles of snow accumulated on the side of the road would offer nothing in the way of a barrier.

As we ascended closer to the resort, I spotted tiny beacons of light coming from a couple of chalets. They looked inviting. For a moment, the sight banished the nagging voice in my head that told me coming to the Alps was a terrible idea.

I'd spent countless hours considering every eventuality of what could go wrong. This included breaking my neck or being swept up in an avalanche and being buried alive. There was also the potential for personal humiliation such as falling arse over tit the minute I arrived. Or I could be a spectacularly terrible skier. I expected both things would be the case.

The minibus stopped. Our driver, a young guy with blonde hair poking out from his red beanie, turned around to tell me it was my stop. I looked out of the window. I saw a huge bar with a wooden terrace. It had orange-striped outdoor heaters and a graffiti sign with "Shack 83" on it.

I got outside and waited as Blondie located my black case from the underneath storage.

"Are you going to be all right from here?" He asked, sensing my inexperience in being in a ski resort.

"Yes, thanks," I said, trying to sound confident.

I walked towards the bar, dragging my case behind me. All I could see were men who looked like Kip. They had bushy beards and woollen hats. The girls all had long hair and bright padded jackets. I was wearing black ankle boots and a duffle coat. I felt about as cool as Paddington bloody bear. 'Shit', this was a bad idea.

I pulled open the bar door. The body warmth of sixty or more people poured out with the thumping beat of techno music. Everyone had the same goggle-marked tanned face. I made my way to the bar and found Kip standing behind it. He was chatting to a cute blonde girl in a bright yellow knit headband who had ordered six tequila shots.

"You made it." He said whilst keeping his attention on the tequilas.

I imagined Kip's bar as a quaint wooden chalet. I had pictured Swedish looking men there drinking tankards of honey-coloured ale. I hadn't imagined Ibiza in the Alps.

"Hi," I said, with a nervous grin stuck to my face.

"This is my mate, Alex." Kip said, pulling his mate over by the back of his jumper. Alex was tall and looked more like an accountant than a ski bum, with his short brown hair and glasses.

"Anything you want, at any time, ask Alex or me." Kip said, smiling.

"Thanks, it's a cool bar," I shouted, struggling to make

myself heard over the music.

"I'm glad you like it. Come, I'll take you to see your apartment, you can dump your stuff, and then we'll come back for a few drinks."

I followed Kip out. Despite the subzero cold, he wore a T-shirt and his woollen, green hat. The apartment block was two streets away from the bar. It smelled of window cleaner, socks, and pot noodles.

"My friend's back in the UK for a week," Kip said. "You'll be staying in her apartment: it's quieter than the bar, and it will feel more like a holiday."

My eyes scanned the apartment. It was the size of Helen's garage. It had a tiny kitchenette, three-foot living space, a bed in the hall, and the tiniest bathroom.

"I realise it's not plush, but you'll have all your meals with me at the bar, and so you'll only sleep here."

"It's great, thank you."

"I didn't think you would come."

"I'm trying to push myself out of my comfort zone."

"I can arrange to do that." Kip had a mischievous smile as he said this, which allayed my fears about coming.

We headed back to the bar. Kip poured me shots all night. At 8 a.m. the next morning, I was expecting a hellish hangover. But amazingly, I felt fine.

"It's the mountain air." Kip told me. "You don't get the same hangover up here."

Kip was wearing a pair of cobalt blue ski pants with a bright yellow ski jacket. I put on the ski outfit I'd borrowed from Helen's friend Sarah, which was white with gold buttons and a fur trim. Think of footballers' wives, but on a TK Maxx budget.

"So, you've never skied before."

"I never liked the idea of strapping myself into two pieces of wood and sliding down a mountain. I didn't even like sledging as a kid."

Kip laughed.

We went to the ski hire shop to hire me a pair of skis, boots and a helmet. We then headed up to the nursery slope.

"Now use me to balance." Kips said once I had the skis on. "We'll traverse across the slope, taking it nice and easy." I leaned into him; I hadn't imagined that learning to ski would involve quite as much physical contact.

"Remember, you are making a pizza slice," Kip said, pushing my legs into the shape of a V and turning my boots in.

After an hour, my thighs burned. Sweat drenched me. I could barely ski as three-year-olds zipped past me. Despite this, I loved it. The wide expanse of blue sky, with the air crisp and fresh. The majestic mountains that surrounded us. The warming heat of the morning sun. I'd never felt more alive.

We skied every day, and miraculously, I improved. I went from the gentle beginner's area to a red run from the top of the mountain. The views up there were breathtaking. Kip was great fun. He spent every day teaching me to ski. Every night, I'd sit at his bar, smelling of deep heat as he poured me drinks and brought me nachos.

On my penultimate night, Kip took the night off work so that he could take me out for dinner.

"You haven't experienced the Alps until you've been to a traditional restaurant."

I put on my jeans and a pink cashmere jumper, and we

walked to a small French restaurant on the outskirts of the village.

"This is typical French food," Kip said as we walked into a small, wooden restaurant. A pair of old wooden skis hung on the wall. A large, stuffed squirrel with two pointy teeth stared down at us from a shelf.

"It's a marmot, they're the Alpe d'Huez mascot." Kip said. "They live in the mountains here, don't worry; you rarely see them."

The waiter host showed us to a corner table for two, and the low lights created an intimate and romantic atmosphere.

"Bonsoir, je vous en prie." The waiter said. He was a tall, reed like man with a large forehead and was wearing a knitted tie. He handed us the menu, and then he brought over a jug of tap water.

"This is quite some place."

"You must experience the more authentic side of the Alps. We should have the local specialty of fondue with a bottle of Savoie wine."

We ordered. I noticed that Kip had abandoned his hoodie and was wearing a smart, dark blue shirt. He had brushed his hair and trimmed his beard.

"Are you converted? Is skiing to become your new winter sport?"

"I don't know, ask me when I can walk again." I said, smiling. "It's been fun, and I can honestly say I'd never have skied if you hadn't invited me out here."

"Why?"

"Money, I suppose, and if you've never done something, you don't know what you're missing." The waiter returned with the wine.

"I can see why you love this place so much."

"Yes, it gets under your skin." He raised his glass. "To skiing and to new adventures."

On the way back to Kip's bar, it started to snow. Flakes so huge and fluffy you could eat them from the back of your hand. It was so quiet that all I could hear was the soft padding sound of our boots in the snow. We pulled down our hats as our faces began to freeze, and Kip linked his arm through mine. It was cute, and as we walked back, I smiled to myself. 'How did a week skiing end up being one of the best holidays I'd ever had?'

We took a slight detour to walk past the local nightclub. A bouncer stood outside. We could hear faint European dance tracks.

"It's a terrible venue. But you can't come to Alpe d'Huez without entering a truly trashy club like the Igloo."

Kip dragged me over to the front door. We paid ten euros and got our hands stamped before going inside. Black paint covered the walls, and there was a red vinyl floor. Green lasers bounced off two glitter balls hanging from the ceiling. A handful of people were dancing. Most still wore their ski clothes. Four men of my dad's age sat at the bar. They had wrinkled mountain skin, tight blue jeans, and flannel shirts. Kip ordered two shots of flaming sambuca. We danced until closing time at 3 a.m. When we staggered back to Kip's, we found the front door locked, and Alex had gone to bed.

"Come in for one last drink?" Kip pulled out the contents of his pockets in search of his keys. He unlocked the front door and stumbled inside. He fell into a table and knocked two bar stalls crashing to the floor.

"Get yourself a drink, I need to pee." He said waving

towards the bar. I poured a whisky for Kip and a rum for me. As I bent down to get a bottle of Coke from the fridge, Kip came back in and started to kiss the back of my neck.

"The final part of any good ski holiday has to be a wild night of sex." Kip was smiling.

"Wild you say?" I laughed teasingly.

"I will do my best."

His kiss was firm and sexy. He unbuttoned my coat and pulled off my pink cashmere sweater. I pulled off his shirt and ran my hand across his toned, sparsely haired chest. He lifted me up, and I wrapped my legs around him as he carried me downstairs. In his room, there was a double futon in the middle of the floor, and there were clothes scattered everywhere. He lay me down on the bed and turned on a small bedside lamp. The room smelled of Kip's aftershave and ski wax. We undressed each other in the frantic way people do when they've been thinking about having sex all night.

"What happens if I start liking you?" I asked as he removed my bra.

"Don't." Was all he said before kissing me again.

THIRTY-FIVE
SEMMY

The day after Semmy's final exam, Margaret woke her up at 6 a.m.

"Morning Semmy." She said marching into her room and opening the curtains.

"It's time to get up. Richard and I are taking you, Hope, and Edna, on a special day out."

A day out with Richard and Margaret was not something Semmy would ever describe as special. She wanted to sleep in peace, so she rolled over, hoping Margaret would disappear.

"Up you get," Margaret said, pulling the bed sheet from Semmy.

Hope slept in her cot at the end of Semmy's bed, and she could hear her gurgling happily as Margaret lifted her up.

"Where are we going?"

"Richard's taking us all on a safari. Have you ever been on a safari before?"

Semmy didn't answer. Did Margaret really expect that her family had ever had the money to afford the fees to go on a safari.

"We'll drive to the park this morning, and then this afternoon we're going to visit the site of the new refuge. Richard thought it would be marvelous to have a photo of you and Hope by your new home as it's being built."

It was too early for Semmy to begin protesting. Her plan was still to take Hope and go back home to her father. She had no intention of moving into a refuge.

"Today is also a chance to celebrate the end of your exams."

Semmy dragged herself out of bed and went into the kitchen. Richard was sat at the kitchen table. He wore camel-coloured shorts, along with a matching cotton waistcoat and safari hat. Semmy thought he looked ridiculous and wondered if this was what all white men wore when they went on safari.

"Big day." Richard said pouring himself a coffee. "A safari, and then we'll drive over to get a first look at the new refuge."

Semmy forced a smile while Edna ran around getting all the supplies of food, nappies, and milk for Hope.

An hour later, they reached the gates of the safari park. The first sight of a majestic giraffe was of it peering down at their jeep. It dispelled all her teenage brooding. She couldn't believe how calm the giraffes were. A line of vehicles drove past them, packed with tourists all straining to take photos.

"I'm getting out to take pictures," Richard announced. They'd reached a clearing where a few giraffes were eating leaves.

"Are you sure?" Margaret said. "These are wild animals; you can't start walking around them."

"I always do this on safari. It's the only way to get a real feel for it."

Richard left the driver's door wide open, and so Margaret leaned across and closed it.

"The man thinks he's Tarzan." Margaret said, looking the happiest she had been in months. Semmy watched Richard march off towards the animals. She thought he looked a lot less like Tarzan and more like a stupid white man who would get himself killed. A giraffe walked over to the jeep, taking six graceful strides, and he was peering down at them all. Richard ran back, red-faced, with his bald head covered in beads of sweat.

"We should get a photo of Semmy with the giraffes. It would look great on the website."

They coaxed Semmy out of the jeep. They told her to smile while Richard took photos of her alone. Then, he took photos of her with Margaret and with Hope.

A jeep designed for safaris, with the roof down, pulled up. A Ugandan guide in uniform was driving. A white man a decade younger than Richard stood with his binoculars next to his wife.

"Great day for a safari, isn't it?" Richard said.

"Perfect, absolutely perfect; seen much?"

"Not yet, we've only just started."

"We saw a fantastic pride of lions first thing, really something." The man looked at Semmy, Margaret, and Edna as though trying to work out the family dynamic.

"Family Day out?" He asked.

"Yes, something like that. My wife and I started a charity recently for vulnerable young girls. Semmy here has come such a long way since we first met and has just completed her exams. We thought it would be nice to treat her." Richard said, grinning with pride.

"Good for you. We have our own charity project that we are involved in. You may have heard of it, it's called the 'Young Future's Programme.'

The man started to deliver a speech about the charity that he must have repeated a hundred times. He finished by explaining the reason they started the charity was to teach their own children how lucky they were. Semmy glanced at his teenagers in the back. A boy and a girl, around her age, staring at their mobile phones. She wondered if starting a charity gave them any idea of how comfortable their lives were.

They said their goodbyes and set off again. For the next two hours, they drove around. They spotted elephants, buffaloes, zebras, and antelopes.

"Next stop the WOMAID refuge." Richard said as Margaret put the coordinates into the car's sat nav and they set off.

"It shouldn't be that difficult to spot a new building of this size," Richard said. They drove past nothing but miles and miles of green fields, trees, and the odd village of huts. Eventually, they came to a road where there was a small trading centre. It had a few concrete shops, one of which sold decorators' paint.

"This is right," Margaret said. "I remember thinking about how handy it would be to have a paint shop around the corner from the refuge."

Richard turned off the main road and onto a smaller track, which was just wide enough for the jeep. They passed people working in the fields. They continued along a bumpy track that knocked Edna and Semmy together on the back seat. A large clearing was the first thing they spotted, with a hole in the ground and a small pile of bricks.

"I don't understand," Margaret said. The mood in the jeep turning from excited anticipation to confusion.

"Where's the building?" Richard stopped the jeep and yanked up the handbrake. "It's supposed to be here."

Richard got out of the jeep, slamming the door so hard behind him that the whole vehicle shook. Margaret followed him out, while Semmy and Edna watched from the back of the jeep. Richard was waving his arms around and shouting, and Margaret looked as if she were crying. The ride home was silent. Semmy wondered what this would mean for their new charity.

THIRTY-SIX
ANNA

A glimpse of daylight peeked through Kip's bedroom, where the blind was an inch too short for the window. I hadn't slept with anyone but Mark for ten years. I thought it would feel weird, and I'd be out of practice. But it was nice. More than nice, it was spontaneous, passionate, and unexpected. I wrapped the duvet around me, opened my eyes, to find that Kip had already left.

I heard a noise from the bar upstairs, so I pulled on my jeans and sweater, expecting to find Kip. I found Alex instead, who was on his hands and knees under the bar, changing a beer pump.

"Kip's gone to the cash and carry to pick up some stock for later." He said. "I was to tell you to help yourself to coffee, toast, or anything else you desire." He looked under his arm at me and smiled.

"Thanks, I don't think I can stomach food right now."

I picked up my coat, which someone had folded and placed on the bar. Despite my headache and feelings of nausea, I couldn't stop smiling. I walked back to the apartment, and the sun was already shining. Families clanked past me in ski boots, with their skis balanced on their shoulders. Their well-rested, healthy, and wholesome faces couldn't be more of a contrast to how I was feeling.

Back at the apartment, I closed the curtains and lay down on the bed and fell back to sleep. By lunchtime, there was still no message from Kip, so I put on my ski gear and headed out solo to the slopes. My legs were too tired to ski, so I spent the afternoon in a café drinking coffee. There was still no message. I was starting to think Kip was ignoring me. I didn't expect him to be one of those guys that loses all interest in a girl once they'd had sex.

At 7pm I went to the bar; Alex was there, and a handful of seasonaires, but no Kip. I sat and drank a couple of beers and ate a plate of nachos. At 10pm I grabbed my coat and was leaving when Kip appeared.

"You're not going, are you?" He asked, following me outside.

"It's late, and I have an early flight in the morning. Listen, thank you for everything this week, for teaching me to ski, and for the meals and stuff."

"I liked you being here." Kip said.

A silence fell between us.

"I like you; you know that don't you?" He was staring at me. I didn't know what he expected of me, did he want me to declare that I liked him too. His phone rang, saving me from having to say anything.

"It's Rose." He said looking at his screen. "She's been trying to call me all day; I need to take it."

He kissed the side of my cheek and then turned away and began to speak to Rose. I wandered back to the apartment, feeling a pang of sadness that the holiday and any romance was over. I was packing the last of my things when there was a knock at the apartment door, and Kip was standing there.

"It's gone." Was all he said.

"What's gone?"

"The money raised for the refuge. Rose said that Richard drove to the site of the new refuge. There was nothing there but a pile of bricks. Now, they can't reach the builders."

"This doesn't make sense."

"Of course it makes sense. Richard screwed up, which I always knew he would."

I want to cry. All that money, all the effort we'd put into fundraising.

"How's Rose?

"Devastated; the Ugandan police have told Richard that these kinds of scams are not uncommon. I imagine they're more likely to happen when you leave an idiot like him in charge."

"So, what happens now?"

"I don't know." Kip looked exhausted; he sat down on the corner of my bed. "When you get back to the office, try to find out what you can about this. I can tell Rose is rattled, but she won't that accept Richard is to blame."

"You really think he had something to do with this?"

"I don't know what to think, but if he has, we need to find a way to prove it."

THIRTY-SEVEN
SEMMY

In the days following the visit to the refuge, Semmy did her best to keep out of Richard's way. He arrived at the house every day looking harassed. He complained to Margaret that the contractors had disappeared, and no one would help him. Margaret tried to reassure him that everything would be all right, but Semmy couldn't see how. She wondered if Rose and Richard would give up on the charity now.

Sydney's father, George, was a police officer in Masindi. He came to the house to investigate the missing money and find out more about the contractors. Sydney and George shared the same big white teeth and easy-going disposition. George wore his police uniform. A khaki short-sleeved shirt with the Ugandan flag on the left sleeve, cotton trousers of the same colour, and a black beret.

They sat in the kitchen with Margaret and Richard on one side of the table and George on the other. Semmy loitered by the door so she could hear.

"How did you come to appoint the contractors?" George asked.

"An electrician that was working at Margaret's hotel recommended them to us." Richard said. "They were called Seyma Contractors, and I met the owner, Patrick, and asked him to provide a quote. He seemed to know what he was doing, and so we signed a contract with him." Richard handed George the paperwork. It had the logo of the construction company and an itemized quote.

"I see, and you say that you've since tried to contact Patrick, but the phone number is not in service?"

"Correct."

"What about the electrician, the man who first gave you the contact?"

"I can't reach him either, he is no longer working at Margaret's hotel."

"Did you transfer all of the money for the build to them?"

"At the end of November. They had asked for payment in full. They lacked the funds to buy the materials and hire the tradespeople without all the money up front."

George shook his head.

"It's not an unfamiliar tale, and the problem is that there's very little we can do. I have been in with the Bank to ask about the account where you transferred the money. They tell me that the account for Seyma Contractors has had all funds withdrawn and is now closed. I'm afraid you have been a victim of a scam, and I would suspect the men involved have left the area. I wouldn't want to give you false hope."

Richard hit his fist against the table.

"Are you telling me we just give up on ever finding the men who did this? Are you looking for money? Is that it? Is it a bribe you're after?"

Semmy expected George to be offended at Richard's outburst. Instead, he listened and then calmly replied. "That's not it. I don't want your money; I am merely telling you that these things happen. In the future, you should ensure your contractors have a good track record. Also, find a local businessperson to act as an intermediary for you."

"We understand." Margaret said, smiling. Richard looked like he was going to implode. George stood to leave and looked across the room at Semmy.

"You must be Sydney's friend from school. Will you be continuing your studies at Masindi Secondary School when the new term starts?"

Semmy nodded.

"Sydney will be pleased. He enjoyed doing the play with you. Despite my concerns, he plans to keep acting. Teenagers can be very headstrong.'"

He looked to Richard. "I will see myself out."

THIRTY-EIGHT
ANNA

I arrived back in the UK with Christmas nipping at my heels like a badly trained terrier. A man carrying Brussels sprouts wrapping paper knocked into me as I walked to the office. I resisted the urge to scream at him. I arrived at work with as much Christmas spirit as a turkey on steroids.

I found Rose sitting at her desk. She wore a black turtleneck top, her hair tied back, and barely any makeup. Her face looked fraught and worried. She looked old.

"Darling, you're back." She said, removing her reading glasses.

I sat down at my desk.

"Is there any news from Richard?"

"They haven't found the contractors if that's what you mean? Richard's still searching for them, and before you say a word, I'm well aware that Kip suspects foul play."

"He's worried about you, that's all."

"I'm not the one he needs to worry about. It's those girls, that young baby, and all the other young women we could have helped." Rose's voice sounded strained and bitter.

"The police have informed Richard that the bank account we sent the money to is closed."

Rose shook her head from side to side.

"Kip was right; what do two old codgers like Richard, and I know about starting a charity?"

"They might still find them."

"It's unlikely. Richard's staying in Uganda, and he may be there for Christmas, which will be fun for me. It's his decision. If he prefers to be out there with Margaret, running around like a headless chicken, well that's up to him."

Rose looked at me with her bloodshot eyes.

"Anyway, tell me, how was the holiday? Did Kip look after you?"

"Yes."

Rose stared at me.

"And?"

"And what?"

"Well, how was the skiing?"

"I was okay; I wouldn't say I was a natural."

Rose continued staring at me as if she were peering into my soul. I recited the usual post-holiday nuggets of information. I commented on the food and the days we spent skiing. I even talked about the bloody weather.

"Did you sleep with him?" she asked. I could tell Rose would not be fobbed off by a lie.

"Once." I said not looking at her.

"And?"

"It was a mistake."

"My God, you young people sure know how to shit one another." She said and I smiled, it wasn't a turn of phrase I was familiar with.

"Let me speak to him." Rose suggested.

"No, please don't it would be way too embarrassing if you asked him about it. There is nothing to say; we were drunk, and it was a holiday thing."

"I'm sorry."

"What for?"

"If Kip has not treated you as gentlemanly as he should have, I am, in part, responsible. I should have raised him to act better."

"He's a grown man. He could act better if he wanted to."

"I suppose. We all act foolishly sometimes; men of Kip's age especially."

Rose looked content to let the conversation drop for now.

"Have you told Robert or any of your friends what has happened?" I asked.

"Not yet, I've told no one. I can't face it. I am being a total coward, as so many of mine and Robert's friends have invested in this charity. I worry about how he'll take the news. Would you mind coming with me to see him?"

"Of course not."

Rose smiled. "I find myself relying on you a lot more than I should, and I realise a lot more than we pay you for."

THIRTY-NINE
SEMMY

Semmy often thought about her father and wondered how he was coping. She'd overheard Margaret and Edna talking in the kitchen one day after school. It sounded as if he'd been at the house again, drunk and looking for money.

"Will you take me back home soon?" Semmy asked. "I'd love for my father to meet Hope, and I can check that he's okay. He must be worried about me."

"One day soon I will take you," Margaret said. "I've got too much on now with my hotel to be driving out to your village and dealing with your drunk father."

A few days before Christmas, Richard and Margaret had returned from another trip. They told her that they had been searching for the contractors again. Semmy could tell they had been drinking. They sat outside on the garden furniture where she and Hope were sitting.

"Could I go home before Christmas to see my father and check that he's okay," Semmy said as soon as they'd sat down.

"Not this again, Semmy," Margaret said. "You must stop going on about this. I have told you I will take you and let that be the end of it."

Her voice had been so harsh and dismissive that Semmy could not hold back her tears.

"What are you crying for?" Margaret said. "I'm not

saying we won't take you, just not today. You know what we've been going through."

Semmy tried to stop herself from crying and didn't want to be childish, but it was so frustrating. Every time she asked, there was always a reason not to take her.

"I worry about him that's all. It will be Christmas soon, and he's all alone. I want to know that he's okay."

"No news is good news," Margaret said.

"Would it make you feel better if I drove over there this afternoon to check on him?" Richard asked, his voice calmer and kinder than Margaret's.

"Yes." Semmy said, jumping up, she could have hugged him, she was so happy. "Hope and I will come with you. He's never seen Hope."

"Hold on," Richard said, waving his hand up and down. "Take a breath. I'm not talking about all of us going over there. It could be unsafe for you and Hope if we get back to your village and your father is not in a good way. We need to handle this carefully and take one small step at a time. I can drive over on my own and see how he is. This will put your mind at rest and enable you to relax and enjoy Christmas. If the visit goes well and your father is in a good place, then we'll arrange for you to see him soon. Does that sound okay?"

Semmy was angry, and disappointed and she didn't hide how she felt. Richard picked up the keys from the table. As soon as the door closed behind him, Margaret turned to her with an angry look.

"You should be more grateful." She scolded. "Richard is doing his best to keep you and Hope safe. You know he grew up with no money and an absent father who was a drinker.

He knows how unpredictable they can be. He knows how much it hurts to want a relationship with someone who can't be a parent."

"Is that true?" Semmy asked.

"Yes, of course it's true."

Margaret's phone began to ring, and she turned away from Semmy before answering it.

"I need to go into town. It appears that there is someone else who may need our help." She announced when the call had finished.

She was gone for less than thirty minutes. She returned, calling for Semmy and Edna with a manic excitement in her voice. From the front door, they saw a woman sitting in the passenger seat of the Jeep. She looked a few years older than Lydia. She had dark, ebony skin, short tufts of black hair, and the malnourished face of a woman surviving on nothing.

Semmy and Edna walked to the passenger side of the jeep. As they approached, they smelled a foul stench that made them want to gag.

"My dear God almighty, what has happened to this girl?" Edna said.

"I don't know; she doesn't speak much English." Margaret told them.

"Where did you find her?"

"Humble Todd, the man from the hairdressers, called to say he found her this morning. She was asleep outside his salon. When he'd approached her, she'd started screaming at him. He remembered the charity and the business card I'd left and thought we'd be able to help."

The woman was so frail, with large sunken eyes and sores on her face, neck, and arms. She wore a long blue dress with puffed shoulders. It was dirty and covered in holes. Her bare feet were swollen, and she had infected mosquito bites all over her ankles. It wasn't just her physical state that made Semmy sad. It was the look on the woman's face. She had the same fear in her eyes that she had seen in Lydia's.

"My name is Kyembo Semmy." Semmy said to her in Luganda.

The woman didn't speak; she just looked at Semmy.

"It's okay." Semmy said, putting her hand out. "You'll be okay."

They walked slowly into the house and sat in the living room. Edna went into the kitchen and came back with a glass of milk.

"Ask her what her name is," Margaret instructed.

"Mwanga Florence." She said, her voice no louder than a whisper.

"Ask her why she is living on the street." Margaret prompted.

Semmy would have preferred not to have asked Florence lots of questions. But Margaret was not going to let the poor woman catch her breath. She discovered Florence was 22 years old. She lived with her husband, Samuel. Florence's mother had told her that the harder your husband hits you, the more he loves you. But she had come to know that this wasn't true. He hit her so hard that he was not driven by anything even close to love. Her home was a village to the east of Masindi. She had one sister, but she was too scared to go there for shelter. She knew it would be the first place her husband would look for her.

Margaret began inspecting Florence by lifting her arms as though she were a child.

"Ask her if she's sick?" Margaret said.

"She had the test, and she has AIDS. Her husband gave it to her."

Margaret said. "Tell Florence we will get her cleaned up, new clothes, and any medicine she needs."

As Semmy told Florence this, tears fell from her eyes. Margaret walked over to the dark wood cabinet in the corner of the room and picked up her phone. She pointed it at Florence. Semmy realised she was taking a photo just as Richard had photographed her and Lydia. Anger and disgust washed over her.

"Won't you ask her before you take her photo?" Semmy snapped.

"Would you ask her if she minds?" Margaret said, her voice laced with sarcasm. Her polite British smile vanished from her face.

Semmy asked Florence who shook her head. It was the same gesture she had made when Richard took her photo. How could she complain given her need for help.

"Let's get her cleaned up," Margaret said, "Edna, fetch some warm water and towels. Semmy go and get something of Lydia's that Florence can wear."

After Edna had helped Florence to wash, she attended to her wounds as well as she could. There was also a poker burn across her right shoulder. It made her look like she'd been branded, just like a farmer brands his cattle.

The noise of the front gate opening announced Richard's return. In the drama of Florence's arrival, she'd given little thought to his visit to her father. Margaret went into the hallway to meet Richard.

"Before you go in you need to know that I have had to

bring home a young woman called Florence. She's in desperate need of the charities help".

Richard opened the living room door and smiled when he saw Florence. He walked across the room to her, extending his hand. Florence stared at him, her body rigid with fear.

"Hello, my name is Richard Greene; welcome to WOMAID. We will look after you."

Semmy translated what Richard had said. As Richard turned around to leave, Semmy asked him.

"How was my father?"

"He's well enough, but I'm afraid to say he's still drinking. It was wise for you and Hope not to accompany me. He still needs time to come to terms with what happened to Lydia."

"Can we not visit him?" Semmy asked.

"In time. Let us talk about a possible visit in the new year."

Richard and Margaret exchanged a look. It made Semmy feel uneasy, she questioned whether he was telling the truth.

FORTY
ANNA

It was a few degrees centigrade above freezing as Rose and I waited for the 10:15 to London's Charing Cross. We were visiting Robert to tell him the news of the contractors and get his advice about what to tell people. We arrived at his home in Kensington. It was decorated like a scene from the Liberty Christmas catalogue.

The exchange-looking girl took our coats and escorted us upstairs. Robert was sitting waiting for us in his drawing room. A log fire burned in the grate surrounded by tasteful, costly Christmas decorations.

"It's lovely to see you both," Robert said, standing up and kissing us on each cheek.

"Darling, I'm sorry to bother you this close to Christmas," Rose said, "There's something I need to speak to you about."

"Go on," Robert said, peering at her over the top of his tortoise shell glasses.

"It's the money for the refuge. I'm sorry to have to tell you we've been the victims of a terrible scam. All the money we raised and sent to the contractors is gone."

Robert's eyebrows pinched together. This was not the news he'd been expecting.

"Gone."

"I'm afraid so. Richard went to visit the site, and there is nothing there. The plot of land is empty, and we've been unable to locate the contractors."

Robert is too high-class for hysteria. His displeasure showed in his eyes and a slight twitch of his mouth.

"I see." He said.

"According to the Ugandan police, it happens more often than you'd think. Small charities like ours are most at risk, as we don't have any local presence."

"I thought you had someone out in Uganda supervising."

"We did, I mean we do. Margaret, she's a friend of Richard's. It seems she was preoccupied with looking after Semmy and Hope, she took her eye off the ball. She also has her own hotel project, and it's obvious now that we couldn't rely on her."

"This is very unfortunate." Robert adjusted the cuffs of his shirt sleeves.

"Richard is staying in Uganda to track down the contractors to try and get the money back. I'm afraid it's not looking good. I can't tell you how embarrassed I am."

"I quite imagine."

Robert stood up and paced the room.

"The trouble is, Rose, that nobody will thank you for the news that you've lost their money. It doesn't matter how blameless you and the charity are. People give to charity to feel good. If a few days before Christmas you start calling to tell them this, they won't thank you."

"These are our friends; they trust us. I can't lie to them."

Robert sat back down in the armchair opposite Rose.

"People have given you money to help Semmy and Hope to have a better life."

He lowered his chin and stared at Rose. It was a rhetorical question, but he still waited for her to answer.

"Yes." She said.

"Well, aren't you giving them a better life? Through our friends' support, you've created a charity."

Rose nodded.

"You and Richard aren't taking a salary, are you?"

Rose shook her head.

"You see, Rose, nothing is black and white. Unfortunately, this scam has affected some part of the money our friends have donated. Yet, the bigger picture is that the charity has fed and clothed the girls. It has paid Anna and Margaret's salaries. It enabled Semmy to go to school and Hope to thrive."

"I suppose," Rose said.

"Can you afford to keep the charity going?"

"Yes, but I'm having second thoughts."

"You shouldn't lose heart, Rose. Are Semmy and Hope still at your house? Are they happy to stay there until we make other plans?"

"Yes, they can stay for as long as they want. We also have a new girl called Florence who has just moved in. She's in a very bad way and in need of our help."

"Good, you need to focus on the fact that you're still doing something miraculous. You are providing a place of safety to very vulnerable young people. In the meantime, my advice would be to build something."

"A smaller refuge?"

"Anything you can afford; a building reassures people that their money has been well spent."

Robert lent forward and in a low voice asked.

"You don't suspect any wrongdoing on the part of anyone involved in the charity, do you?"

His question hung in the air; I looked across to Rose, who smiled her most perfectly poised smile.

"Not at all." She said.

Robert looked relieved. He lent back in his chair.

"Good, now remember, send only good news. People aren't interested in the day-to-day issues of a charity such as yours. This is a minor blip, and one that will soon be forgotten."

We left Robert's. I wondered what it's like to have so much money and confidence in what you do that the loss of £200,000 is just a blip.

FORTY-ONE
SEMMY

On Christmas Eve, Margaret drove Semmy and Florence into town to visit the market.

"What will you give me for these?" A small Ugandan woman asked. She held out a handful of tomatoes, each a different shade of orange, red, and green. Her stall was like all the others. It was a plank of wood suspended on top of half a dozen crisscrossed sticks. The only thing on the stall were tomatoes, a table full of them ripening in the midday sun.

"Where are you from?" The stall holder asked Margaret.

"The UK"

"I like the UK very much. Where in the UK do you live?"

"I used to live in Surrey." Margaret said.

"My uncle lives in Oxford; do you know this place."

"Of course, now if you'll excuse us." Margaret led Florence and Semmy forward through the crowds.

Women carried tall pots or baskets on their heads. This left their hands free to pick up goods while their babies slept on their backs. Men sat around chatting or selling bunches of produce. The produce was small enough to hold, like sweet potatoes and carrots.

"Now keep up with me," Margaret ordered as they marched past two women dancing outside a shoe repair stall. The stall proprietor was clapping to the loud drumming music playing on his radio. A motorbike cut past them, and the crowd of people parted like the sea and nearly knocked Florence to her feet.

"Are you okay?" Semmy asked, as she took hold of her arm to steady her.

"I'm fine, I worry that someone will recognise me and tell my husband." Florence said.

"Keep your head down and we'll soon be going home. Margaret never stays long at the market."

They stopped at a stall piled high with second-hand western clothes. It looked like a job lot bought from somewhere in Europe.

"Yes, please?" the woman behind the stall asked. Margaret picked up a pair of jeans and held them up against Florence.

"Do you like these?"

"Yes." Florence said. Margaret picked up a t-shirt.

"And this?" The t-shirt was pink and had a butterfly on the front.

Florence nodded again. Margaret continued to pick up clothes as if she was shopping with her teenage daughter.

"How much for all these?" Margaret asked the stall holder.

"15,000 shillings" (£3.20) the woman replied.

"That's too much, I'll give you 10,000 shillings."

The woman on the stall knew she could pay more. Margaret told Semmy that the only way to win respect from the local people was to show she wasn't a stupid tourist. She paid 10,000 shillings, but Semmy wasn't convinced the woman now respected her.

On the way back to the jeep, they passed a large metal cage. It was full of squawking chickens. The chickens were all flapping their wings in every direction.

"Give me that one and that one," Margaret said, pointing at two birds.

"D'you want me to kill them?" the stall holder asked. Margaret nodded. The man grabbed the two flustered birds and twisted their necks until they stopped moving. He threw their scrawny, limp bodies onto his rusty scale.

"5,000 shillings."

"These should taste good for our Christmas lunch." Margaret said, paying the man and taking the birds.

Margaret, Semmy and Florence arrived home to find Richard in the garden. He was shooting a line of beer bottles with an old hunting rifle that had belonged to Rose's father.

"Whatever are you doing?" Margaret asked, when there was a second of silence between the sound of the gun.

"I'm just keeping my eye in," Richard said, putting the gun down. "I used to be a pretty good shot back in my army days."

"Who are you planning on shooting?" Margaret asked.

"I'd happily shoot the contractors if I ever got my hands on them. It might also be an idea for you to learn how to use it. It would give you a way to defend yourselves if Florence's husband or Semmy's father ever turn up spoiling for a fight."

Margaret laughed, but Semmy was horrified. The problem with Richard was that she never knew if he was being serious.

FORTY-TWO
ANNA

Mum and dad arrived from France on Christmas Eve. They spent the first hour complaining about the journey because of the snow. I mentioned I'd skied in France. This set Mum off on another rant. She scolded me for finding the time and money to go to the Alps but never to them in Brittany.

My dad was carrying his latest manuscript around the house with him like it was a newborn baby. It's a historical work based on the Bayeux tapestry. He took up writing at 52 and had his first novel published when he was 57. It was semi-autobiographical about an English man living in France. It's full of British clichés, which to my shock and dad's delight, the book buying public thought was charming.

Mum works as a bi-lingual wine exporter for a Swedish millionaire who owns a vineyard in the South of France. It suits her as she gets to pack and label boxes like it's an Olympic sport. For mum the purpose of work was always to keep busy.

On Christmas morning, all our attention was on present opening. Lunch was surprisingly calm. Mum and Helen cooked and served dinner without bickering at each other. It was late in the afternoon after everyone had been drinking, that the questions began.

"Are you still working for that charity?" Mum asked.

"Yes,"

"Well, you can't go on living with your sister forever. Isn't it time you got a proper job so you can afford to move out and get a place of your own?"

"It is a proper job."

"From what I read, there are many dodgy charities these days. They are all run by friends of politicians and not worth giving your money to."

Mum reads the Daily Mail even though she's in France, so she's always reliably uninformed. I'd already decided not to talk about my job, the missing money or Mark. If we could avoid each of these, we may at least be able to spend Christmas being civil.

"Well, you've done your bit." Mum said as if working for a charity was something you ticked the box of but could never be a serious career choice.

"What about Mark?"

She knew this topic would wind me up. I'd been clear that it was over between us; I was happy with that decision, and there was nothing more to discuss. Like Helen, she never liked him, she thought he was too showy. I hadn't told her any of the details of our break-up because we're not a go into detail type family.

"What about Mark?" I said in a tone that demonstrated my reluctance to share.

"I wondered if he'd managed to wheedle his way back to you."

"No."

"You need to get out there and start dating again. Over 30 is a difficult age for a woman; men will start to wonder why you're single and what's wrong with you. If you're going to settle down, it needs to be with a sensible man, not someone who can't commit."

I thought of Kip and smiled to myself.

Dad was fine not quizzing me about Mark, my lifestyle choices, my job, or my status as a single woman over 30. However, by Christmas evening he was so drunk that he started to call Tim, Mark, by mistake. I felt like I was in some bloody BBC sitcom.

By eight pm, Mum had managed to take control of the TV. Dad was asleep in the armchair, and Tim was helping the boys build their new Lego toys. Mum switched on the film Titanic, despite Helen and I protesting that it was too long. I stared at the screen as Mum rustled away in the tin of Quality Street in search of orange creams.

"So, is there no news about Mark?" she asked.

"No, I thought we'd covered this."

"He doesn't want to try and get back together with you?"

I shrugged my shoulders.

"If he does, what will you say?

I could tell this was how the rest of the evening was going to go. Mum would have one eye on the film and the other peering into my life.

"I'm going out," I said, standing up and obscuring Kate Winslet in the process.

"Where are you going?" Helen said as though I'd taken leave of my senses.

"It's Christmas day; you can't go out on Christmas day." Mum said.

"I'm going to see Rose, she's alone and I want to pop over and check she's okay."

"But you've been drinking and she's only your employer, we're your family. Does she not have family of her own."

"They're all abroad and I can walk there and get a taxi back. I'll be home before the film ends; I promise."

Helen looked at me as if I were deserting her on the actual Titanic. I stepped out of the house and sighed with relief. I needed a change of scene to clear my head. At least going out gave Mum a reason to berate me about something other than my poor life choices.

FORTY-THREE
SEMMY

In the past, Christmas at Semmy's homestead would include a visit from her aunt Grace. Grace would come with her husband and three children. Some years her uncle Clement and his family from her mother's side would also visit. They would somehow fit into their two sleeping huts. Semmy's father would kill one of their chickens for lunch.

The gifts would always be handmade, like a basket, a woven mat, or a dress. Semmy's uncle Clement had brought the family a calf a few years ago. Semmy's mother was so pleased. She took such good care to raise the cow. It provided the family with fresh milk when Semmy was young. Sadly, the cow passed away, and they couldn't afford to buy another one.

Christmas with the charity didn't bring gifts of calves. Richard did surprise them all with a present. Semmy received an Oxford English dictionary to help with her continued studies. Hope had a large teddy, so soft and fluffy with glittery blue glass eyes. Edna's gift was a new basket for her bike. Florence had toiletries, a bar of soap and a carton of talcum powder. It was Margaret who had the most sparkling and expensive gift, a necklace. The prettiest thing, a precious red stone hanging from a gold chain.

"I don't know what to say." She blushed as Richard helped her to do up the clasp around her neck. "I didn't think with everything that has been going on with the refuge that we would bother."

"Nonsense! Christmas is still Christmas, regardless of everything else. You all deserve to be a little spoiled today." Richard picked up Hope and waved the teddy bear in front of her.

After the presents, Edna went home to be with her family. Florence and Semmy walked to the local church. When they returned two hours later, Margaret and Richard had cooked a traditional Christmas lunch like they had in the UK. The only difference was that they had chicken, not turkey and there was no cranberry sauce.

At dusk, Richard and Margaret went to the Masindi hotel to keep drinking. Florence and Semmy sat on the veranda and sang Christmas carols. Carol singers were known as "nightingales" in rural villages. They'd move between people's homes singing carols and receiving small tokens of appreciation. Semmy knew no nightingales would knock on the gates of a house like this. She thought of her father, and for a while she even convinced herself that she could hear him calling her.

That night, Semmy lay awake unable to sleep while Florence slept in the bed that had been Lydia's. The sound of the jeep announced the return of Richard and Margaret. She could hear their muffled voices as they came in the front door.

Semmy turned over to try and get some sleep when she heard footsteps climbing the stairs. They were too heavy to be Margaret's and she wondered why Richard had not gone back to the hotel like usual. A few minutes later a faint metal noise of her door handle turning made her heart sink. A shard of light came in from the hall and Richard's silhouette was in the doorway.

"Are you awake?" He whispered, closing the door behind him.

She did not answer. He came into the room and stood over Hope's cot. He was there for several minutes looking at Hope and not speaking.

"What do you want?" Semmy said.

"Can you not sleep?" He asked.

"No."

"Do you mind if I come and sit on your bed?"

She didn't answer. As he sat down, he made the bed sag. Semmy lay as still as she could, hating the fact he was in her room.

"You know I've started to look at you and Hope as my family." His words were slow and slurred. "I always wanted a family of my own, especially a daughter, but it never happened. I am so happy that now I have you and Hope to take care of. No matter what happens, I will never let you down. I will love you like you are my own children." He reached his hand out to touch hers, and she pulled it away.

"You don't need to be afraid of me."

Semmy wanted to scream at him to leave. But she feared he'd scold her for overreacting. His hand reached out again, and he stroked her leg over the bedsheet. Despite the darkness of the room, she could see him staring at her. She started to move away fearing what he would do next when Margaret appeared in the doorway.

"What on earth are you doing in here?" she shouted.

"I wanted to see my girls."

"It's late and you're drunk; it's not appropriate for you to be in here."

Richard stood up and tapped the edge of the bed.

"Goodnight, Semmy". He whispered.

Semmy didn't speak. She pulled the sheet up around her and prayed he didn't return.

FORTY-FOUR
ANNA

It was past eight on Christmas Day when I arrived at Rose's house. I rang the doorbell and waited. I rang again, still no answer.

"Rose; Rose; are you there?" I called through the letterbox.

"ROSE," I shouted with a growing sense of urgency. I thought for a moment something terrible could have happened. What if she'd had a heart attack or a stroke and was lying helpless and alone.

I peered through the glass of the front door and saw a figure moving slowly towards me. Rose opened the door. She wore a pastel pink dressing gown. Her hair was in curlers, and she had smudged black makeup around her sleepy eyes.

"Darling, how long have you been standing there?" Her voice was croaky.

"Not long." I lied, shivering, "Are you okay?"

"Of course I'm okay." She snapped, warning me against treating her like an old woman.

"Come in."

She held open the door. I stepped inside her hall. A single string of Christmas lights hung around a large hall mirror with two sprigs of holly. The lounge had no Christmas decorations. There was an eclectic mix of furniture and artwork that was enough to feast your eyes on. Rose's belongings were an accurate reflection of her. There were ornaments and tribal masks from her travels in Africa. Bright and romantic oil paintings of flowers and landscapes. Pastel pink velvet curtains hung over the two large windows. A deep pile cream rug was on the floor, and a large pink sofa with scatter cushions.

"Drink?" Rose asked, picking up a bottle of gin from a 1970s glass hostess trolley. She tilted the bottle up to the light and noticed it was empty. She threw it into the gold trash bin in the corner of the room.

"I don't know why I drink this stuff." She muttered, kneeling by a tall wooden dresser to take out a new bottle. "Gin always makes me feel depressed, Christ, its Christmas, we're all bloody depressed."

I smiled.

"Anyway, not that I'm not happy to see you, but don't you have nephews to entertain or aren't there party games you should be playing?"

"I escaped."

"Ah I see, using me as an excuse."

"Kind of; how's your day been?"

"Darling, I haven't bothered to get dressed all day. I've eaten smoked salmon washed down with champagne and watched TV." She poured me a large gin and tonic, adding two cubes of ice and a slice of lemon.

"Have you spoken to Richard?" I asked.

He called me this morning. He went on, as he always does, about how stressful it is. He's trying to track down these contractors."

"Don't you believe him?"

Rose let out a deep sigh. "I don't know what to believe. Every time I call the house, him and Margaret are always off together somewhere. Whenever I do speak to him, he tells me he's busy and yet it sounds to me like the only place he's being busy is in the pub. I've started to wonder if there isn't more to him wanting to be out there."

"Like what? You don't think there's something going on with him and Margaret, do you?"

"I don't know. He was living with her and helping her renovate her hotel before I came along. Who knows if there was more to it than they ever let on."

"He married you, why would he do that if he and Margaret were together? Besides, I've seen photos of Margaret, and I've heard the way you talk about her. I don't think you have anything to worry about."

"That's very sweet of you to say, but there's nothing worse than being an old fool."

"Which you are not."

A knock at the door made both Rose and I jump.

"Whoever could that be now?"

"Shall I go for you?"

"No, you stay put." Rose said, putting down her glass and pulling the cord of her dressing gown tightly around her waist.

"The sight of me in curlers will frighten anyone away."

The backs of her slippers clicked along the floor as she padded her way down the hall. I listened as the door opened and Rose exclaimed.

"Darling, I can't believe you've come."

I felt like an intruder. Christmas day was for family and friends. It isn't for employees trying to escape their nosy mothers. The living room door opened, and Kip walked in. He was wearing his green woolly hat and a yellow puffer jacket. He looked very pleased with himself.

"Looks like we've both had the same idea about cheering up the old girl." Rose knocked him playfully on the arm.

"Enough of the old. I don't know what the fuss is about. I'm sure you've both got better things to do than to visit me."

She put her arm around Kip's middle and pulled him close to her. There was a teary glaze to her eyes revealing how happy she was to see him.

"You should have come earlier, I'd have cooked." She said.

"That's exactly why I'm late." Kip said laughing and throwing his jacket onto the back of the sofa. He leaned down and gave me a kiss.

"Merry Christmas Anna."

Rose walked to her drinks trolley. She picked up her gold pineapple ice bucket and said she needed to fetch more ice.

"How are you?" Kip asked sitting down next to me on the pink sofa.

"I'm okay."

"I'm sorry I haven't called or messaged you since you came back from skiing."

"Why would you?" I tried to sound like I hadn't noticed.

"It's this time of year, it all goes a bit crazy, and I meant to - I guess I wasn't sure how things stood between us after what happened."

"You don't need to explain yourself; I'm a big girl, I can handle a one-night stand."

Rose walked in with some more ice.

"I should be going and leave you to catch up." I said.

"Nonsense, you've just got here." Rose said. "Stay and have a drink with us." She handed Kip his drink and raised her glass for a toast.

"To good health and new beginnings."

"To good health and new beginnings," Kip and I repeated.

"Perhaps this Christmas isn't turning out to be so bad after all." Rose smiled.

"See you don't need Richard; in fact, isn't life better without him." Kip said.

Rose looked up at me.

"I'm sorry," Kips said, holding up his hands. "I came here to cheer you up, not to talk about Richard."

I stayed long enough to be sure that the Titanic would be well and truly sunk by the time I got home. I ordered a taxi and when I got up to leave, Kip followed me out.

"It was good to see you tonight." He said looking at me with those big brown eyes. "Do you have to go? It's not that late, and Rose has plenty of room if you wanted to stay."

"I need to get back; besides you and Rose need some time to catch up."

I opened the taxi door.

"I'm going to be here for a couple of days if you fancy hanging out. We could go and try to catch a movie again?"

"My parents only arrived from France yesterday. They want to spend time with my sister and me. I'll let you know if I can. Goodnight, Kip."

I got into the taxi and left, although my hormones were screaming at me to stay. I was a 30-year-old woman with a schoolgirl crush. I felt like such an idiot. I got back to Helen's relieved to find everyone had gone to bed and I could escape any further questions until the morning.

FORTY-FIVE
SEMMY

Semmy avoided being alone with Richard on the days following his drunken visit to her room. He'd broken an unspoken rule. Their bedroom was their private, safe space. To sit on her bed like that, and touch her, it had made her uncomfortable. Semmy and Edna were in the kitchen. They overheard Margaret telling Richard that the house was too crowded for him to stay again.

Time dragged in the days that followed Christmas. Semmy found she had too much time on her hands without school. She missed Sydney and wondered how he was spending the holidays. Florence was there for company. With her medicines and Edna's food, her health improved every day. Sitting on the veranda, playing with Hope, they talked about their lives as children. Despite her twenty-three years, Florence still seemed so young. Being married at fifteen with a husband who never let her leave the house had kept her isolated.

Occasionally the conversation would drift to the future. Semmy was optimistic about her life. It would involve finishing her education, meeting a nice man, and raising a family in a house like the Greene's. Florence would never talk about what she wanted. It was almost like she'd abandoned any belief that her life could be good.

By the middle of January, Richard returned to the UK. Semmy was pleased to see him leave. The following day

Margaret received a phone call that she had been waiting weeks for.

"I've had the best news," she announced at breakfast to Semmy, Florence, and Edna. They were sitting around the kitchen table, enjoying bowls of porridge. My solicitor called. He told me I've won the civil court case. I am to inherit everything in my late husband's will."

"Who else would have had it?" Edna asked, looking confused.

"It doesn't matter; all that matters is that justice was served and what was rightfully mine stays with me."

"Will you be rich now?" Semmy asked.

"Not rich, but I'll have the money I need to finish the hotel."

"Will you leave WOMAID?"

"Not to start with, it will take time to get the hotel up and running. Besides, Richard has plans to build another refuge, so he'll need my support."

Margaret looked at her watch.

"I have to get on, I have so much to do." She said scurrying out of the house.

FORTY-SIX
ANNA

It was the middle of winter; Richard returned to the office wearing a navy fleece gilet over a white short-sleeved shirt. He looked remarkably well-rested from what he had claimed to be a stressful stay in Uganda.

"How are we all?" he said, dropping his suitcase onto the office floor and extending his arms for his wife to greet him.

Rose looked up at him from behind her desk but didn't move.

"I bring great news." He said pulling out his mobile phone and scrolling through. "Here, a photo of Hope with her first tooth." He waved it in front of me and then showed it to Rose, who gave his screen a cursory glance.

"I'd begun to think you had emigrated to Uganda for good," Rose said, not smiling.

"I was trying to sort out the bloody mess with the contractors and support Margaret."

"I heard you've been doing a lot with her."

"What's that supposed to mean?"

"I have plenty of friends in Masindi. Friends who saw you and Margaret propping up the Masindi hotel bar."

"So, we can't go out for a drink together."

"No, not when you tell me you're too busy to speak to me on the phone. What am I supposed to think? Edna said that on Christmas night you were so drunk you slept at the house with Margaret."

"I didn't sleep with Margaret; I slept on our couch."

There was a momentary pause in hostilities. Richard looked perplexed by his wife's anger. Rose was tight-lipped and fuming.

"What about Semmy's father, Albert?" Rose asked. "Did you go and see him?"

"Yes, the man is still in no fit state to take care of himself or the girls."

"Did he not want to see Semmy and Hope?"

"He didn't say, and I didn't offer."

"What if he drinks himself into oblivion and Semmy loses him too?"

Richard pulled at his chin with his hand, irritated by Rose's questions.

"I don't care what Albert does, and frankly, if he drinks himself to death, it would be a blessing. Semmy and Hope are better off without him."

Rose shook her head.

"It's time we changed things up around here. From now on, I'm taking charge. I'm going to oversee the building of the new refuge. I'll appoint the contractors; I'll transfer the money, and there will be a direct line of reporting to me."

"If that'll make you feel better. I can see I'm not wanted around here today; I'm going home to get changed."

Richard picked up his case and stormed out of the office, slamming the front door behind him.

"Are you okay?" I said.

Rose looked up at me.

"You'd think by my third husband I would have learned how to manage them, but it never gets any easier."

FORTY-SEVEN
SEMMY

"Are you ready to go into school to collect your exam results?" Margaret said as Semmy pushed her eggs around her plate too nervous to eat breakfast.

They set off with Margaret driving too fast as usual. A red dust cloud sprayed off the road and coated the pedestrians on their way to work or school. She slammed on the brake as a man was herding his cows from the road using a thin whipping stick and his own determination.

At the school, there was a crowd of people already forming. In some cases, entire families had come. Many had worked hard and sacrificed much for their child to have a good education. Collecting exam results was a big deal.

Semmy got out of the jeep alone and told Margaret she'd been back shortly. Walking through the crowd of waiting siblings, parents, and grandparents was hard. A lump of sadness and regret stuck in her throat, which she tried to swallow away.

She saw the children from her class all gathered around the notice board. It hung under the sign of the school motto "In God we trust, as we strive for excellence". They clambered over each other to see their results printed on a page of names pinned onto the board. Semmy walked over, desperate to know what she'd got but not brave enough to push her way through to see.

Her classmates announced their grades to each other. Their loud celebrations and commiserations did nothing to calm her fears. Like a wave reaching its peak and then descending, the children dispersed. At last, Semmy was alone at the board.

Her eyes scanned the list of names. She could see the name of every one of her classmates, but not her own. She ran her eyes back down the list again and again, but she couldn't see her name. Did they lose her paper? Did she not have a grade?

"So did you pass?" A voice came from behind her. Semmy turned around to see Sydney. He looked so handsome, smiling down at her with his big brown eyes and shiny white teeth.

"What are you doing here?"

"I came to see you, it's a big day and I wanted to know how you'd got on."

"My name isn't here."

Sydney cast his eyes across the board.

"This is you." He said pointing to her name in the middle of the list. "You've passed and received a good grade."

Semmy looked at her name and turned to hug Sydney. He laughed at her outburst of excitement.

"You shouldn't be so surprised. Now you can start at the secondary school; we'll spend our lunchtimes together again."

Semmy walked back out of the school with Sydney. Her smile was as wide as her face.

"Thank you for coming today; it's good to see you."

"I'll see you next week when school starts."

Semmy climbed into the jeep and told Margaret the news about her results.

"See, I told you that you'd have nothing to worry about."

On the journey back, Semmy stared out of the window. She watched women with babies strapped to their backs as they fetched water or worked in the fields. They look tired. This was the life that waited for her if she returned to the village. Raising Hope as a single mother and nursing her father when he was old and sick. Semmy knew she shouldn't be in such a hurry to leave the charity just yet.

FORTY-EIGHT
ANNA

It was early February, and I was alone in the office when Robert called.

"I'm glad I caught you, Anna. I've had some information that I need to discuss with you."

"Really", I said, intrigued.

"After you and Rose came to visit me before Christmas, I asked a friend of mine to run a few checks on Richard. It was to give me some peace of mind that there was nothing about the missing money that should be a cause for concern."

"I see; go on."

"Richard is something of an enigma and there are two things that are of concern. Rose said he'd had an extensive career in the army and yet there's no record of him ever serving in the British army. The second is a claim by a man called Tom Reynolds. He posted on Facebook that his mother invested in a water filter developed by Richard Greene. According to Tom the water filter was a scam and Richard stole his mother's money.

I don't want to worry Rose at this stage as it could be quite innocent. We all know better than to believe everything we read on Facebook." Robert continued, "I've reached out to Tom Reynolds. He's happy to meet, but I am in Courchevel skiing for the next week. I wondered if you might drop him a line. He lives not far from Tunbridge Wells."

I phoned Tom and explained that I worked for Richard

Greene. I said I wanted to know about his connection to him and the water filter. The next day we met for lunch in a small café in Lewes high street. The café was an independently run place with a glass display unit filled with fresh salads, pies and pastries.

Tom was the only man on his own in there, and at six foot three, he towered over me as I approached him. He wore a brown sweater, jeans, and boots. I would put him in his early thirties. He had short red hair, a pale white freckled face, and light blue eyes; he looked kind, gentle, and trustworthy.

"Thank you for coming to meet me."

"I'm only too happy to." He replied. "I want to do everything I can to stop Richard from ripping anyone else off."

"Well, I'm not sure he's guilty of that." I laughed. "Think of my visit as due diligence on behalf of one of the charity's trustees."

"I hope I am wrong, although I doubt I am. Shall we get lunch first and then talk?"

We ordered two salmon and broccoli quiches with a side of green salad.

"Could you tell me about Richard?" I asked.

"He met my mother Celia six months after my father passed away from cancer. She was in a difficult place. It had been a long illness, and she'd retired to take care of him. When he died, she lost her husband and her purpose. She was only 65, there was no longer work to distract her, and I was away living and working in London.

My father had spent most of his life at Brighton University working as a physics professor. He frequently attended undergraduate science events. At these events, young scientists pitched their latest ideas and had the chance to connect with mentors or sponsors.

Mum continued to attend these events after my father died. I encouraged her to go, to get out of the house and keep busy. When my father had been alive, he had often mentored students and from time to time he would sponsor them."

Tom looked up at me and smiled.

"We're not talking big sums of money; I should stress. On a lecturer's salary, my parents were never wealthy. They would give a few hundred pounds here or there for certain bits of equipment."

I smiled encouragingly.

"It was at one of these events that my mother first met Richard. I'd assumed, from the way that she spoke about him, he was a student. She told me all about his water filter. It made water safe for rural African communities. She said it was brilliant. I thought he'd be around twenty and was looking for a project sponsor. We were excited by the potential.

Neither my mother nor I are scientists. She attended these events to provide some sponsorship. It was her way of honoring my father's memory and it made her feel good to be useful.

It was only after I met Richard that I realised he wasn't a student. He'd attended the event as a visitor and had happened to meet mum there. I was suspicious about why a man of his age couldn't raise funding for his invention. Especially, if it was as promising as he claimed it to be."

"Was he there to raise money?" I asked.

"He was there as a donor. He told my mother he was a

retired philanthropist, and he was there to support young scientists. I asked him about what he had supported, and he was always very vague. He said he couldn't discuss them for fear of disclosing too much before all patents had been filed. I asked him to tell me the name of the students. I was curious to know if we had supported any of the same academics. He refused to say."

"To begin with he never mentioned needing money for this water filter. My mum and I were under the impression that he had money. He told her he'd developed a prototype and invested over £100,000 in it. His plan was to sell it to third-world governments and overseas charities.

It all seemed plausible. He was the right age and he talked with such passion and confidence. When he did ask my mother for support, it was small amounts to begin with. As the sums of money increased, he offered her shares. As soon as the filter was commissioned, he reassured her she'd received all her money back, with interest.

I thought he was a little odd; but he made my mum laugh. I hadn't seen her happy for so long, I wanted to believe the best in him."

"So, what happened?"

"Nothing, and that was the problem. Every other week he said he had a meeting with UNICEF or Oxfam who were interested. He would always come back with the same news; they loved the technology and wanted to commission him to develop it for use. However, there was always one more test or regulatory certificate they required. My mother ended up giving him close to £100,000."

Tom looked at me and shook his head.

"I didn't know she was giving him this much. I asked to

go through her accounts one day, and when I discovered what she had given him, I demanded to see his invention. I arranged for an old colleague and friend of my fathers to come with me. Richard showed us a machine which looked like something he'd put together in his garage. The worst of it was, the water came out no different from when it went in. He waved some patent in our face, claiming this proved the validity of his invention, but it was worthless. What he'd invented was no more effective than adding a simple water purifying tablet."

"What happened?"

"Richard became defensive and aggressive. He insisted that his invention would save thousands of lives. It was my dad's friend who wasn't qualified to understand the technology or its potential. To this day, I'm not sure if Richard was deliberately misleading us or deluding himself about what he'd created. He couldn't accept that his invention was worthless."

"Did your mother get any of her money back?"

Tom laughed, "I wanted to take him to court, but a lawyer advised me not to. My mother had given the money in good faith, and there were never any guarantees it would succeed."

"Were Richard and your mother ever more than friends?" I asked.

"No, thank God. She enjoyed his company, and she thought him harmless. She wasn't ready for anything romantic. To this day, she tells me that she believes Richard had only good intentions. I suspect it's a more palatable reality for her. The last thing she wants is to accept the fact that she allowed herself to be conned within a year of being widowed."

"Is she still in contact with him?"

"No, after she told him she wouldn't give him any more money, he stopped contacting her."

Tom looked up at me.

"Look, I've no proof that Richard tried to defraud my mother. It's suspicious to me that once she refused to give him any money, he disappeared. I posted a comment on Facebook to alert anyone else that he approached for funding. This is where your trustee must have read about it."

I thanked Tom for his time and returned to the office. I had an uneasy feeling that Kip was right about Richard being behind the missing money. I just still didn't have any proof.

FORTY-NINE
SEMMY

Margaret was just weeks away from the grand opening of her hotel. It was all she could talk about. You'd have thought it was the event of the year, which for a small town like Masindi, it was. Margaret had arranged for the local MP to come and cut a ribbon and for the local press to attend.

On Semmy's first day of starting secondary school, Margaret said she'd pick her up from school. She'd take her and Florence to visit her new hotel. They could have dinner there; it would be a good way to mark the new term.

Semmy changed into her smart new uniform. It consisted of a maroon skirt, a white blouse, a maroon blazer, a tie, and new shoes. It had been less than two months since she was last at school, but she felt two years older. Margaret had taken an obligatory photo for the WOMAID website. Semmy was too excited at the prospect of her first day and seeing Sydney to mind.

At lunchtime, Semmy waited for Sydney under the mango tree. The tree stood between the primary and secondary school. It was the end of the dry season, and there had been no rain for months. The usually lush green playing field had turned into a brown and dusty expanse.

"Hello," Sydney said, beaming down at her.

"Hello," Semmy smiled up at him, her stomach doing somersaults.

"How's your first day at secondary school?"

"Good, the school is so much bigger; I keep getting lost." She laughed. "I like the fact I no longer feel like the new girl. The subjects look good, and I even have drama this afternoon."

"I'm writing a new play and I'm hoping the school will let me perform it at the end of term. There's a part that I've written with you in mind. A young woman named Namono who grew up in a remote village. She travelled to a local town where she reinvented herself. Namono had to overcome great tragedy and hardship. The name Namono means, she who is beautiful."

Semmy blushed and couldn't look at Sydney as he spoke.

"Will you read the play at least?" he asked.

"Of course." Semmy said as the bell rang causing them to part ways.

After school, Margaret collected Semmy with Florence already in the jeep. They drove straight to Margaret's hotel. It felt to them like they'd stepped into another world. A place she had only seen in magazines where wealthy people had their holidays. Instead of hotel rooms, guests would lodge in white circular concrete huts. Each hut had a double bed dressed in white linen and draped with a mosquito net. There were two white wooden bedside tables on either side of the bed. A green wooden wardrobe stood in the corner of each room, and a rocking chair. The rooms all had ensuite bathrooms with sparkling new white toilets, sinks, and baths. Bamboo bathmats sat on the real wood floors. Outside, each hut had coloured paving laid out in a geometric pattern.

"What do you think?" Margaret asked.

"I don't know what to say," Semmy said, casting her eyes around everything. "It's so nice and new looking. How many people will you need to run this place?"

"Plenty, I'll be hiring next week. That is part of the reason I have brought you here. Florence, I did think you might like to apply for a role. We need someone to help in the kitchen and we need cleaners. What do you think?"

"I would like that, thank you," Florence said.

"When your English has improved, we can consider you for a front-of-house job such as the receptionist."

"I could help on weekends," Semmy said.

"If you can keep up at secondary school, I'd be happy to give you weekend work," Margaret said. "If you can earn your own money, then no matter what happens you can take care of yourself."

FIFTY
ANNA

It was my first day back to work, after my meeting with Tom Reynolds. Rose and Richard were already in the office. Rose asked me about my weekend as I removed all trappings of winter clothing, my gloves, hat, and scarf. I wanted to tell her about Tom Reynolds and his mother. I knew if Richard found out I'd been gossiping about him, I was sure he'd sack me. I had to find proof of him taking money from WOMAID, but I didn't know how I could do this.

The atmosphere in the office was still as frosty as the weather. Rose no longer radiated vibes of a newlywed in love. Her tone with Richard displayed some irritation. That niggling bite of criticism that you'd expect from a couple that had been married for a lifetime.

It was approaching the financial year-end. Rose asked me to reconcile the money that came into the charity account with our donation records. We tracked all donations received by the charity on Excel. They all matched. However, I noticed only one donation of £500 from Martin Wilby. He'd purchased a silent auction prize of a bottle of House of Commons port at the fundraising dinner. There was no other donation. I checked and rechecked. Richard was in his office reading the paper and drinking coffee. I went into ask him about it.

"I was checking the bank accounts. There's only Martin Wilby's silent auction money showing as received. He told me at the event that he'd sent a donation of £10,000," I said.

"The man's a charlatan," Richard looked up at me from behind his desk. "You can't believe a word he says. I'm quite sure he told you he'd donated that money to impress you. If he'd have sent us the money, it would have been in our bank account."

"What if it got lost in the mail?"

"Trust me, Anna, he hasn't sent us anything."

"Shouldn't I email him and check?"

"No. If you have spare time, get me another coffee." He handed me his Chelsea football mug and returned his attention to his paper.

I made Richard's coffee and then returned to my desk. I didn't trust Richard, and I couldn't see the harm in emailing Martin. If he hadn't sent any money, then he could ignore my email or say he'd made a mistake.

I emailed Martin. His response was prompt. He'd donated £10,000 on the 12th of October, into the bank account provided. He forwarded the email from Richard. Richard had asked Martin to pay the money into the account of R Greene, and he had provided his personal account details. This was the proof I needed. I finally had something to show that Richard was a liar.

"Rose, I have something I need to tell you," I said.

"Is there a problem?" She asked.

I turned to look behind me to check that Richard remained occupied in his office. I then explained in hushed tones how Martin's money went to Richard's personal account.

"Maybe Richard hasn't seen it." Rose tried to sound upbeat, but there was hesitation in her voice. I wondered if she felt like Celia Reynolds. Admitting to herself that she'd made a mistake was more painful than the mistake.

"You'd think he'd notice £10,000 appearing in his account," I said. "There's something else," I continued. "I met a man called Tom Reynolds. His mother gave Richard £100,000 towards his water filter invention. Apparently, it never worked. Tom's convinced Richard conned his mother out of her money."

Rose rubbed her forehead.

"I know Kip has told you that he has his suspicions about Richard; what if he's right?" I said as Richard walked into the room.

"What are you ladies busy whispering about?"

"I have a headache coming on that's all." Rose's voice was strained. "I must have been staring at the screen for too long. I need to go home and lie down."

"I'll take you."

Rose stood up from her desk and as she walked past mine to leave, she looked me in the eye. I couldn't be sure, but it looked like she was telling me she believed me.

Richard was out of the office for less than an hour. He returned, slamming the front door behind him.

"What have you been saying to Rose?" he yelled.

"I don't know what you're talking about."

"Don't lie to me. Rose was questioning me the whole way home. She asked about a missing donation from Martin Wilby and started going on about Tom Bloody Reynolds."

"I contacted Martin." I said.

"I specifically instructed you not to. I'm your boss. If I tell you not to do something, you fucking well listen to me." Richard shouted his face close to mine.

"Rose is already nervous after the contractors disappeared. I'm going to get this charity back on track and I don't need you screwing things up for me. I'm booking tickets for Rose and me to fly out to Uganda tomorrow. Rose wants to see the girls and get things started with the new refuge. There is no time like the present. I'd seriously consider if you want to continue working here. I would have no problem finding a replacement."

He turned and started to walk back into his office and then he stopped.

"For your information Tom Reynolds is another stupid kid. He didn't like his mother spending time with me. He was just like Kip, he hated to think that his precious nest egg was being spent on anything other than him. His mother believed that I was trying to do something good for society. I told Rose this, so whatever it is you think you're trying to do, it won't work."

FIFTY-ONE
SEMMY

Semmy didn't see why Richard should need to return to Uganda so soon. It was only weeks since he'd been there for his Christmas visit. She was however pleased at the prospect of seeing Rose again.

They arrived looking tired and unhappy as if they'd spent the journey fighting. Rose arrived wearing a light pink dress. Her hair was covered with a dusty pink scarf and large black sunglasses concealed her eyes.

"Darling, come and give me a hug," Rose said, looking her over and smiling.

"You've grown so much, and you look more and more like your sister every day." She turned and looked at Florence.

"It's so wonderful to meet you at last." Rose put her hands on Florence's shoulders and looked her straight in the eye. "I've heard so much about you and the help you're giving with Hope. It sounds as if you're a tremendous asset to the charity."

Margaret appeared at the top of the stairs.

"Hello, Rose," Margaret said, descending the stairs with barely a smile.

"Hello, Margaret."

"To what do we owe the pleasure of your company?"

"I've been wanting to come out for months, and yet Richard chose to have his extended Christmas stay without me. I am here to oversee the plans for the new refuge. It would be very embarrassing, not to mention expensive, if we were to have another problem."

Richard walked through the front door, carrying their cases. He had a red face. His white linen shirt had wet patches under the arms and down his back.

"I'll put the cases upstairs." He said, his voice tense. "Rose would like to sleep in her own house. I hope you don't mind relocating to your hotel."

"Of course," Margaret said. "Edna's already made up your room."

Edna walked in, carrying Hope on her left hip.

"Who have we here?" Rose said, extending her hands to take Hope. Rose looked lovingly at her chubby arms and legs exposed in her cotton blue dress.

"Look at you?" Rose said misty eyed." You're even more adorable than I could have imagined."

"I will set up some tea for you outside on the veranda," Edna said. "After your long trip, you must be tired."

"Yes, thank you; that would be wonderful. Every time I travel, I'm reminded that I'm getting older, and a nine-hour flight takes it out of me a lot more than it ever used to."

Outside, the mid-afternoon sun was beating down a pleasant heat. It bathed the back of the garden in sunlight.

"The garden's looking nice," Rose said as she cast her eyes over the green lawn and blossoming flowerbeds. Margaret sat with her beige sun hat sitting loosely on her head. A red stress rash was visible up the side of her neck. Edna brought out a tray of tea.

"How are plans for the grand opening going?" Richard asked.

"You know how things are out here," Margaret smiled.

"The cottages have been decorated. There are a few snagging issues, and I need a descent plumber and electrician. Finding good tradespeople is a challenge."

"I could always drive over and take a look for you," Richard said.

"What do you know about water or electrics?" Rose asked mockingly.

Margaret looked at Richard and smiled.

"Your help would be appreciated."

"We could both come over to the hotel; I'm curious to see what you have been able to achieve with the money we pay you." Rose sipped her tea, keeping her eye on Margaret.

"It's not just my salary that has paid for the hotel."

"I'm sorry," Rose said, "my husband convinced me to employ you as he said you needed the work."

Margaret picked up her tea and looked offended.

"If you wish to come, you are of course welcome."

"I'd like that. I have felt so out of touch with everything over here." Rose said. "With only my new husband and you, his friend having any involvement with what has happened. Neither of you have any good explanation for what went wrong with the contractors. There's been the racist assumption that it's to be expected in a country like Uganda. I would think every country has people that are ready to rip you off. Common sense checks and staying on top of the work are usually enough to prevent this."

"It's not us being racist," Richard said. "The police told us that these cowboy contractors target small charities all the time. Do you really think Margaret and I have anything to do with that money disappearing?"

"That's not what I said."

"It's what you implied. We started this charity to help vulnerable girls living in the area. I'm not going to steal from them?"

"I thought Margaret, we could discuss what your role at the charity will be moving forward. I worry you're not able to oversee the building of the new refuge, given your hotel commitments. I had thought it was time to review the situation."

"With pleasure," Margaret replied. "I've done my best, but I shan't stay where I am neither wanted nor appreciated."

"Have I offended you?" Rose asked, her voice was unapologetic.

"I object to your inference that I am somehow to blame for what happened to the missing money. You like to think you're a great philanthropist, having started WOMAID. The truth is you don't have the foggiest idea of the time and commitment it takes to make a difference.

I have been here every day. I ensure Semmy gets an education and develops into an independent young woman. The baby that you hold with such care and delight is a healthy and contented baby that I helped nurse. Florence sees the doctor and gets the medicines and support she needs so she can live with her HIV and AIDS." Margaret spits the words at Rose.

"Now, if you'll excuse me, I have better things to do with my time than sit here and listen to this nonsense. I will expect you sometime tomorrow at my hotel." With that Margaret left.

FIFTY-TWO
ANNA

The day after Richard and Rose's departure to Uganda, I received an email from a man called Colin Jenkins. He'd come across the WOMAID charity website and wanted to learn more. He had until the end of the tax year to make his annual charitable contribution. He asked if someone from the charity would be able to meet him at his place in London.

I had limited experience with donor meetings. I wasn't a natural fundraiser. The thought of sitting alone with a stranger and selling the charity filled me with dread. I emailed back to say that Rose and Richard would be happy to meet him on their return from Uganda. His response was.

'For personal reasons, I need to make my decision about my charitable donations this week. If no one from the charity can meet, I'm afraid I will have to leave donating to WOMAID.'

I was tempted to send an email thanking him for his interest and asking him to contact us again next year. However, my conscience wouldn't allow it. I had to go and meet him. What was the worst that could happen, he didn't donate, and I made a fool of myself.

The next morning, I stood nervously outside his modern apartment block in Hackey, south London. I looked down the list of names by the entrance buzzer. Colin's flat was the penthouse. A woman in her mid-thirties, carrying a small fluffy white dog, emerged from the building. I walked in and took the stairs to the top floor. The exercise helped to calm my nerves. Colin answered the door in tight grey jeans, a white V-neck T-shirt, with bare feet. He was the same age as Richard, only trying far too hard to appear younger. He'd pulled his thinning white hair into a small, tight ponytail. In the centre of his chin, he had a small patch of white hair. It was so small it could have been an area he'd missed shaving.

"Anna." He said extending his hand. He smiled and revealed two capped front teeth that protruded, giving him a rabbit-like look.

"Come in." There was a trace of a Somerset accent. He smelled like a teenage boy who'd overdone the aftershave.

Inside, his apartment was a canvas of different shades of grey. It looked expensive and bland. A bachelor pad for a man with more money than taste. There were no photos, ornaments, or homely touches. The only pictures were a couple of abstract prints.

"Nice place." I said to be polite.

"Thanks, it's simple, but I like things simple."

"What will you have to drink, tea, coffee or diet Coke?"

"A diet Coke would be good, thanks."

He motioned for me to sit on his grey box-shaped sofa. I sat down, readjusting my skirt and ran through my sales pitch in my head. He returned with a glass of Coke and sat on the box-shaped armchair that was across from the sofa.

"Anna, why don't you start by telling me a little bit about your charity?" His voice was soft, like a hypnotist. He was disarming with his slight build and calm manner. Yet, there was an unnerving undertone that made me wary.

"The charity is WOMAID, which of course you know." I coughed. "Rose and Richard Greene started it when they were on holiday in Uganda last year. They took in two young girls; Lydia, who was 17, and her 15-year-old sister Semmy. WOMAID gave the girls a safe place to live. Lydia died in childbirth several months later. The charity continued to support her sister and Lydia's baby that survived. A 24-year-old woman called Florence also lives there. She is living with HIV and AIDS."

"I see. So, you are raising money to support them?" He asked in his soft voice.

"We are raising money to build a refuge. A place where the girls and women can be independent and create new lives for themselves."

"I see."

"The refuge will support up to 10 young women in the area that need a safe place to live."

Colin nodded.

"Tell me about the charity founders?"

"Rose grew up in Masindi. She knows a lot about the difficulties that young women face in remote areas of Uganda."

"What about Richard? What's his role?"

I hesitated for a moment. I'm conscious his role could be to corrupt everything we're working to achieve.

"What's the matter?" Colin asked, leaning forward in his chair. "Is Richard not a good boss?"

"No, I mean yes." I felt hot. I was wearing the same outfit I'd worn to see Martin. My black pencil skirt with tights, a white blouse, and black blazer. My clothes felt tight, too formal, and uncomfortable. I removed my blazer and straightened my skirt as Colin sat back in his chair watching me.

"So how much do you need to raise?"

"One hundred thousand pounds."

"That doesn't seem much, not when you consider what you're providing for these girls."

My heart had a brief flutter of excitement and relief. Perhaps, my fundraising skills weren't entirely absent.

"You know, Anna, that all charities claim to be incredibly worthwhile?"

"Yes."

"I ask lots of charities to come and see me, as my philanthropy is very important to me. I must make sure that I'm having the most impact. I need to know that my donation will be well deployed and make a real difference."

"I understand. Your support will make a huge difference to Semmy, Hope, and Florence, and to many more girls and women in the future."

"Would I be able to come out and meet these girls, see the refuge that I've contributed to?"

"Yes, of course." I was sure Rose and Richard would be happy to offer philanthropic tourism if it meant a large donation.

"Good," Colin clasped his hands together. "I need to find my cheque book."

"Great." I sat back with a huge smile on my face. I had no idea how much he intended to give, but I was imagining a sizeable amount. I couldn't wait to see the look on Richard's face. He was not going to be so quick to sack me now.

Colin returned with his cheque book and a pen. He sat down next to me on the sofa.

"One last thing I've forgotten to ask."

"Yes."

"What is it that these girls have done that has led them to needing the charities help?"

"The girls and women are all victims of physical or mental abuse. They are with the charity because they were unable to live at home. Semmy's father is a violent drunk. Florence's husband hit her with a burning poker."

"Please don't think I'm being insensitive. I'm just trying to understand what a woman such as Florence must do to make her husband beat her?"

Colin's question wasn't normal. He stared at me, his rabbit teeth hanging over his stupid little beard.

"I can arrange a further meeting with Rose or Richard when they are back in the UK." I said, standing up and pulling down my skirt.

"I don't want to meet Rose or Richard. I'm having a perfectly enjoyable time hearing from you. Please, Anna." He said, patting the sofa. "Sit down; I am trying to learn more about your charity that's all."

I sat back down.

"So, you'd like to make a donation?" My voice was shaky.

"I've always wanted to support you. How much I give will depend on you. I'm trying to work out the level of help the girls need."

I'm starting to freak out. He's playing mind games. I knew my sixth sense about him was right.

"Let me help you, Anna, as I can see this situation is confusing. Would you say the women you support need my help enough that you'd do anything to help them?"

"Yes, of course I want to help them."

He moved closer to me on the sofa, so his arm and leg are touching mine.

"What are you doing?" I looked at him; he could sense my fear.

"Come on, Anna. You know as well as I do what I mean. You've come to this meeting in your short skirt, with cute little kitten heels and pretty lip gloss. You hoped that if I found you attractive that I'd be more generous."

My heart is pounding through my ribcage.

"Well, Anna, I do find you attractive. I'm prepared to give you money. I need to understand from you how far you're willing to go for me to be generous."

"I need to go." I stood up with thoughts of rape flooding into my brain. He grabbed my arm and pulled me back onto the sofa. He pushed his spiky mouth onto mine and used his arms to restrain me. All I could feel was his tongue against my lips. His vile breath was disgusting and suffocating. I managed to free my arm.

"Get off of me." I screamed.

"The girls you support have suffered a lot worse than a kiss. Are you going to run off after just one kiss? You shouldn't be quite so squeamish, or maybe you're not quite as committed as you claim to be?"

He held my arm for a second longer, staring into my eyes, and then, he let go of me. I ran to the front door. I knew he was behind me, but I had my hands on the catch, and as I pulled the door open, the lift opposite opened. A tall man was stood inside with spiky brown hair wearing a cartoon character t-shirt.

"Hold the lift," I shouted.

"If you leave, you know I can't donate," Colin said behind me.

I ran into the lift; my adrenaline was pumping, and my

legs were shaky.

"Are you alright?" The cartoon t-shirt man asked. He had a kind smile framed by a square jaw with cowboy stubble.

"Yes," I said, staring at Colin as the lift doors closed. We reached the ground floor, and I looked around to check he hadn't followed me down the stairs, then I ran.

On the train home, I took my phone out to call Helen. I remembered it was half term and she was in Disneyland with the kids. One word of what happened, and she'd be on the next Eurostar train home armed with a giant Mickey Mouse. I considered calling Rose and Richard but what could they do. I called Mark. He told me he'd be waiting for me at Tunbridge Wells station.

I stared out of the window as sweeping views of the Kent countryside flicked past me. I recounted every minute of the meeting. Was there anything I said, or did that made him act like that? At the station, Mark was stood on the platform. He was dressed in jeans and his black barber jacket. As I stepped off the train, he pulled me into him, and I let him. I wanted someone to hold me; I needed to feel safe.

FIFTY-THREE
SEMMY

On Rose's first full day in Masindi, she insisted Richard take her to see Margaret's hotel. She asked Semmy to go with her. Florence stayed behind to look after Hope whilst Edna went into town to pick up groceries.

Semmy sat in the back of the jeep. The last time she'd seen Rose and Richard, they had seemed very much in love. It was different now. There was a tension between them.

At Margaret's hotel, there was a new sign for 'Brown's Safari Lodge'.

"That's a grand title for a hotel where the only wildlife you are likely to see is a street dog," Rose commented.

Richard ignored Rose and spoke into the intercom on the wall. A few minutes later, the gates opened, and they drove into the car park.

The reception of the hotel was an open wooden structure. It had a large wooden desk with a computer, a telephone, and a vase of red spiky flowers. Moses, the Ugandan boy who was Semmy's age, came to greet them. Richard asked him to run and fetch Margaret. The boy disappeared for a few minutes before reappearing with Margaret at his side. She was wearing jeans with a plain white T-shirt and open-toe sandals.

"This place looks very different from when I last saw it," Rose said. "A year ago, you had four lodges all in a very diabolical state. From what I can see, it looks like you have at least eight and all refurbished."

"I've extended. It was always the plan to add more rooms so we could cater for the safari groups."

"How entrepreneurial of you," Rose said.

"Would you like a tour as you're here," Margaret offered.

"Thank you."

They walked around each of the lodges. Rose touched the bedding or ran her hand against the smooth new bathroom fittings.

"You've only recently received your husband's inheritance. I'm surprised that you've been able to do so much. It can't be on the small amount we pay you to work for the charity."

"I have other means," Margaret said.

"Such as what? If you don't mind me asking."

"A bridging loan, I take it you've heard of them?"

"Of course."

They left the lodges and walked into the restaurant. A simple room with four large tables and chairs to sit up to 16 guests. They sat down at a table; Rose perused the surroundings her face tense. Richard asked Moses to fetch them all some mineral water.

"What do you think?" Margaret asked directing her question to Rose.

"I think there has been a serious level of investment. As I alluded to earlier, I'm surprised you have achieved so much."

"I'm pleased you don't think it looks cheap," Margaret said, glancing at Richard.

"No, it's not cheap. Do you not have any guests?"

"Not yet. Our official opening date is a week Saturday, if

you're still here, perhaps you can attend."

"We'll be here." Richard said like a man with two wives.

"Shall we discuss what happens in terms of your employment at WOMAID." Rose said. "It seems now might be a good time to discuss ending your employment with us."

"Rose, we need to discuss this," Richard said, looking annoyed. "We have the girls to think about. We can't expect Edna to take care of them on her own. We need someone in Uganda that we can rely on."

Rose turned her attention to Richard. "I'd love to have someone that I could rely on. As you have both magnificently demonstrated it is not either of you."

Moses comes out of the kitchen carrying a tray of glasses and a large bottle of chilled mineral water.

Richard looked as if he were ready to protest.

"Richard, please don't waste your breath on my account." Margaret said, "Let your wife run the charity. I can see she has already made up her mind. I'm only too happy to step down and I've no desire to outstay my welcome. Now if you'll excuse me, I have a hotel to run. Please finish your drinks and see yourselves out." Margaret got up and left the restaurant.

Rose and Richard walked back to the jeep, with Semmy keeping a few paces behind them.

"I thought we were trying to get the charity back on track with this trip," Richard said. "It wasn't about firing the one person who's kept everything going."

"Is that what she's been doing?" Rose said. "You told me without our support she would never open her hotel. It doesn't look like she's struggling. Her new hotel looks like she's had a windful. At the same time the charity has lost

£200,000."

"You're being ridiculous."

"What am I supposed to think?"

"You can't go around accusing Margaret of stealing our money. She's a good friend of mine."

"Your friend," Rose said. "Is that all she is? I noticed how quick you are to jump on a plane to visit without me. You walk around this place like you own it. When we get back to the house, I want you to pack your things and go."

"Go where? I'm your bloody husband; I'm not going anywhere."

"I've had many husbands," Rose said, staring at Richard. "I thought I'd suffered the worst of them but then you came along."

"This is ridiculous. We've only been married a year and you're calling it quits over some missing money?"

"It's not just the money. I agreed to start the charity after you told me that raising funds was your thing. You bragged about your water filter invention and the money you'd raised for it. You let me believe it was providing fresh water to people in remote African villages. That wasn't true, was it? It never worked and instead you stole £100,000 from a widower."

"The water filter wasn't a con. There were teething problems that was all."

"I don't want to hear it, Richard; I don't want to be around you anymore."

"This is my charity, as much as it's yours," Richard said.

"Without my house, my friends, and my money, I can't see you have very much to offer," Rose said walking back to the jeep.

FIFTY-FOUR
ANNA

We got back to Helen's; I went upstairs to get changed while Mark poured me a large glass of red wine. He said he needed Colin's address so he could run some checks on him at the police station. In the meantime, I was to try and relax and not worry.

Mark was gone for several hours. He returned with a cut on his left cheek and a black eye.

"What happened? Did you go and see Colin? I thought you were going to make enquiries at the station and report him."

"I know how these things go. Some junior officer will come and take a statement. If they have the time, they'll meet with Colin. He will deny everything. It will be your word against his. Nothing will get done. This way it's sorted." Mark walked over to the kitchen sink, picked up a glass from the draining board, and pushed on the tap.

"What if Colin reports you?"

"I don't care. I'm more worried about you. You look pale, Anna, when did you last eat?"

I shrugged my shoulders.

"You've got to eat. I'll order pizza."

I lay on the sofa and watched TV as we waited for the food. I still didn't feel hungry when it arrived, so I just picked at the burnt, cheesy bits on the bottom.

"I need to lie down," I said, feeling exhausted.

Mark didn't want to leave, but I insisted. I lay down in bed but didn't sleep. Two hours later, my phone rang, and Richard's name flashed onto the screen.

"What the fuck happened?" He screamed down the phone at me. "I have just received a call from a man called Colin Jenkins. He tells me he was potential support until your thug of a boyfriend went over to his place and attacked him."

"Colin attacked ME." I screamed down the phone. It was typical of Richard to take a stranger's side over his own employee. "Colin wanted me to go and see him as he claimed he wanted to donate money to the charity. The bloke is a fruitcake. He started asking me these weird questions and then he tried to kiss me. I thought he was going to rape me. I called Mark to come and pick me up because I was so freaked out."

"Anna, do you have any idea what will happen if it gets out that a charity worker's boyfriend beats up a potential donor? He was being friendly."

"He was more than friendly," I screamed down the phone.

"That isn't what Colin tells me." Richard's voice was angry and aggressive. "I've got enough to deal with right now with Rose, I don't need you making things difficult. Colin has told me that either you resign from the charity with immediate effect, or he'll go to the police and report Mark."

"Can I speak to Rose?"

"No, we're just on our way back from Margaret's hotel and she has a migraine."

I hung up the phone in disbelief. I couldn't believe Richard would not consider my side. I had no choice; I had to resign. If Colin reported Mark, they'd suspend him. I couldn't allow him to lose his job because of me.

FIFTY-FIVE
SEMMY

Semmy was relieved to get out of the jeep once they'd returned to the Masindi house. Richard was in the process of telling Rose, for the third time, that he would not get a divorce. Rose was insistent that he pack his bags and move out immediately.

"Florence we're home." Semmy shouted as soon as she was through the front door.

"Florence?" She shouted again.

From the kitchen she could hear voices. She ran down the hall and that's when she saw her father. He was sitting at the kitchen table, wearing his red and black checkered shirt. Hope was sat on his lap. Sitting opposite him was Florence.

"Father, what are you doing here?" Semmy asked. She felt the strangest mix of emotions at his presence; she was happy, frightened, and confused all at the same time.

"I'm here to take you home," he said.

Richard appeared in the kitchen followed by Rose.

"What the hell are you doing here?" he shouted, making Hope cry.

"I'm taking my daughter and granddaughter home. I know I've made mistakes," Albert said, his voice slurred. "There are times when I've not been a good father, and I thank you for all you've done but, I need them home now."

"Hello, Albert," Rose said, pushing past Richard and holding out her hand. "It's good to meet you at last. I'm

Rose, and this is my house."

"I'm sorry to barge in to your home like this. I've been here several times before. A white woman has been here, she refuses to let me see my own daughter; it's not right."

"I understand," Rose said in a calm voice. "I can take Hope from you, she seems a little distressed."

"She's okay." Albert said holding her more tightly.

"They're not going anywhere with you," Richard shouted. "When will you learn that you can't come here drunk and demand to take them home? Semmy and Hope have a life here. Semmy has just started secondary school. She's not going to give up her future because you need her home."

Richard took out his wallet and began waving banknotes in front of Albert.

"Take this and go home."

"I don't want your money; I want my family."

Semmy knew her father was drunk. He smelled of drink and he hadn't washed in weeks. His long grey beard was covered in grey, and his eyes looked like he'd not slept for weeks. If she returned home with him, she'd have to quit school. Her life would consist of taking care of her father and Hope. She didn't want this. Yet, she couldn't bear watching her father beg Richard for permission to have them home.

"It's okay, we'll come with you father," Semmy said, putting her hand on his shoulder.

"Is this what you want?" Rose asked.

"It's for the best." Semmy said helping her father to stand.

"Have you gone mad?" Richard shouted. "You're not leaving, nor is Hope."

"You cannot stop them from going them home, and nor should you," Rose said turning to Semmy. "Go upstairs and pack a bag of things for when you get home. We can bring the rest of your stuff another time."

Semmy ran upstairs and put a change of clothes, a couple of toys, and toothbrushes in a bag for her and Hope. When she returned, Albert was waiting in the hall holding Hope. Rose was with him, but there was no sign of Florence or Richard.

"Thank you," Semmy said, hugging Rose. "We'll never forget all you have done for us."

"You are welcome here anytime."

Semmy stepped out onto the porch with her father next to her and Hope in his arms. They walked down the steps, past the WOMAID jeep and the immaculate lawn. Hope had stopped crying and was looking at Albert. There was a moment of calm and quiet as they walked along the path. It was only when they reached the gate that they heard Rose shout.

"What are you doing, have you lost your mind?"

Semmy turned to see Richard standing outside the house. He was holding the old hunting rifle that he used to shoot tin cans. The same gun he'd joked to Margaret she should use to protect herself from Albert.

"Albert, stop or I'll shoot," he shouted.

Semmy looked at her father. "I worry that Mzungu will try to kill me."

"I'm warning you, Albert, you cannot leave, I will stop you."

They kept on walking. Rose continued screaming at Richard to put the gun down. They reached the gate and

Albert put up his hand to push it open. That was when they heard the gunshot. A loud, deafening sound that made Semmy's stomach turn. Anxiously she turned to see if her father or Hope had been hit. They were fine. Instinct made her turn around. Had Richard meant to miss them? Was he planning to shoot again? That's when she saw Rose lying on the ground at Richard's feet. A pool of blood was growing around her.

"We need to go back. Rose has been shot," she said.

"We can't go back, the man's crazy; he'll shoot us." Albert said.

They started to run, out of the gate and towards home.

FIFTY-SIX
ANNA

"Rose is dead," were the first words Kip said when I answered the door to him.

"What?" It was 9 a.m. on Saturday morning and I was still half asleep.

"Richard has killed Rose. He shot her outside her Masindi home with her old hunting rifle."

"I don't understand." I said.

"What don't you understand, Anna?" Kip shouted, "Rose is dead."

It didn't seem possible. How could someone take a trip to their family home with their husband and then end up dead.

"Come in." I said to Kip who followed me into the kitchen. We sat down at Helen's kitchen table. He looked like a different person. Anger and grief had drained him of all colour. Every ounce of playfulness was replaced with a deep sadness and a palpable hatred.

"What happened?" I said, passing him a cup of coffee.

"Richard called me last night to tell me that there had been a terrible accident. Yesterday they had been out visiting Margaret's hotel and when they returned home, Albert was there. He was drunk and insisted that Semmy and Hope went home with him. Richard and Rose pleaded with Albert to leave. According to Richard he was shouting, upsetting Semmy and Hope and then he forced them to leave with him.

Richard was frightened for their safety. He tried to stop Albert from leaving. As a last resort Richard took out the hunting rifle that they keep at the house. He said he wanted to scare Albert. He shouted a warning to him that he'd shoot if he didn't stop, but Albert kept on walking.

Richard and Rose shouted numerous times but still Albert would not stop. As he was about to leave the property Richard fired the gun. It was intended only as a warning shot, but Rose stood in front of it."

Kip looked up at me his eyes full of confusion.

"Can you imagine Rose doing something like that?"

"Are you asking if I think Rose would step in front of a gun to stop her crazy husband from shooting a man and his two children?"

Kip nodded.

"It's exactly the kind of stupid, big-hearted thing that Rose would do. She wouldn't think for a second that her husband would pull the trigger."

Kip began fiercely rubbing his forehead with his fingertips.

"What happened after the gun went off?" I asked.

"Richard called an ambulance but by the time it arrived, Rose was already dead. Albert left with Semmy and Hope."

"Was anyone else there, Florence or Edna?"

"Florence was in the house, and Edna was out. We've only his version of events, and we know what a fucking liar he is."

Kip stood up and began to pace around the kitchen.

"I don't know what to do. I want to go out there and strangle the man until I get the truth out of him."

We sat in silence while Kip drunk his coffee and I tried

to process all he had said.

"Let's go to Rose's house." He said.

"Why?"

"I don't know, I can't just sit around here all day, or I'll go mad. Maybe we'll find something at her house, which will give us some answers."

When we arrived at Rose's house, I had the weirdest feeling. I felt like she'd be there, and fling open the front door, wearing her pink slippers, with her hair in curlers and smoking a cigarette. She wasn't, of course. Inside, the house smelled of her perfume. It was so quiet, too quiet.

"You go upstairs, and I'll take a look downstairs," Kip said.

Upstairs, Rose's bedroom, had a mirrored wardrobe running the length of her bedroom. I opened the first door and saw the shimmering ball gown she wore to the fundraising dinner. I closed the door and bent down to look under the bed. There were boxes filled with her things. Shoes, scarves, hats, but nothing of Richard's.

The next room was her bathroom and then a small study room. There was an antique writing desk with a wooden flap folded out. It was a deep red wood with a white pearl flower motif on the back. A white sealed envelope with the word 'confidential' written in Rose's handwriting was sat on top.

"Have you found anything?" Kip asked.

"Only this," I held up the envelope.

Kip took it and opened it. I watched as his eyes scanned the document inside.

"It's a letter to her solicitor. It's dated three days ago; she must have written it before leaving for Uganda. It confirms her request in writing that he amend her will to make me the sole benefactor. Do you think she suspected he might do something like this?"

"I don't know, maybe, there's so much I need to tell you," I looked at Kip.

"Before Rose left for Uganda, I discovered a donor called Martin Wilby had donated £10,000 to WOMAID in October. He'd paid the money into Richard's personal bank account. Richard never told Rose he'd received it. I told Rose about it, and I know she confronted Richard. He had made some excuse, but I don't think she would have believed him. I also found out that he'd previously conned £100,000 from a widower called Celia Reynolds. It was for a water filter that Richard invented and never worked."

"Why didn't you call me and tell me all of this?" Kip asked.

"I was going to. I told Rose and the next day she was flying to Uganda with Richard. Then yesterday a man called Colin Jenkins called the office. He said he wanted someone from the charity to go and see him. He claimed he intended to donate a sizeable sum. I went to see him, and he tried to attack me instead. I called Mark and told him what happened. It was a stupid mistake as Mark went to see Colin and beat him up. He then threatened to press charges against Mark unless I resign."

Kip looked at me in disbelief.

"You mean to tell me in the last 48 hours Rose found out Richard was lying, she changed her will, you were attacked by a stranger, and now Rose is dead."

"Yes, that's about the size of it."

"This is all Richard's doing." Kip said opening cupboards and pulling out the contents onto the floor.

"What are you looking for?" I asked.

"I don't know." He said slumping onto the floor holding his head in his hands.

"How can one man come into our lives and cause so much misery. He appeared out of nowhere arriving in Rose's life and bragging about what a successful man he was. Yet, there's nothing of his here. It's like the man didn't exist before meeting Rose. Does he not have any possessions? How do you get to seventy years old and have nothing?"

Kips eyes scanned the top of the wardrobe. He jumped up onto Rose's wooden study chair and removed two cardboard boxes. Tucked behind the boxes was a brown leather case. It was dusty and old. Kip put the case down on the floor and pulled back both clasps. A heap of random papers and photographs were thrown together inside including photos of Richard.

The first photo we saw was of Richard as a child. He had a weird smile even then. His hair was cut with a wonky fringe, and he wore round NHS glasses. He was wearing a brown buttoned duffel coat that was two sizes too small. A woman, his mother, I suspect, was standing next to him. Her clothes were drab and functional. They both wore the same soulless expression as if a stranger had taken the photo.

I picked up another photo of a younger athletic-looking Richard with short brown hair. He was wearing a khaki soldier's uniform and lying on the grass beside a blonde woman. I turn the photograph over, on the back, it reads, 'Me and my Maggie Brown, Kenya 1981'.

"This is Margaret Brown." I passed the photograph to Kip. "Rose had begun to suspect that there was something going on between them. I wonder looking at this photo if she was right."

Another photo caught my eye and made me feel sick. Richard, as a young man dressed in an army uniform with his arm around the shoulder of another man. The other man is shorter and thinner. Even in his twenties, he had rabbit-like teeth.

"That's the man that attacked me," I said, jabbing my finger at the photo. "Richard must know Colin Jenkins."

"You must have gotten close enough to the truth that he wanted to get rid of you." Kip said. "I wonder what Rose said that forced him to want her dead?"

"Perhaps she threatened to expose him."

Kip picked up the case. "I'm getting on the next flight to Uganda. I'm not going to let Richard get away with this. Will you come with me? I'm not sure I can do this on my own."

I nodded. If Richard was as bad as we suspected, I'd be happy to do anything to make him pay.

FIFTY-SEVEN
SEMMY

It's late when Semmy gets back to her village, she's hungry and tired but doesn't complain. She takes Hope into their sleeping hut. There's a hole in the wall where the mud has washed away and the moon shines in. It was always Semmy and Lydia's job to fix the holes.

Semmy lays Hope down on Lydia's sleeping mat. Wearing only a cotton pink dress she worried her niece will get cold in the night. She wraps Lydia's bed sheet around her and inhales the faintest smell of her sister. The thought that Lydia should be returning home with them is too painful to acknowledge. Ignoring this thought Semmy turns her mind to sleep.

Her worries flit between thoughts of Rose and what will happen to her and Hope now they are home. Sleep must have come in some form, as she's woken by the noise of dogs barking and the cockerels crowing. The sound of the neighbour's children playing outside drifts in, and the chatter of people setting off to fetch water from the bore hole. Noises of home that she'd missed. It's only now Semmy realises how much. Living at the Masindi house was comfortable, but she never once heard the neighbours.

Hope wakes up and looks startled by the unfamiliar surroundings. Her eyes fix on Semmy, who distracts her by tapping the newspaper cuttings that hang above her head. Lydia and Semmy would hang the cuttings from the thatched roof of their hut with string to decorate it. Photos of their favourite Ugandan pop stars and fashion outfits they liked. There were a couple of pictures from around the world. Lydia had chosen a picture of the Statue of Liberty and always promised she would visit it one day.

The noise of Albert getting up and sitting on his usual stone by the fire makes Semmy rise. He's sat with his pen knife stripping wood to make kindling.

"Did you sleep?" Albert asks when he sees her.

"A little. Do have any ugali? I need to feed Hope?"

Albert tilts his head in the direction of the kitchen hut. Semmy bends down to put Hope on the ground, she stops when she notices how dirty it is. There are piles of leaves, old maize shells, and empty plastic bottles littering the floor. It was her job to sweep the compound every morning before school. It looked as if her father had not swept it in weeks.

In the kitchen hut, Semmy finds the bag of maize flour, their staple food and one of the few they could afford. They've enough for a week if they eat only one meal a day. Hope's demand for food grows louder, her cry telling the whole world there's a baby at their home now. It won't take long before people will start talking.

Albert lights the fire, and Semmy puts on a pan of water to boil. She sits on a stone next to her father. He looks older than she remembers. His wrinkled black skin sags around his mouth and across his forehead. His body slumps forward as if his head's grown too heavy for his neck. He looks at her, and she remembers him as the kind man from her childhood.

The water takes ages to boil. Hope's screaming gets louder. Semmy stands and rocks Hope in the same way Edna did, but her crying doesn't stop. When the water boils,

Semmy adds the ugali, turning it over in the water with a wooden spoon. She keeps adding the flour until it forms a thick, doughy mix, then covers the pan with a metal lid. They wait some more. Having lived at the Masindi house, Semmy had gotten out of the habit of waiting.

When the ugali's ready, there's no honey to sweeten it or milk to make it creamy. Hope complains at every mouthful, but she's hungry enough to eat it.

A rustling sound comes through the bush as Albert's sister, Aunt Grace, walks in. She has a small, thin frame like Semmy's. She wears a bright green African dress, and her black hair's concealed beneath her headscarf.

"You've come back." Aunt Grace says her eyes full of tears. "It's so good that you've come back for your father, he has missed you so much." Her eyes fell onto the baby.

"This is Hope," Semmy said. Aunt Grace held out her hands to take Hope.

"She's beautiful, and I swear I can see Lydia in her face."

Aunt Grace looked across at Albert, "You see," she said. "Did I not tell you Semmy would come home? He said you'd stay away now; you'd like the modern things like the nice clothes, the TV, the different food."

"Tis no matter what I said." Albert shook his head and waved his hand to signal to Grace to stop talking.

"We're African; we are patient and forgiving people. Let us not talk of what happened and let us think only of our future."

"I can't wait to show people my great-niece," Aunt Grace said smiling.

"There is to be no talk about Lydia; you hear me," Albert said. "We'll tell people that Hope was an orphan at the charity. Semmy brought her home so she can live in a Ugandan family. There is nothing more to say about it. Do you understand me?"

Semmy understood that her father would never get over the fact that Lydia was pregnant out of marriage. She wondered if he'd ever accept Hope as part of their family.

FIFTY-EIGHT
ANNA

Finding Richard's photos had convinced Kip and I that Richard and Margaret were having an affair and Richard had arranged for Colin to attack me. It was timed perfectly so that the only person I could call was Mark. A man I had frequently described as hot headed.

Kip booked us on the next flight to Uganda that left the following evening from Heathrow. Helen returned from Disneyland that afternoon. I provided her with a summary of recent events and watched as she had a mini meltdown. What if Richard tried to hurt Kip and I? I reassured her I'd be fine, but I was nervous.

We got a taxi to the airport and Kip called Edna to say we were coming out. She informed him that they'd taken Richard to Masindi police station. He was there answering questions.

Kip stared at the in-flight entertainment and drank beer the whole flight. We landed at four in the afternoon and stepped off the plane onto the tarmac. The heat was exhausting and clung to us like a mobile sauna. Inside the terminal building, we joined a queue of tourists waiting to get their entry visas.

Every other tourist seemed to be American. They were loud with cross pendants hanging from their necks. I thought that going to Africa to save lost souls was a thing of the 19th century. It appeared I was wrong.

A chubby, pasty-faced post-adolescent American stood in front of us. He wore a blue baseball cap and had a large red rucksack strapped to his back. Three large maps stuck out of the top.

"I love going out to the remote schools." He said to a young woman next to him. "You're going to love it; most of these kids have never seen a white person before, they want to touch your skin."

He swung around grinning at me, his protruding maps knocking Kip in the face.

"Hey man, I'm sorry about that."

Kip nodded.

"I've been to Uganda twice before," The American continued so loudly that I couldn't help but listen.

"It's just amazing how friendly everyone is. These people have nothing, literally nothing, but they would give you everything they own. I've brought a map of the world and a map with all the American states on it, as most of them don't even know where America is." He swung around to smile at me and knocked Kip again.

"Can you watch your bag, please?" Kip said irritated.

"My bad, sorry." The American continued, "I used to bring sweets, but then I worried about giving the kids sugar. You don't want to get kids addicted to sugar when they can't afford to buy it. I also worry about their teeth as they don't have dentists like we do."

He hit Kip for a third time.

"Hey, get your maps out of my face or I'll be forced to stick them up your FUCKING ARSE!" Kip shouted. The spotty American turned to face the other direction. He then began slagging off the Brits and how uptight we are. It was a merciful change from hearing about his Ugandan experiences.

Kip had booked a hotel in Kampala for the night. Our taxi to the hotel was an old white Mitsubishi hatchback. Nine out of ten cars in Uganda were white, old, and Japanese. Our hotel looked like it had been built in the 1970s in the days of Idi Amin. There was dark wood paneling on every wall and fake marble flooring. It was quiet as if we were the only guests staying there. A young porter took my bag up to my room. I gave him £5, which was worthless, but as I didn't have any Ugandan money or dollars, I didn't know what else to do.

My room gave me a Saturday Night Fever vibe. Black glossy tiles covered the ensuite bathroom. The sink and bathtub had flecks of glitter. I kicked off my sweaty trainers and lay on the bed, my head whirring about everything that had happened. I ordered a plate of chicken and chips in my room with a can of Coke. I didn't sleep much. I got up at 7 a.m. feeling like a zombie, my eyes black and my hair out of control with post-flight static.

In the dining hall for breakfast, I was the only white person in there, and Kip was nowhere to be seen. The other guests were all dressed in smart business suits. A young male waiter asked me in a very softly spoken voice how I'd like the chef to cook my eggs. I was starting to realise that most Ugandans were softly spoken. Their speech was more rhythmical. It was soothing and much nicer than being screamed at. I ordered an omelette with diced onions and peppers. I washed it down with coffee so thick it laced my throat with bitterness.

After breakfast I found Kip pacing the reception area.

"Are you ready?" he asked.

"Yes." I said.

"I've hired a four-by-four so we can drive ourselves to Masindi."

"You're going to drive, have you ever driven in Uganda before? Wouldn't we be safer in a taxi?"

"We'll be fine." He said looking impatient.

I followed Kip to the jeep. Outside the hotel, the traffic was already close to gridlocked. At the first roundabout, a traffic policeman in a light blue uniform was directing the traffic using only his hands and a whistle. He beckoned us forward, even though there were now four lines of traffic where there should be two.

"See what could be easier than driving out here." Kip smiled. It was the first time he looked like he'd stopped thinking about Richard since we'd left the UK.

We drove across the capital of Kampala. There were a handful of modern buildings. Most of these were international banks. They demonstrated Uganda's precarious foothold on the 21st-century global economy.

The shops were wooden or concrete shacks advertising phone credit or barber services. Butchers had slabs of meat hung outside, attracting flies. There was even a man selling a 1970's three-piece sofa in beige velour, like my Nan used to own. Depressingly, there were plenty of shacks selling coffins.

Outside of the city, the smell of burnt firewood drifted into the car. I turned on the radio to hear a health announcement. It was about protecting yourself against HIV and AIDS and knowing your status.

"How are you feeling now we're here?" I asked Kip.

He looked across at me.

"Okay, that's a stupid question. I know how you feel,

shit, angry, guilty, and pissed off. There's nothing I can say to make things better. I'm sorry about that, but can we not spend the entire journey sitting in silence, please?"

"I can't get my head around the fact that Rose is dead. She's been my only family my entire adult life. Without her, I've no one."

"You're not alone. I'm here, aren't I? I know it's strange for you to have to rely on anyone but yourself. You can lean on me for as long as you want. I'll help you get through this."

Kip smiled.

"I don't deserve you or your kindness. I'm sorry for the way I reacted the last day of your holiday in France. The morning after we got together, I freaked out. One minute we were mates having fun together. The next we were in bed, and it was intense. I meant what I said about liking you. I like you too much to fuck everything up."

"You don't have to worry, we're still friends."

"You know I've never been in a serious relationship before. I've never actually said the words I love you to anyone, apart from Rose. I've been close a few times. I'm scared that when I finally say it, I'll screw things up."

"For someone who seems so confident, you don't have much faith in yourself, do you? The way you strut around your bar and swagger your way down the ski slopes. I'd never have guessed such insecurities lurked beneath the surface."

"Are you taking the piss?"

"No, it's just you're not special in being scared. If weren't just a little bit scared, you'd be an arrogant twat. I also don't blame you for not falling in love. I had ten years with Mark. I don't regret them but I kind of wished I hadn't tried to settle down so quickly. Coming out to France to see you made me realise what I'd missed out on."

"Do you think you and Mark will get back together?"

"No, never. The trip with you changed that." I looked at him. "Not because I slept with you, and it was so amazing I couldn't possibly sleep with any man but you. It was more I finally knew I'd be okay on my own. I didn't need Mark. I didn't need anyone."

We drove past an athletic man on a pink bike with a forest worth of sticks tied to its back.

"There are some things you never get to see back home," Kip said, and we both started laughing.

We drove for another hour before pulling over at the side of the road. Kip bought us corn on the cob from three women who were cooking it on charcoal stoves.

"Service stations Ugandan style." He said.

It tasted amazing, like the corn had been picked fresh that morning. Back in the jeep, the motion and the heat coming in through the windows put me to sleep; I woke up as my head knocked against the window. We had reached the red earth road with giant potholes that led to Rose's Ugandan home.

FIFTY-NINE
SEMMY

Semmy woke up early again. Hope and her father were asleep, so she walked to the borehole. Early morning was the best time to collect water. It was not too hot, but the sky had enough warmth to make the walk pleasant. At the borehole children and women were already crowded around. Semmy spotted her best friend Mercy.

"Semmy, is it really you?" Mercy said, as if she were a ghost.

"Yes," Semmy embraced her friend.

"I kept asking your father where you are, and all he would tell me was that you were away studying."

"I went to a charity that paid for me to go to a school in Masindi."

"Did you pass your exams?"

"Yes, did you?"

Mercy shook her head. "The exam was hard don't you think?"

"Yes." Semmy said feeling sorry for her friend.

"I heard about Lydia. You must miss her so much," Mercy said.

Hearing her best friend talk about her sister brought tears to Semmy's eyes. It felt like a new wound inflicted where an old one had barely begun to heal.

"She took sick when we were away."

"What made her sick? Was it malaria?"

The water pump became free. Semmy stepped forward to fill her jerry can and avoid answering any more of Mercy's questions.

"I've missed you," Mercy said. "It wasn't the same at school without you. After I failed my exams, my father said I had to stay home. I spend my time helping with the farm and taking care of my brother and sister."

Semmy had to bite down on her bottom lip to stop her tears. She wanted to tell her friend everything. How Lydia had died. That she has a niece that requires her to be like a mother. She even wanted to tell Mercy about Sydney. The first boy she had kissed and how lovely he had been. She knew she couldn't. She feared what her father would say or do if he'd heard she'd spoken of these things.

When the jerry can was full, it took all her strength to lift it. She'd grown weak living as a Muzungu.

"I can help you," Mercy said, and Semmy felt embarrassed.

"I'll be fine. I need to get back home now. I'll come and see you soon?"

"You promise," Mercy smiled, but there was something in the way she stared at Semmy that made her uncomfortable. It was as if she were looking at someone completely different.

Back at her homestead, Albert was awake, and Hope was crying. He did nothing to comfort her. Semmy dropped the heavy water onto the floor and went to check on Hope. The routine began again. Boiling water, preparing the ugali, and comforting Hope until it was ready.

"What will we eat, when the ugali is gone?" Semmy asked.

"You'll not starve. We have land we can plant again, and

we can grow food. It will take time, as the ground is hard and there are lots of weeds, but I'm positive things will be okay now you're home. Today we'll go out to the field and start digging."

"What about Hope?"

"Strap her to your back, like your mother did when you were young."

Semmy fed Hope the ugali and then took her bed sheet and made a sling to support her. On the walk to the field, Hope's feet dug into Semmy's back. They started to dig, but the earth is as hard as stone, and the weeds were stubborn.

At lunchtime, they returned to the homestead. Working in the heat with so little food was exhausting for Semmy. She lit the fire and cooked a little ugali. Enough to stop Hope from crying and she stole a few spoons for herself. Physically she'd adjust. Her stomach would shrink, and she'd get used to a diet of rationed food. Her strength would return from fetching water and working the land. Even her sleep would improve when her body became used to a mat, not a soft mattress.

Emotionally, the adjustment would be harder. Living back at home without Lydia for company. The changing mood of her father and the demanding needs of a newborn. Even reacquainting with her old friends would take time.

Her mind wandered to Sydney. Was he waiting for her in the playing field under the tree? Was he wondering what had happened to her? She thought of the play he'd written. Another girl would play the role he wrote for her. It seemed foolish to her to think of such things, but she wasn't ready to forget her life in Masindi just yet.

SIXTY
ANNA

I recognized Rose's Masindi house from photos I'd seen. The tall black security gates and her long driveway framed by flowerbeds. Her quaint brick house, with the red-tiled roof that glowed orange in the sun.

Edna appeared on the front steps as we pulled up. She wore a red, patterned, Ugandan-style dress. Her hair braided in neat lines from her forehead to the nape of her neck. Kip smiled as she walked down the steps to greet us.

"It's so good to see you again," Edna said hugging Kip, "Rose was like a mother to us all. We miss her very much."

"Edna, you haven't changed a bit. This is my friend, and Rose's right-hand woman at WOMAID, Anna."

Edna took both of my hands in hers.

"It is so good to see you at last."

"I take it Richard's not here?" Kip asked.

Edna shook her head. "No, come inside and I can tell you what I know."

"What about Margaret?"

"She hasn't been here. I called to ask her if she knew anything about Semmy. She said I mustn't worry. Richard would take care of everything as soon as he had finished sorting out what happened." She took a handkerchief from her skirt pocket and wiped the palms of her hands.

"I'm worried about the girls. Hope, she's such a sweet little thing, and I wonder how Semmy will cope with her on her own. And Florence, she's not been here since the shooting. I think the whole thing frightened her so much that she ran away. She'll be getting sick without her medicines."

"Let me worry about Semmy, Hope, and Florence," Kip said, putting his arm around Edna. "We'll make sure they're all okay."

Edna smiled. "You must be hungry; come, I'll make you some food."

We followed Edna up the steps, and into the hallway. The hall was painted cream with a shiny real wood floor. I stopped to look at the photos on the wall. There was one of Rose with her sister Nadine as children. Another of their parents with the workers from their sugar plantation. There was even a photo of Kip as a teenager; his mother beside him, he had wild and unruly hair even then.

"That was just before my mum died," Kip said, looking over my shoulder.

"Your mum was very pretty."

"Come and sit out the back," Edna said, taking us through the kitchen and outside to the veranda. We sat on wicker chairs overlooking the immaculately kept garden. The sun was low in the sky, providing a lovely warmth.

"It's too long since I've been here. I should have come before now."

"Rose would like the fact that you're here now. It's so green and quiet. I never expected Uganda to be so green."

"That's why it's known as the fruit basket of Africa."

Edna came out with a tray of beers.

"Will you sit with us," Kip said.

"I was going to fetch you some food."

"It can wait. I need to talk to you about what happened.

How was Richard on the day of the shooting?"

"He was a man in shock. I came home as the ambulance arrived. All he kept saying was it had been a stupid accident."

"Do you believe him?"

"Why would Richard have shot Rose?"

"I don't know. We think Rose was planning to leave him. Did she say anything to you?" Edna looked unsure of what to say.

"Speak freely, Edna, please," Kip said.

"I knew Rose wasn't happy. She didn't get on with Margaret, and she hated Richard spending all his time with her. I told her that he'd stayed over at Christmas, and she said she should never have married him."

"What is happening with Richard? Are the police investigating this as a murder case?" Kip asked.

"I don't know. A nice man, a local officer, George Lutaya, is overseeing the case. His son went to school with Semmy. He told me that Richard had admitted to firing the gun that killed your Aunt Rose. George was aware that Semmy was staying here as her father had a problem with drink and could be violent. Richard said he was protecting Semmy and Hope. He said he only meant to scare Albert. I think the police believed him."

Kip was shaking his head.

"The man's a compulsive liar."

"George says it will be sent to the local court for a judge to decide on which charge is brought and any sentencing. They were holding Richard at Masindi police station. Bail was set at $10,000 and it's been paid."

"Who paid it?"

"I don't know, I think it must have been Margaret.

George is driving out to see Semmy and her father tomorrow. He'll take a statement from them and come back to me with any news."

"Do you think Richard will come back here?" I asked.

"I don't know," Edna said, "if you're worried, you could book into the local hotel; I can give you the details."

"There's no need," Kip said. He looked at his watch. "Edna, would you like me to run you home?"

"I need to get you something to eat."

"We'll be fine," Kip said, "I'm grown up now, I can fix us some food."

Kip showed Edna out and returned with the same pensive look on his face.

"Don't worry, Anna. I'll stay up all night if it makes you feel any better. That man is never stepping a foot inside this house again."

"Do you think he's going to get away with it?"

"Not if I have anything to do with it."

SIXTY-ONE
SEMMY

Another day of working in the field and progress was slow. Semmy returned home exhausted and couldn't see how they would get the land ready for planting in time. Maize seeds had to be in before March when the rains came. March was only a couple of weeks away.

Semmy began to put the water on to boil. Hope had fallen asleep on the walk home and she lay her down in their hut. Albert said he needed to see his friend Joseph. He hadn't said what he was going to see him for, and this was the first time he'd left Semmy at home alone. She worried. Joseph was his friend who brewed the beer and a visit to his house would always mean he returned home drunk.

Supper time came and went, and still her father hadn't returned. Semmy put Hope to bed and stayed up sitting alone by the fire. She had never felt so lonely, and the homestead had never been that quiet. She stared into the dying embers of the fire until she heard her father's footsteps. He stumbled into the clearing. Swaying and unsteady on his feet, he looked up at her, startled, as if he'd forgotten she was home.

"Semmy," he slurred, quickening his speed to reach her. That's when he tripped face first over a large stone. He fell so that his head was in spitting distance of the fire, close enough to tinge the ends of his hair.

Semmy jumped up and helped bring him to his feet. He was too heavy to lift. Without Lydia to help her, he toppled backwards and caught her lip with his elbow as he fell. Semmy felt no pain, but she could taste the blood in her mouth. She ran her tongue over her cut lip. Albert was far enough from the fire. She's let him lie where he was. He could sleep off the drink until the morning.

The following morning, Albert was still lying by the fire. He woke as Semmy started to boil the water and feed Hope. He looked up at her, his face full of worry and confusion.

"You didn't hit me; you fell," she said.

"Fell?"

"When you came home from Joseph, you tripped over that stone," she said, pointing to the offending object. "You were so close to the fire that I thought you might catch alight, and so I tried to move you. I wasn't strong enough, and as you fell again, you caught me with your arm."

He touched his hair; the ends were brittle.

"I'm sorry." He said.

Semmy wanted to scream at him. She wanted to tell him that he had no right to go out drinking when they had no money. That she was tired and hungry and needed him to help her. Her life at home was not going to be spent picking him up when he got drunk. She dare not say any of this. Instead, she fed Hope, strapped her to her back, and they set off to the fields.

Hope was heavy on Semmy's back. The sun was relentless, and the prospect of another day spent digging made Semmy want to cry. A neighbouring family had hired two oxen to plough their field. Semmy watched as these two muscular animals pulled a wooden plough and churned up the land. They made it look so effortless compared to their laboured progress with a fork and spade.

Semmy was lost in her own thoughts when she looked up to see George, Sydney's father, walking towards them. He was wearing his black beret at a right angle across his forehead. His beige shirt and trousers were neatly pressed. The Ugandan flag was sewn onto his sleeve, and a gun was holstered in the belt of his trousers.

"My name's George Lutaya." He said to Albert his smile a mouth of white teeth. "I'm in charge of the investigation into the death of Rose Greene."

"Is she okay?" Semmy asked.

George shook his head. "I'm afraid not. I'm sorry to have to break this news, but she was killed the day that you left the Masindi house. Richard Greene claims it was an accident."

George opened his small black notebook and began to read from it.

"Richard's statement is that you, Albert, arrived at the house uninvited, you were drunk and abusive to both him and his wife. Richard asked you, repeatedly, to leave the house, but you refused. You then forced Semmy and Hope to leave against their will. For protection, Richard took out his hunting rifle and threatened to shoot you if you failed to stop. Still, you did not stop. At this point, you were at the gate of his property. He fired a warning shot, and Rose stood in front of the rifle."

Semmy looked at her father. Neighbours who were tending to their land nearby had stopped digging and were stood watching them. The women had their hands on their hips and their children asleep on their backs. The men leaned on their spades or forks, watching. Only the farmer with the oxen continued working.

"I was a little drunk, but I didn't abuse anyone," Albert said, "Semmy wanted to come home with me; I didn't force her. They had kept her against her will."

Semmy could see that George was looking at her, but she didn't speak.

"Did you see Richard with the hunting rifle?" George asked.

Albert nodded.

"Did he warn you that he'd shoot if you didn't stop?"

"Yes, but if we had stopped, he would have forced Semmy to stay. He had no right to keep my family from me."

"Richard Greene says that you didn't want to leave with your father, Semmy. Is this true?"

George will know from Sydney all about how her father drinks. He'll know he's violent and this is why Semmy was taken to stay with the charity. She's sure he'll even be able to smell the brew on him from the night before.

"What happened to your lip?" George asked.

"I fell." She said running her tongue over where it had swollen up.

George looked at Albert in disgust.

"Did either of you see what happened to Rose?" he asked.

"I turned around after the gun was fired. That was when I noticed Rose was lying on the floor," Semmy said.

"Why didn't you return to her?"

"We were afraid to."

George nodded and made a note in his book.

"Richard will need to appear in court in front of the local magistrate. It will be up to a judge to decide whether he meant to kill his wife. I daresay you'll be called as witnesses.

Can I take a contact number so I can reach you?"

Albert gave George the mobile number for Aunt Grace. George leaned forward to look at Hope strapped to her back.

"Do you have what you need for her?"

"Yes, thank you," Semmy said tears stinging the backs of her eyes.

George left and Semmy returned to work on the field. She spent the next hour thinking how sad it was that Rose had died at the hands of her new husband. She also wondered what Sydney would think when he heard she was back working in the field.

SIXTY-TWO
ANNA

Edna arrived early the next morning to prepare our breakfast. I hadn't slept much, and I'd heard Kip up and down for half the night. Edna served us fried eggs and toast, followed by a plate of fresh pineapple, papaya, and mango. I ate like I hadn't eaten in a week, while Kip drank coffee.

"You have to eat," Edna chastised him. "What else can I prepare for you, porridge maybe, or some rice?"

"Edna don't fuss, I never eat breakfast." Edna looked at me like there must be something wrong with a man that does not eat.

"What are you going to do today?" she asked.

"Can you tell us how to get to Margaret Brown's hotel? I want to go and see if Richard's staying there."

"I warn you, don't expect a warm welcome from Margaret."

"I don't care what kind of welcome she gives me." Kip drank the last of his coffee. "Are you ready?" He said as I rushed to eat the last of my pineapple.

Despite the tragic circumstances of my visit to Uganda, I still marveled at how beautiful it was. The tropical-coloured flowers that greeted us as soon as we opened the front door. The warm breeze that bathed us in African sunshine and the feeling that life had gone back in time.

We drove to Margaret's in silence. I stared out of the window. Fruit sellers with giant stalks covered with green bananas sat at the side of the road. Women wearing colourful dresses walked past with water or baskets of fruit on their heads. Men congregating, deep in conversation at every street corner. An absence of cars made the place quieter. I'd never visited a place where so many people walked or rode bikes. It was also the colour of the town I noticed. Every shack and building were coated in the red dust of the road, giving everywhere an orange hue.

Margaret's hotel was located at the edge of Masindi town on the road out to the famous Murchison Falls. When we arrived, the front gate was locked. The only person around was a young Ugandan man. He wore blue overalls and was sweeping the path with a broom made of thin sticks.

"Mrs. Brown is not here." He informed us.

"Do you know when she'll be back?" Kip asked.

The boy shook his head.

"What about Richard Greene; is he here?"

Again, the boy shook his head and said nothing.

We drove into town looking for signs of Margaret, Richard, or Florence. We had photos from the WOMAID website that we showed to people. No one had seen them. We drove back to Margaret's hotel and this time the gates were open. Margaret was sat at the reception desk dressed in beige trousers and a peach short-sleeved shirt.

"Can I help you?" She said.

"I'm Kip, Rose Greene's nephew." Kip held out his hand while Margaret raised her eyebrows in surprise.

"That must mean you are Anna." She said getting up and shaking my hand.

"We've come to see Richard. Is he here?"

"He's out." Margaret said.

Kip's eyes searched the cottages and trees behind Margaret.

"If you don't believe me, you're welcome to look around," Margaret said.

We walked past circular lodges to a restaurant. On one of the walls, there was a photo of the current Ugandan President Museveni. On the other, a giant map of Masindi National Park.

"I like what you've done with the place," I said.

"Thank you. Maybe when people realise traveling to sub-Saharan Africa isn't half as dangerous as they've been led to believe, I'll make my fortune." She smiled, but there was little humour in her face.

A young Ugandan man walked past, carrying a mop and bucket.

"Moses, is my friend Richard here?"

Moses looked confused as if it were a trick question.

"Have you seen Richard this afternoon?" she said.

"No, Miss Brown."

Margaret turned to Kip and said, "Are you satisfied he's not here?"

"Where is he?"

"He had a few errands to run."

"I need to see him; I have to understand what happened with my aunt; he owes me that much."

"I'm very sorry for your loss. Rose was a unique woman, and it's a terrible thing that has happened. Richard has had a lot to come to terms with. He's distraught and could be facing prison time for what happened. It was a stupid bloody accident, and he should have known better. Firing off warning shots from a gun is asking for trouble."

Margaret spoke with sincerity, but her words did nothing to placate Kip.

"I don't believe Richard is distraught. I think he meant to kill Rose," he said. "He married her for her money, and he started the charity to get rich. I assume you knew all about his little scam."

Margaret rolled her eyes and sighed.

"What makes you think Richard intended to kill Rose, or that I had anything to do with it?"

"We found a photo of you with Richard in Kenya. My aunt was suspicious about the time he spent over here with you."

"Richard and I dated in the 1970s. Whatever your aunt suspected; we weren't having an affair. As for my working at WOMAID, I did this to help those two girls, Lydia and Semmy."

"Why did you pay Richard's bail?"

"He's a friend of mine and he was good to me when no one else was. The poor man has lost his wife in the most awful of circumstances, it's the least I can do."

I showed her the photo of Colin Jenkins and Richard together in Kenya.

"Do you know this man?"

"Yes, he was stationed in Kenya when Richard and I were there; I forget his name." Margaret said, looking confused about why this photo had any relevance.

"His name is Colin Jenkins. Last week, he contacted the charity, and when I went to see him, he tried to attack me. I think Richard was behind it."

"Why would he do that?"

"To get rid of me. I'd started discovering things about

Richard's past, and he wanted to try and stop me from asking too many questions."

Margaret shook her head.

"Can you hear yourselves? Has everyone around here gone mad? It's very simple. The charity was poorly set up and run. Rose and Richard didn't know what they were doing. I should have been more vigilant, but I was rather busy getting my own hotel ready. Unlike your aunt, I don't have a nest egg for my future. If I don't open the doors on this place soon, I have nothing. I was also rather busy taking care of Semmy, Florence. and Hope. As for Colin Jenkins, Richard hated the man. He wouldn't ask him for anything. I suspect that a more sensible explanation would be that Colin found out about the charity. He asked to see you to taunt Richard. As for why he attacked you, that's what Colin does to women. He's a cretin of a man."

A red heat rash appeared on the left side of Margaret's neck.

"If you'll excuse me, this has taken quite long enough, and I have a hotel to open."

"You plan to go ahead with the opening despite what's happened?" Kip asked.

"I don't see how delaying the opening of my hotel will help anyone. I trust you'll find yourselves out. And one more thing, next time you plan to visit, please have the courtesy to call beforehand. I do hate unannounced visits."

Back at Rose's house, Kip took two beers from the fridge and handed me one. We sat outside as the sun started to set, and the mosquitoes began to bite. Kip found some citronella candles that he lit around us. It was so peaceful. We sat listening to the geckos as the night sky and stars surrounded us. Kip seemed calmer. I wondered if seeing Margaret had helped.

"Do you think Margaret's telling the truth about her and Richard?" I asked.

"I don't know. She's so different from Rose. Her manner, the way she looks."

"She's scary, where Rose was so sweet."

"It could be why my aunt was an easy target. I don't know, she seemed genuine."

Edna brought us a goat curry with rice.

"You get off home," Kip told her. "Take tomorrow off, we can manage."

Edna smiled and left to return to her family.

"I wonder what Rose would say if she could see us sitting here together at her house," I said.

Kip smiled. "She'd be delighted. Did you know she'd phoned me after you had come back from France."

"I made her promise she wouldn't. What did she say?" I asked, feeling beyond embarrassed.

Kip smiled. "She told me that I should treat you with respect and that you were a lot more sensitive than you let on to being. She was worried about me hurting you. After your breakup with Mark, she said you didn't need me messing you around. She was very fond of you, Anna. Never underestimate how much she enjoyed having you as part of the charity."

"I'll miss her."

"I was thinking we should host something in her memory at the house. We could invite the people she knew locally who want to pay their respects. We could see if George could get Semmy to come back for it. Who knows if we put up posters, it's possible Florence might show up."

"It's a great idea."

We sat up past midnight talking and drinking. It felt like when we'd been in France together. When we went inside, Kip locked the back door behind us.

"Do you think Richard will come back here?" I asked.

"No, but I don't want you to have to worry about it."

He went to the cupboard and took out two glasses and poured us both a water. He stepped towards me and placed a kiss on my left cheek.

"What was that for?"

"I'm grateful you're here; this would be a million times harder on my own."

I smiled.

He kissed me again this time on my lips, and he held his face millimeters from mine.

"What?" I said.

"I don't know. I want to spend the night with you, Anna. Only, I know I'm not in a good place, and I don't want to screw you around."

"I'm a big girl, Kip. I can sleep with you, and forget it ever happened in the morning."

He smiled, and then he kissed me again.

SIXTY-THREE
SEMMY

A week after George had come to speak with Semmy and her father, he returned to their homestead. He had agreed to drive Semmy and Hope to a memorial lunch at Rose's house. George reassured Albert that she'd be gone for a few hours, and he'd be there the entire time.

The first person Semmy met on her arrival was Kip. Throwing his arms around her, he told her how pleased Rose would have been that she was there. He wore a blue t-shirt, and yellow shorts, and had red sunglasses on top of his head. It seemed, to her, a strange outfit for such a somber occasion.

Around thirty people had gathered in the garden. Most, Semmy didn't recognize. They were white and old; Semmy assumed they must be ex-pat friends. Edna came over, and a smile of joy spread across her face.

"I've missed you both." She took Hope into her arms.

"Where's Florence?" Semmy asked.

"We don't know. No one has seen her since you left. We've looked for her and placed signs about the memorial in the town. We hoped Florence would come if she were able, but there's still no sign of her."

Kip introduced Anna and Semmy. They already felt they knew each other so well, and yet it was the first time they'd met. Life at WOMAID had been challenging for them both, in different ways. Anna having had to deal with Richard's ignorance and old-fashioned views of how a charity should be run. Semmy in Uganda trying to build her life without Richard exploiting her.

"I can't believe I finally get to meet you," Anna said. "Thank you for all the letters you've sent and the photos. I'm sure having to write all the time and pose for the photos could be annoying."

"I didn't mind. I'm sorry about how things ended."

"How's it living with your father again?"

"He's pleased we're home. He doesn't say so, but I can tell."

"What about your studies, can you continue with them?"

"No, not yet. At least I have a qualification."

Kip stood up and announced that he wanted to say a few words about Rose.

"Thank you for coming. I must warm you, I'm not a gifted orator like Rose. She knew what to say, and when she spoke, people felt at ease and wanted to listen. It was one of her many talents."

Kip took a drink of beer and looked up, his eyes were red and tearful.

"Rose loved this house, this country, and the people she met here. When my mother died, she took me in and loved me unconditionally. She guided me throughout my whole life, without judgment. Not judging is hard. Rose understood that it's human to make mistakes. She never looked for people's weaknesses. She looked for what made people special. Rose had a talent for spotting a person's unique strengths."

Kip raised his beer towards the sky.

"To Rose. May she always be remembered for her smile and her sense of style. Most importantly, her belief in the inherent goodness of us all."

"To Rose." Everyone said raising their glasses. Edna was next to talk by leading grace.

"Lord, we count our blessings. Give us the strength to live as the sorrow of Rose's parting sits heavy on us. She was a true angel, and we know that you will have welcomed her with open arms. Lord, thank you for the food we eat in celebration of the life of Rose. May we continue to be grateful for all that you do, now and forever, Amen."

Edna had prepared a buffet lunch of rice, curries, and stews. Semmy, Anna, George, and Kip took their food and sat down together. Kip positioned himself between Semmy and George.

"Are there any developments in the case against Richard?" he asked.

"The postmortem has confirmed that the bullet entered her chest and hit her heart. It was impossible to save her."

"What happens next?"

"A court date will be set this week. It will be up to a judge to decide what happens."

Kip turned to Semmy.

"Are you able to tell me what happened the day she died?"

"I couldn't help Rose; I wanted to, but my father was afraid that Richard would shoot him."

"I understand it must have been terrifying. Did you see him with the gun?"

"Yes, Rose was shouting at him to put it down, but he wouldn't listen."

"Did Rose try to stop you from leaving?"

"No, she knew how much my father wanted us to be home with him. She was going to stop the charity."

"What makes you say that?"

"She sacked Margaret and told Richard she wanted a divorce."

"I see." Kip looked at George.

"Do you know about this? Doesn't this show he had a motive?"

"It shows they were having problems with their marriage. This doesn't mean he meant to kill her. Given the occasion, it might be best if we leave the questions about the shooting."

Kip nodded.

"How is life back at home?" He said to Semmy. "Do you have enough money? We still want to help you. If there's anything you need."

"Thank you, but my father is nervous about the charity, after all that happened. He only let me come here today because George was to chaperone us. We're digging the land to start farming again. Also, my neighbour, Mrs. Wintonze, is in a savings and loan scheme. Have you heard of these?"

Kip shook his head.

"It's when a group of people save money together. There is one in our village. When you've saved enough, you can take out a loan to help you to start a small business."

"That sounds like a great idea. What kind of businesses do people have?"

"Mrs. Wintonze borrowed money to buy a second-hand sewing machine. She makes and sells school uniforms. She's made enough money to pay school fees for her two eldest children."

"What business would you start?"

"I don't know."

"You have to think of something that people want and no one else can give."

"What about being able to use a computer?" Edna said. "I bet there aren't many people in your village who know how to use one."

"That could be your business?"

Kip smiled at Semmy.

"I'm serious. Start a computer business. You could take Rose's computer back with you. We're not using it, we have laptops. It will sit in the corner of Rose's living room gathering dust for the next twenty years. Can you get solar panels to run it?"

"My father's friend Joseph has a TV that he runs from solar panels."

"Come with me."

Semmy followed Kip into the living room. He started unplugging the computer from the wall. He called her over and insisted that she see how it all fitted together. He removed the blanket from the back of the sofa and wrapped it around the screen to protect it.

"Now take this home and see if you can do something with it." Kip said smiling.

George drove Semmy, Hope, and their new computer back home to the side of the road leading to their village. Semmy knocked at her father's friend, Joseph. He agreed to strap it onto his moped to take it the final distance along the path to their homestead. Albert was sitting outside his hut, making kindling, when they returned.

"What is that?" He asked.

"Rose's nephew Kip gave it to me. It's so I can start a business teaching people how to use it."

280

"What use will people around here have for a computer?"

"It can tell them if it will rain, so they know when to plant their seeds. It will even tell them what price maize is selling at, so they don't get ripped off when they come to sell it at the market."

"How do you know such things?" Albert asked.

"They taught me at school."

"How will you get it to work without electricity?"

"I'll get solar panels like Joseph."

"With what? I told you we don't want anything to do with that charity. These Mzungus are always filling your head with their ideas. Why can't you take a husband and raise a family like all the other girls in the village?"

Semmy knew her father would never understand. She'd watched her parents farm their small piece of land their whole lives. They struggled every day to have enough food or to buy the little luxuries that they wanted, such as soap and meat. She didn't want that life for herself or for Hope.

SIXTY-FOUR
ANNA

When Robert heard the news about Rose's death, he'd said he'd continue investigating Richard. The day after her memorial, he called to say he had more news.

"I've discovered that Colin Jenkins and Richard did their army training together in Kenya. According to their records, they were both dismissed from the army at the same time. It appears that Richard fabricated his entire army career."

"What was he dismissed for?"

"Gross misconduct. Colin and Richard had a day's leave whilst still training in Kenya. They had hired a car and drove to the capital city, Nairobi. After spending a day drinking in a bar, they started talking to two local Kenyan girls. The girls were 15 years old. Richard and Colin claimed they'd said they were 16.

They left the bar and headed to a national park on the outskirts of Nairobi. It was late, past midnight, and the girls had requested to be taken home. Richard and Colin had refused. Insisting the girls stayed out drinking with them. Colin started trying to kiss one of the girls. The girl tried to push him away, but Colin wouldn't let her go. Richard tried to intervene, and Colin threatened him with a knife. According to the records Richard left. He drove to the nearest bar and called the police. By the time the police arrived, Colin had raped the girl."

My heart sank as Robert relayed the details of what had

happened. I could picture that foul-mouthed and rabbit-toothed thug praying on an innocent girl.

"Did they go to jail?"

"Colin made a plea for diminished responsibility. He claimed a 12-hour training marathon had affected his judgment. He received a five-year sentence at Nairobi prison and served three. The army dismissed Richard after he pleaded guilty of giving alcohol to a minor."

"What about the girls?"

"There's no record of what happened to them. If you were being kind, it would explain why Richard was keen to start a charity supporting young women." Robert said.

"If you were being a cynic, it's possible he has a thing for young girls." I said shuddering at the thought.

After the call from Robert, we decided to drive back to Margaret Brown's lodge in search of Richard. The front gates were open. Red and yellow balloons floated outside.

"It must be her grand opening." I said as we pulled into the car park.

Moses was standing at the entrance with a tray of drinks, welcoming guests. Inside there was the sound of music and people chatting coming, from the restaurant. We followed the noise, and that was when we saw Richard. He was standing with his back to us, talking to two old white men.

"I should have done this a long time ago," Kip shouted. Richard turned around as Kip lifted his right hand and punched him in the face. It landed hard enough to knock Richard off balance and send him crashing onto the floor. The guests parted to stare at Kip.

"What do you think you're doing?" Margaret screamed as she ran over.

"Get out of here now." She started pulling at Kip's arm as Richard lay on the ground rubbing his jaw.

"I know the truth about you, Richard. How you manipulate, lie, and exploit people to get what you want. Your day is coming. If not in court, then I'll make sure you pay for what you have done."

Margaret called over a couple of large Ugandan guys and was instructing them to throw Kip out. They put their hands on his shoulders, and he brushed them off.

"I'm leaving." He shouted.

We returned to the jeep with Kip red-faced.

"Do you feel any better for that?" I asked.

"The only time I'm going to feel better is when that man is locked up or dead."

SIXTY-FIVE
SEMMY

Semmy went to visit her neighbour Mrs. Wintonze about joining the savings and loan scheme. Mrs. Wintonze was a large lady with stern features. Her presence let the world know she'd take no nonsense from anyone. She was older than Semmy's mother would be by a few years. They had lived in the village ever since Semmy was born.

Mrs. Wintonze had one concrete dwelling that her husband had built with a kitchen and sitting area. There was four mud and wattle huts that she and her six children used for sleeping.

"Tell me where you've been all this time." She asked Semmy. "Your father will not talk about it, and he has been in a very bad way. It's not good for a man to have so much time on his own. He needs his family to keep him focused. I heard of your sister's passing and went to the funeral. I'm sorry for your loss, your father said she was sick."

Semmy had never been a good liar, she told Mrs. Wintonze all she could that was true.

"A charity in Masindi took us in. They paid for me to go to school, and for us both to live in their house with them. When Lydia got sick and passed, we brought her body back to father, but we agreed I would stay there to complete my studies. I passed my exams and so I am home now. The charity gave me a computer. It is so I can start a computer business in the village. I have learnt how to use one and I can teach others. I want to join the savings and loan scheme to save money to buy some solar panels."

Mrs. Wintonze stared at Hope.

"What about the baby? Is she yours?"

Semmy did not answer.

"I've known your father his whole life. He's a very proud man. I can see the child was not fathered by an African man, but she has your features, yours, or Lydia's."

Semmy continued to look to the floor and said nothing. Mrs. Wintonze shook her head.

"Do you have money to save?"

"I have a little." Semmy opened her hand showing Mrs. Wintonze the money that Kip had given her when she'd left.

"My father does not know I have this. He would take it from me and spend it on the brew. I want to save most of it to buy a solar panel and the rest to buy food."

"Very well. We have 20 people in our group. I am one of four who run the scheme. It is mainly adults but, we could make an exception. You'll have to come to the group every week for a meeting. We save together and those who want to borrow must present their business plan. Do you understand?"

Semmy nodded.

"It's very important you only borrow what you can pay back. I will help you, so you understand what the costs of your business are going to be. You are smart, you will pick it up okay."

"Thank you." Semmy said with tears in her eyes. "Why are you being so nice to me?"

"I have a daughter your age. If she ever found herself raising a baby with a father who drank, this is what I'd want her to do. You'll be fine, you know that. There are plenty of people in this village that will look out for you."

Semmy wiped her eyes.

"The next meeting is on Monday at 4pm." Mrs. Wintonze said smiling.

SIXTY-SIX
ANNA

The day of the court case arrived. Richard put in a plea of involuntary manslaughter. If the judge agreed, he'd be free. He could live his life as if nothing had happened.

The Masindi court room was a small concrete building in the centre of town. It looked as unassuming as any small-town council building. Inside, the décor consisted of white walls and dark wood paneling. There were two large wooden desks at the front, one for the prosecution and one for the defense. The judge sat on a throne-size chair at the front. Kip and I sat on benches at the back of the room with half a dozen strangers. Margaret was there; she looked at us when we arrived, but she didn't smile.

Richard was seated at the front, wearing a black suit that was too big for him. Either he hadn't been eating, or he'd borrowed it from a larger man.

Richard's solicitor was a tall Ugandan woman in her early thirties. Her long hair was braided and fell down the entire length of her back. She wore an expensive-looking navy suit. It was a smart move for him to appoint a female defense lawyer. It made him seem pro-woman.

Representing the state was a slim man with a shaved head, grey suit, and pale pink tie. He looked older and had the air of a man that was going through the motions more than invested in the case. He presented the facts. Richard and Rose had returned home to find Albert in their kitchen.

Albert was drunk and insisted that the girls leave with him. He explained that the girls were staying at the charity as their father was unable to take care of them. Depicting the events, he avoided any emotional language. He spoke in a soft voice that made him sound as if he were describing an altogether more relaxed occasion. His expression remained neutral, even as he explained how Richard had taken the gun and shot Rose.

Richard's solicitor stood up next. She explained how Richard and Rose had met. Their romance had resulted in marriage within six months of meeting. They were staying at Rose's family home during their honeymoon, and it was then that Richard had encountered Semmy.

He and Rose had taken Semmy and her sister Lydia into their home and established WOMAID. She was so convincing about Richard's saintliness; I even began to believe her.

When the coroner presented the result of the autopsy, Kip broke down in tears. The worst part was the description of how a single bullet had ruptured her coronary artery. It had cut off the blood supply to her heart. Had the bullet entered two millimeters to the left she'd have survived.

There was a break for lunch. Kip and I sat outside the courthouse, not having the stomach for food. We didn't talk much and before long we were called to take our seats once again.

Richard took the stand in the afternoon. The prosecutor asked about his relationship with Rose. The formation of the charity and the money they'd lost to contractors.

"Did Rose hold you responsible for what happened?" the prosecutor asked.

"She was very upset, but she didn't blame me."

"How would you describe your marriage?"

"It was wonderful," Richard said, and Kip's body tightened next to me.

"Wonderful? There have been several statements given to the police claiming the contrary."

Richard rubbed his bald head.

"Rose was temperamental, hot-headed and passionate," he said. "I said our marriage was wonderful to me, but it wasn't perfect."

"What was the mood like between the two of you on the day that Rose died?"

"We had been arguing."

"About what?"

"Rose didn't like me spending time with Margaret. We had gone to visit Margaret's new hotel, and Rose seemed annoyed at how well it was doing. Rose thought Margaret had not overseen the building of the charity refuge properly. I think there was some resentment that Margaret had done so much with Semmy and Hope, whereas Rose had not."

I looked across the courtroom at Margaret, who sat staring stoney-faced looking at Richard.

"Rose would have wanted to be more hands-on," Richard continued. "The charity had meant a lot to her, and she was unhappy that things hadn't gone as she'd planned. We'd intended for our trip to Uganda to help her feel more positive about the charity's future."

The prosecutor then asked Richard a series of questions related to their return to the house. What were Richard's thoughts and reactions to finding Albert there? Could he explain why he got the hunting rifle? Why did he chase Albert outside? He tried and failed to establish any motive as to why Richard could have wished to kill his wife.

Richard kept up his performance of a wounded man, grief-stricken by what had occurred. Watching him answer the questions, it was easy to believe that he'd acted out of compassion for the children in his care.

Richard's solicitor stood up next. She focused her questioning on Rose's state of mind.

"Did Rose think that you and Margaret were stealing the charity money?"

"I think it was something she had thought about when she was feeling low."

"Did she have any evidence of this?"

"No."

"What was your relationship with Margaret Brown?"

"We were friends."

"Did Rose every get jealous of your friendship?"

"Yes, she suspected we were having an affair."

"Were you?"

"No," Richard shook his head. "I loved my wife; we'd just got married."

"Rose's medical notes show that she was taking antidepressants. Were you aware of this?"

"Rose suffered with her nerves and could get anxious."

I looked at Kip, who was leaning forward in his seat.

"Was she ever depressed?"

"Sometimes."

"Suicidal?"

"My wife struggled with mental illness."

"Is it possible that the day she stood in front of the gun that she was not of sound mind?"

"It's possible. She'd complained about how exhausting she'd found the flight."

"You repeatedly shouted warnings about firing the gun to stop Albert from leaving. Rose understood that there was a risk in putting herself in front of it. Yet, she did this with tragic consequences."

"I'm afraid so," Richard said.

Kip stormed out of the courthouse. The inference, by Richard's solicitor, that Rose's death was due to her, "not being of right mind" was insane.

"I don't get how Richard's solicitor spews this bullshit," Kip said. "Richard wasn't a loving husband and a generous man. Rose wasn't a depressed and suicidal woman. The man is a ruthless psychopath who cares about nothing or no one."

SIXTY-SEVEN
SEMMY

Semmy had got up early to go to the river. She wanted to wash the clothes they would be wearing in court. George was picking them up early the following day to drive them to the courthouse. Aunt Grace met her at the river. As Semmy washed the clothes, her aunt talked excitedly next to her. She thought it was a privilege to be called to give evidence. They'd be the first members of their family to see the inside of a courthouse. Semmy didn't share her excitement.

When Semmy returned home, she found Joseph's moped was parked at their compound. Hearing Joseph and her father in her bedroom hut, she'd assumed they were looking at the computer. Perhaps Albert was coming around to the idea that an internet business could work. Joseph appeared with Semmy's computer monitor in his hands.

"What are you doing with my monitor?" She asked.

"Let him be Semmy," Albert said, motioning with his hand that she was to keep quiet.

Joseph walked past Semmy.

"You cannot give him my screen father. I need that," Semmy said, panic in her voice.

"Father, it's not yours to give. I need that screen. Don't you see the computer is useless without it."

"Enough, Semmy, remember who you're speaking to. Joseph can make use of the screen, and we need the money to buy seeds."

"We can borrow the money for seeds. I didn't tell you, but Mrs. Wintonze will help me. She says I can join her savings and loan group."

Joseph began strapping the screen onto the back of his bike. Semmy went up to him. She pleaded with him not to take it.

"Move away and do what I tell you," Albert shouted.

Joseph was a smaller, gentler man than her father. However, he was also a businessman for whom making money was always his priority.

"Your father and I have made a trade; I'm sorry."

He left with Semmy's monitor; Albert followed him on foot. Semmy was angry and frustrated. Was her father so short-sighted? Could he not bear the thought of her making things better for them all.

She took the dress she'd washed and her father's shirt and hung them out in the sun to dry. Hope was hungry and needed food. Semmy lit the fire and fed Hope, but her mind was elsewhere. What would she tell Mrs. Wintonze? The money that Kip had given to her could help pay for solar panels. It wouldn't pay for a monitor as well. Would her father get seeds or spend the money on beer?

Albert staggered back into the compound after dark. Semmy had already put Hope to bed. He'd left in a foul mood; she was nervous of his temper when he was drunk. Waiting in her hut, she hoped he'd pass out.

"Semmy." He shouted from outside her hut. "Semmy, you get out here now."

Semmy came out of her hut before his shouts woke Hope.

"You disrespected me in front of my friend, d'you hear

me?"

"Yes father."

"What did you say?"

"I said yes Father, I'm sorry I was only…"

Before Semmy could finish speaking, Albert hit her. It was a punch hard enough to knock her to the floor. She stood up but knew there was no reasoning with him. His own demons and heartbreak filled him with too much rage. He wouldn't even know what he was doing.

Semmy started to cry. He hit her three more times. Each time she felt like the life was being smashed out of her. Tiredness stopped him. He lurched into his sleeping hut, and she heard his body crash to the floor. Semmy sat up alone by the fire for another hour or so. Her face was bloody and bruised, and her lip had started bleeding again.

Aunt Grace arrived early the next morning to take care of Hope while they were at court. She looked at Semmy's swollen and bruised face and let out a cry.

"How can I go to court looking like this?" Semmy asked.

"I don't know, but you have no choice," Grace said.

Albert emerged from his hut. He looked at Semmy's face and then at his sister.

"I know." He says his voice gruff and hoarse. "Save your words."

"When will this stop?" Grace shouted. "Do you want Semmy and Hope to leave again. They will, you know. They'll leave, and next time they'll never come back."

"I said, save your words," Albert said, rubbing his head.

When George arrived, he looked at Semmy's cut face.

"Did you fall again?" He asked, glaring at Albert.

She shook her head.

"Are you okay to stay here?"

"My father was nervous about appearing in court. He got too drunk. When he came home, he didn't know what he was doing."

Albert kept his head bent down, not looking at George.

"It won't happen again, will it, brother?" Aunt Grace said, bouncing Hope on her lap.

Albert grunted, but still didn't speak.

SIXTY-EIGHT
ANNA

Kip woke up in a foul mood for the third day of Richard's court case. I could tell by the black circles around his eyes that he'd barely slept. He didn't join me for breakfast, preferring to take his coffee and sit outside watching the birds on the lawn.

Today, Semmy and Albert were being called as witnesses. Kip hoped the judge would see that Richard didn't need the rifle to threaten Albert. Semmy had said, at Rose's memorial, that life at home was an adjustment. She didn't say anything about her father drinking or being violent.

We arrived at court, and it was the same few people sitting in the back benches and Margaret. Albert was called to the stand. He gave his name and confirmed he was Semmy's father. It was the first time I'd seen him. He looked nervous and had a vulnerability which I hadn't expected. He wore a clean blue shirt with black trousers. His face was unshaven, and his eyes were bloodshot.

The prosecuting solicitor stood up. He was wearing the same pale pink tie and grey suit that he'd warn on the previous days. An air of going through the motions and being slightly uninterested in the case continued to radiate from him. He began by asking Albert about the events leading up to Semmy and Lydia living with the charity. He then focused his questions on the day of Rose's death.

"Did you at any time threaten Semmy or anyone present

at the house?"

"No."

"Did you witness Richard grabbing the gun?"

"No, Semmy and I had left the house and Richard had disappeared."

"Did you hear Richard shouting to you when you were leaving the property?"

"Yes," Albert said.

"Did he warn you that he had a firearm and was going to shoot?"

"Yes."

"Why did you not stop?"

"I was too scared to know what to do."

"Were you aware that Rose was outside the house?"

"Yes, I could hear her telling Richard to put the gun down."

"Did you turn and see Richard when he fired the gun?"

"No, I only turned to see when he had made the shot, and at that moment, Rose had already been hit."

Richard's solicitors stood up next. Her well-polished appearance and perfectly tailored power suit could have made her seem intimidating to Albert. However, a wide, friendly-looking, smile lit up her face.

"How are you this morning?" She asked.

"I'm fine." Albert said.

She began by establishing the events leading up to the day of the shooting. Presenting the facts carefully and sensitively. Albert's action in trying to force Lydia to get rid of her unborn child wasn't an act of cruelty. On the contrary it demonstrated his concern for his daughter. He admitted he was not educated and had not known the medicine he bought was dangerous. The loss of his wife was presented as a tragic loss to the family. It was understandable at such desperate times that a man would turn to drink.

Her manner was so disarming. I could see Albert starting to relax. He didn't suspect she was extracting admissions of his own failings to build a case for why Richard saw him as a threat.

"Albert, did you consent to your daughters staying in the care of WOMAID?"

"I did."

"Did you worry that the charity mistreated them?"

"No."

"Is it true." She asked, "that you'd been to the house previously seeking money?"

"Yes."

"Did the charity allow you to see your family on these occasions?"

"No."

"What reason were you given for not being able to see them?"

Albert looked at the judge, who reminded him that he was under oath.

"They told me I could see them if I returned when I was sober."

"Yet, you ignored this. Were you drunk when you visited the house on the day Rose died?"

"Yes."

"Are you ever violent when you've drunk?"

Albert hesitated.

"It's a simple enough question. Have you ever hit your daughters when you've been drunk?"

"Yes."

"No further questions."

They showed Albert out of the courtroom and brought in Semmy. I wanted to cry the moment I saw her. Bruising and swelling covered the left side of her face. The bright-faced 15-year-old I'd met the week before at Rose's memorial, had vanished. Instead, a sad, nervous, and embarrassed girl walked in, staring at her feet.

The prosecuting solicitor stood up. He asked Semmy several questions confirming what the judge already knew. Semmy reasons for being in the care of the charity. The events on the day of the shooting. His questions were not probing, and I could sense Kip's increasing frustration.

Richard's solicitor stood up. In the same way as she'd questioned Albert her manner was warm and open.

"How would you describe your time living at Richard and Rose Greene's house and in the care of their new charity?"

"It was nice," Semmy said, "they have a lovely home, and we've always been comfortable and well-looked after."

"Am I to understand that you completed your primary exams with a good grade as a result of staying there?"

"Yes, I'd just started attending Masindi secondary school."

"Did you intend to stay at the charity to complete your studies?"

"That was the plan."

"Were you surprised to see your father and learn he wanted to take you home?"

"Yes."

"Did your father appear drunk or agitated?"

"He was getting upset and angry as Richard didn't want us to leave."

"Your father thought Richard was stopping you from leaving. And was he?"

"No, not really. I think Richard was worried about whether we'd be okay at home. He thought we'd be better off staying with the charity."

"But your father forced you into leaving with him?"

"No, I wanted to make him happy."

"Does it make you happy being at home?"

It was a horrible question delivered at exactly the right time. Could Semmy really stand in court with her face cut up and bruised, claiming that living at home made her happy.

Semmy didn't answer the question. Richard's solicitor left her question hanging for long enough to make her point.

"Did you hear Richard warning your father that he would shoot him?"

"Yes."

"Did he say he'd shoot him or that he'd shoot?"

"I don't know, I think he said he would shoot."

"Do you concede that it's possible he was intending to shoot the gun in the air. To fire a warning shot, but not try to shoot you?"

"Yes, I didn't imagine he'd shoot at us."

"Why is that?"

"He said we're like family to him."

"I have one final question. I can't help noticing the cuts and bruises that are on your face today. Were these inflicted on you by your father?"

"Yes," Semmy said, nodding.

The court was adjourned for lunch. Kip and I walked

outside knowing in our hearts that it was over. We had hoped that the testimony of Albert and Semmy would show them as a loving family. A family pulled apart by a man who interfered in their lives for his own gain. Instead, their appearance had done the opposite. The questioning had painted Richard as a man who cared deeply for the girls. A man led by compassion and not hatred.

That afternoon we were called back into the court to hear the judge's verdict. Kip sat at the edge of his seat willing a verdict of murder.

The judge told the court that, without an eyewitness, it's hard to be certain about what happened. In these cases, he had to consider the facts and evidence he had. It was clear that Semmy and Hope had been well cared for by the charity. The degree to which Semmy and Hope needed protection on the day that Rose had died was unclear. Yet, Albert had a history of drinking and being violent. It was understandable that Richard believed the girls to be in danger.

There was no motive for why Richard would've wish to kill his wife. They were newly married and shared a passion for their philanthropy. One heated argument was not grounds for murder. He would receive a charge of criminal negligence. He would serve a non-custodial sentence and receive a fine.

Kip looked at me.

"Is that it? He's got away with it?"

I nodded. "I'm afraid so."

SIXTY-NINE
SEMMY

Semmy hated every minute of being in court. It was humiliating. Her life displayed as one of misery and desperation. A pregnant sister who died in childbirth, a father too drunk and violent to take care of her. Richard the good Samaritan who had changed her life. It was everything she hated about being with the charity.

George drove them back to the homestead, where Grace was sitting with Hope. Semmy went straight into her hut to lie down; she didn't feel like talking to anyone. She stared at the pictures that hung from the roof. Was this it for her now?

The next day, she and her father went to the field to continue digging the land. Albert had acquired some maize seeds. Semmy wasn't sure if this was from the sale of the monitor. She didn't care; she was relieved that they were going to start planting. It would take a few months before they could harvest, but it was something.

After returning home from the field, Albert said he had to go out. Out meant drinking with Joseph. There was nothing that Semmy could do but wait. As she put Hope to bed, her mind started calculating the odds of her father returning happy. The stress of appearing in court was over, and she hadn't disrespected him. In theory, she had no reason to suspect he would come home drunk and be violent. Sitting up alone watching the flames of the fire, there was still a nervousness about her body. A fight or flight reflex, which would always be a part of her life at home.

She heard the rustling of the bush and the noise of someone approaching.

"Is that you, father?" She said, looking to the edge of the compound. It didn't sound like Albert. The pace was too quick and purposeful. It was dark, and so Semmy struggled to see. She could make out the shape of a man approaching. As she took in his size, stature, and bald head, she realized it was Richard. He wore the same suit that he had worn in court.

"Don't be afraid." He said, his weird smile visible in the light of the fire.

"What do you want?" Semmy asked.

"I wanted to see you and Hope."

"They let you go?"

"Of course they let me go," Richard smiled. "You never doubted me, did you. You know I'd never do anything to harm Rose."

Richard's eyes darted around the compound.

"My father will be back soon."

"Can I sit?" Richard said, motioning to the large stone by the fire. Semmy nodded, and Richard sat down, stretching his legs out in front of him.

"You've lost weight." He said staring across the fire at her. "Your cheeks are sunken, like the first time I saw you; are you not eating?"

"I'm fine."

"Do you have food? I can give you some money," he said, putting his hand inside his pocket and pulling out some notes.

"We have all we need," Semmy said, not looking at him.

"Come closer. You don't need to stand so far away from

me. We're still friends, aren't we?"

She moved two steps closer.

"That's better; I want to talk to you, that's all. You know you and your sister were the reason we started the charity. If I hadn't been driving along the road on the day that you got knocked over, our lives would be very different."

Semmy continued staring at the fire.

"The judge agreed that the shooting was a terrible accident. It means I can continue with the charity. I'd like to take care of you and Hope, if you'll let me. I can help you to complete secondary school. Who knows, you're a bright girl, you could even attend Makerere University, one day."

"I'm grateful for all you've done for Hope and me, but we can't take your help anymore."

"Wouldn't it be nice to never need to worry about your father coming home drunk? I bet you miss the nice house and all your lovely clothes. I can give you everything you could ever wish for."

"You must leave, my father will be home soon. He'll be angry if he finds you here."

Richard stood up and Semmy thought he would leave. Instead, he wandered into her hut, where Hope was sleeping. He stood watching her like he did when he came to her room on Christmas Day.

"How is she?" Richard asked. "I've missed her so much."

It was dark in the sleeping hut. Semmy couldn't see Richard's face. She didn't trust him alone with Hope. Yet she hated being alone with him in the dark.

"Let's sit back around the fire," she said, and Richard followed her out and sat back down on the stones.

"I've got something to tell you." Richard said. "It is going to be difficult for you to hear, but you need to know the truth. I met your sister before I ever met you."

"What? How could you?" Semmy asked her mind trying to understand why Richard was lying to her.

"She used to go to a bar in town that I used to go to."

Semmy felt sick. Could this be true?

"It must have been soon after your mother died that Lydia started coming into the bar. I was living with Margaret and was new to the area. The bar was mainly used by ex-pats, but there were a few locals in there too. I'd buy Lydia a drink and something to eat in exchange for her company."

Semmy was trying to work out why Lydia had never mentioned knowing Richard. If he treated her to meals and she spent time with him, why did she claim to hate him so much.

"You must understand she never came to the bar in her school uniform. She'd always told me she was 18."

Richard looked at Semmy.

"What are you saying?"

"I realise this must be difficult to hear, and I know how this must sound. I was living with Margaret, and we were friends. I was lonely and your sister was very kind to me. It happened one time, that was all. She never came into the bar after that time. I didn't know where she lived, I knew nothing about her but her name."

"What happened one time?" Semmy said.

"She was an attractive young woman."

Semmy started shaking her head.

"You're lying. Lydia would never do such a thing?"

"She was seventeen, a young woman. Plenty of women

at that age are sexually active. For all I knew, she could have had lots of boyfriends."

"STOP." Semmy screamed. "Stop lying. Lydia would never sleep with you. If she had, she would have told me. She would never have stayed in your house."

"How could she tell you? She was ashamed of her pregnancy. If Lydia wasn't pregnant, your father would never have sent her away. When I brought you home, I recognised Lydia. She looked at me and shook her head. It was a sign. I was to say nothing of knowing her. I respected her wishes. There was a small chance that the baby was mine. It was only when Hope was born that I knew. The colour of her skin, the look in her eyes."

Semmy thought about Lydia's hatred of white men. The look on her sister's face when she saw Richard at their homestead. The lightness of Hope's skin.

"You have to go," Semmy said. "I want you to leave."

"I can't. I'm Hope's father, and I want to be there for her. I'm never going to leave her."

Semmy heard her father approaching. Richard didn't notice until he was standing right above him.

"You're not welcome here; do you understand?"

"I need to explain something to you," Richard said, standing up and facing Albert.

"I don't want to hear anything from you," Albert shouted.

"It concerns Hope," Richard said.

"He's lying, father," Semmy shouted. "He's trying to take Hope and me away again."

Albert looked at his daughter.

"He told me he'd keep coming back. He's never going to

leave us alone."

Semmy's words had the desired effect. The rage descended on her father as quickly as if she'd snapped her fingers. He raised his fist and started to punch Richard. He hit him as if his life and the lives of Semmy and Hope depended on it.

Richard tried to fight back. He hit out at Albert, but it was useless. Semmy watched until Richard lay unconscious on the floor of their compound. Albert fell to his knees, exhausted.

"Have you killed him?" she asked, looking down at Richard's body.

"No, he's still breathing, but he won't be bothering us again. I'll go and get Joseph to help me drag him out of here. We'll leave him on the roadside; a good Samaritan may pick him up and take him to the hospital."

SEVENTY
ANNA

Without the court case as a focus, the pain and grief of Rose's death seemed to consume Kip. He'd been to Margaret's hotel several times in search of Richard. She was adamant that Richard wasn't there. According to Margaret, the last time she saw him was when he left the court, which was over a week ago. She was worried about him and had reported him missing to the police.

I felt a little sorry for her. She was determined to see the good in Richard. The truth was that he'd probably left her in search of another Rose or Celia Reynolds that he could con for money. I didn't say as much, but I certainly wasn't concerned for his well-being.

Kip and I had been in Uganda for over a month. Sleeping in the same bed, making love most nights, and then behaving as friends. This had changed after the court case ended. Kip hardly ever came to bed, preferring to stay up all night watching Netflix.

I mentioned over breakfast that I was thinking about returning to the UK.

"Really, why?" He'd asked.

"I think it's time. Besides, you don't need me hanging around."

He handed me his credit card like I were still an employee and told me he'd pay for my flight. I knew Kip wasn't in a good place and wouldn't beg me to stay. I did however expect some emotion from him.

His actions confirmed that I was right to leave as soon as I could. I wasn't his girlfriend, and he'd made it clear the first time we got together not to start liking him. The death of Rose had brought out his vulnerable and serious side. I had been a playful distraction to him, that was all. I was the idiot that had thought I could sleep with him but not get attached. Feminism gave me the freedom to be promiscuous. It was my own emotions that trapped me into falling in love.

Kip insisted on driving me back to the airport. It was 6 a.m. when we'd left. I got in the jeep to leave and struggled to fight back tears. The sky was lit by an orange sunrise that made my heartache seem worse. I focused on the smartly dressed commuters walking or cycling to work. The bikes had undergone so many repairs that none of the parts matched. I smiled at the industriousness of up-cycling everywhere in Uganda.

"You know you can stay for longer," Kip said as we were driving out of Masindi. "It's not like you have a boss that's going to complain if you're not back. WOMAID will remain closed until further notice I'm afraid. I can't see Richard returning to it. Not now he hasn't got Rose to raise the money."

"I know, I need to get back. I have to start job hunting. It's okay for you. You'll leave here and return to your life in the Alps. I'm still sleeping in my sister's spare room."

"What will you do?"

"I don't know, anything that will enable me to save some money and get my own place. Even if it means I have to do a job I don't give a shit about."

"Promise me, you won't do that? You're good at what

you do."

"It's not that easy. I thought working for your aunt would be the start of a new career. It's been life-changing but not in a good way."

"Who knows, you could find yourself a nice new bloke. A man in uniform, doing his bit for society. You could get a nice house. A year from now, you could be married and pregnant."

"You're such a prick, Kip. Why are you acting like this?"

"Acting like what? I'm not criticizing you. Far from it. I'm the fuck wit who works behind a bar for a living and sleeps above his work. I'm as stable and committed as a wet fart. Shit, Anna, I'm saying whatever you do, make sure you're with someone better than me."

"Well, marriage and kids are a million miles from what I want right now."

"What do you want?"

Kip looked at me and a part of me wanted to tell him the truth. The man I wanted was him. The fuck wit who ran a bar and couldn't commit if his life depended on it. I didn't say that, of course. I had my pride.

"I want to get home and clear my head of all the bullshit that has consumed my life for the past few months. That's what I want."

We drove in silence until we reached the outskirts of Kampala, and the traffic slowed to a walking pace. We crawled past the trading sites. Bright, painted shop fronts and huts that advertised haircuts and phone credit.

At the airport, Kip took my suitcase from the boot.

"Thanks for coming with me. I'll never forget how you got me through this."

We stood staring at each other.

"I'd better go."

We hugged each other. Neither of us wanted to let go, and it felt like we'd never see one another again.

I checked my bag in at the British Airways desk. Through security, I wandered around the small parade of shops. There were overpriced safari t-shirts, bottles of waragi (a Ugandan spirit) and soap stone carvings of rhinos and elephants. I got my two nephews a t-shirt each. I spent the flight watching two romantic comedies. I drank four mini bottles of white wine and cried.

I felt ridiculous. I hadn't been this upset when I left Mark, and that was after ten years. I'd known Kip for five minutes and felt distraught. I told myself that when I returned home, I'd be fine. I'd get a new job and keep busy. Everything to do with Kip, Rose, and the charity would soon be a footnote of my life.

I got back to Helen's feeling exhausted.

"Are you okay?" Her face was a picture of maternal concern.

"It was a long flight that's all."

"Boys, come and see Auntie Anna; she's just come back from Africa." Ben and Lewis walked in and stared at me.

"Did you see any lions?" they asked.

"No, not this time."

"Crocodiles?"

"No, I saw plenty of geckos."

"Geckos, do you mean like we've seen in Spain?"

I nodded, and they screwed up their faces.

"I got you a t-shirt each." They looked even less impressed than they were about the geckos.

The next day I went into the WOMAID office. It felt strange and deserted. The soul of the charity had disappeared. It was now a boring old office with useless furniture and stationery. I turned on my computer and I had 120 unopened emails. I put the out of office on to say I'd left the charity and posted the keys back through the door as I left. I couldn't believe it was finally over. Our dreams of providing a safe refuge for young women in Uganda had come to nothing. The worst part was we couldn't even protect the woman that had started it all.

SEVENTY-ONE
SEMMY

Semmy and her father had woken early, the morning after Richard had come to visit. They'd returned to the roadside where they'd left his unconscious body. He was no longer there. What had happened to him and whether he was okay, was things they'd never know. Yet, they agreed between them not to tell anyone of his visit.

Semmy also never told her father about Richard's claim that Hope was his child. Hope being born out of marriage was a big enough challenge for Albert to deal with. He'd never accept Hope into the family if he knew about Richard. Was it possible that her niece was born because of a desperate one-night stand, if that's what you'd call it? Semmy didn't know what to call it – would rape be more accurate? She couldn't bear to think about it.

The force and brutality with which Albert had beaten Richard was also something they didn't discuss. Albert could have killed Richard. The truth was a part of Semmy wished he had. She'd be glad to have him out of their lives forever. Yet, seeing that much rage coming from Albert had scared her. If he was being honest with himself, it had shocked him too. Before his wife died, he'd never laid a violent hand on another human being. Lately, it was the only emotion he showed.

In the days following Richard's visit, Albert never left Semmy or Hope alone. He stayed by her side in the field, and when they returned home, he'd sit by the fire all night. Not going out meant he wasn't drinking. Semmy knew it was difficult for him. Making kindling for the fire kept his hands busy and his mind distracted.

It was midday, several days later and Hope was crying for food and the sun was too hot to work. Semmy and her father returned home from the field for lunch as usual. They walked into their clearing to find George and Kip were waiting for them. George wore his smart khaki police uniform. Kip was wearing long cotton green trousers and a yellow t-shirt. His hair fell over his face, and his eyes were covered with his usual, red-framed sunglasses.

"We're sorry to intrude on you like this," George said, walking over to Albert, and shaking his hand. "Given the time of day we'd assumed you would be returning home. This is Kip; he's Rose's nephew."

Albert shook Kip's hand.

"It's been a week since the court case finished," George said. "The judge ruled that the death of Rose was an unfortunate accident, and so the case is now closed."

Semmy and Albert had known the verdict from Richard's visit, but they'd acted suitably surprised by the news.

"Please sit," Albert said, motioning to the stones around the fire. "Put some water on, so our visitors can have a drink." He said to Semmy.

"No, please, don't trouble yourself," George said as Semmy started to unstrap Hope from her back.

Semmy looked at her father, who nodded, and so she sat down with them.

"Since the trial, Richard hasn't been seen. We wondered if he'd been here to visit. He seemed particularly fond of you and Hope." George said to Semmy.

"We've not seen him, have we, father?"

Albert shook his head.

"The Masindi house has passed to Kip. If Richard does intend to remain in Masindi, he will need to find somewhere else to live."

"Are you staying in Uganda?" Semmy asked Kip.

"I haven't finalized my plans. I have a business in France, which I need to return to. This was the reason I wanted to come and see you today."

Kip looked at Albert.

"I appreciate, sir, that you don't know me. I can only imagine the impression you have of people like me trying to help. I don't wish to take your daughter away from here or anything like that. I only wanted to see if Semmy had started her computer business. And, if there was anything else she needed."

Semmy looked at her father.

"She doesn't need any help." Albert said his tone unfriendly.

"What my father means is I no longer have a business."

Albert turned his attention to Semmy, but she ignored him.

"I'm sorry, my father sold the monitor that you gave me. I joined Mrs. Wintonze's savings and loan scheme so I could save the money for solar panels, but I can't afford a monitor too."

"Semmy what have I told you about disrespecting me." Albert said.

"That I mustn't do it. That you'll punish me." Semmy stood up and looked at her father. "Living here without any chance of earning any money or finishing school is punishment enough. I've been hit and humiliated, and I'm sure that will continue until you marry me off for a dowry and I leave home. George and Kip are good people. I won't lie to them."

It was the first time Semmy had spoken to her father in this way. A defiance that he'd seen a thousand times with Lydia, but never with Semmy. It was as Grace had said. He would lose her if he didn't change.

"Would you like me to help?" Kip asked.

"Yes." Semmy said, her eyes welling up with tears. "I don't want charity; I'll pay you back."

"I can lend you as much as you need. All I want is to make something right out of what has happened. If nothing positive comes from the charity, it will all have been for nothing. Worse than nothing. It will have been to make Richard money. I can't bear that thought. It will haunt me."

Kip looked at Albert.

"Will you allow me to lend Semmy the money she needs?"

Albert nodded.

"I'll leave it with George, who will give you what you need."

George took a small Nokia mobile phone from his pocket.

"If you will allow it, Albert, I've purchased this phone and added credit. In this way, Semmy or you can message me when you need."

"Thank you," Albert said, taking the phone.

Kip and George left and Semmy prepared herself for her father's temper, but to her surprise he said nothing. He just sat down and returned to his attention to stripping wood to make his kindling.

SEVENTY-TWO
ANNA

I started job hunting as soon as I got back to the UK. I applied for a few roles at International Development Charities. In every case, I received emails to say there were candidates with more experience.

In early April, Kip flew back to the UK with Rose's body. He'd arranged a service at the local crematorium. He'd phoned to asked if I'd accompany him in the funeral car to save him arriving there alone. We met at Helen's. He wore a black suit with his hair and beard neatly trimmed, like the night of the fundraising dinner. He seemed sad but calm, like the anger of what had happened was slowly subsiding.

"It's bloody freezing." He said rubbing his hands together.

"You've been living in Uganda for too long; that's all."

"It's the middle of spring isn't it supposed to be sunny? In the Alps, it's lovely weather by this time of year."

"You know what the UK's like."

"I'm starting to remember now I'm here."

He looked at me and smiled.

"Sorry about calling on you again. It's pathetic, isn't it, having no one to accompany me to a family funeral. If I asked a mate from France, then they wouldn't have known Rose. I can't be with someone today that didn't appreciate how great she was."

"It's okay, I'm glad to be here."

We got into the funeral car behind the hearse. Rose's coffin sat on a sea of her scarves with the word "Aunt" displayed along the top in pink flowers.

A crowd of Rose's friends were waiting outside the crematorium. Most of them were around Rose's age. Many I recognised from the fundraising event. They all wore bright dresses covered in colourful flowers. Kip took hold of my hand as we got out of the car and followed the coffin inside. We sat at the front alongside Robert and his wife.

The service followed the familiar format of hymns and speeches. The only time Kip let go of my hand was when he stood up to make a speech. Afterwards, the reception was held in the Hotel du Vin, a grade 2 listed mansion in the centre of Tunbridge Wells. A formal and elegant setting for a wake, with antique furniture and a sense of historic grandeur.

"How are things going?" Robert asked Kip once all the guests had been greeted. "Has anyone heard from Richard."

"The man appears to have vanished," Kip said. "No one has seen him since the day of the court case. It's strange but not surprising. He inherited nothing from Rose, so he's probably gone to find another woman from whom he can get rich."

"What about WOMAID?"

"I've notified the charities commission of Rose's death and Richard's disappearance. There's still some money in the charity account that needs spending. It will be up to us as trustees to decide if the charity continues."

"Should we at least build the refuge?" Robert asked.

Kip shrugged his shoulders. "Someone needs to oversee its construction, or we'll run the risk of losing all the money like last time. That is if that's what happened, and Richard didn't steal it. Besides, who will run a refuge? Margaret is busy with her hotel, and even if she wasn't, I wouldn't ask her."

Robert nodded. "I understand. Are you heading back to France?"

"I must; my business partner Alex has been running things alone for long enough. We must assume Richard's not coming back. I'll call in a few days so we can discuss what to do next."

Before long the food and drinks were cleared, and the last guests had departed. There was a stillness and inevitable quiet that descended like a shroud. The lively chatter of mutual memories was replaced with nothing.

Kip sat down next to me.

"Thank fuck that's over," he said, running his hand through his hair.

"It went well, there were lots of people; the food was good, and people seemed to enjoy themselves." I said.

"Enjoyed themselves, it was a fucking funeral!"

"Okay, it's a lame thing to say, but I don't know what you want to hear."

"It's okay, you don't need to say anything. The truth is I'm talked out."

"Where are you staying?" I asked.

"I've booked a room here at the hotel. I couldn't face going back to Rose's."

"You could come back to Helen's with me. She wouldn't mind."

He smiled. "I'd assumed the way you left Uganda that you'd had enough of me."

"No, if you must know, it was the opposite. I'd started to like being with you too much. It turned out that I wasn't as cool with having a no strings attached relationship as I thought I'd be. I needed to get away from you before I embarrassed myself by saying or doing something stupid like declaring my feelings."

"You're kidding me?"

"No," I said staring straight at him. "I wish I were."

His smile dropped, and he looked confused. He picked up my hand and laced his fingers through mine. We sat like that for a long time. The waiting staff began setting up the room for their next event.

Kip lay his head on my shoulder.

"We'll stay in touch, won't we?"

"Of course."

"And you'll come and see me on the slopes this winter?"

"If I get a job, then yes." I stood up. "Will you be, okay?"

He looked up at me, his dark eyes sad and serious.

"I had no idea how you felt. You should have told me."

"I was never going to do that. Besides, you had enough to deal with."

I bent down and kissed his cheek.

"I'll see you in France sometime." I said before leaving.

SEVENTY-THREE
SEMMY

By the end of June, Semmy had been living at home for four months. She finally started to feel settled. Her friendship with Mercy had returned to the same trust and intimacy they'd always known. Hope was happy in her new surroundings. Her great aunt Grace enjoyed caring for her. Albert had not had a drink for two weeks. He'd sit up with her by the fire each night talking. It wasn't the easy conversation she'd had with her mother. Yet, it was a start.

Albert had even begun to pick up little bits of work around the village. Small jobs, like helping neighbours at harvest time. It meant he had some money for food, and he even gave Semmy money for her savings.

Semmy had purchased a new monitor, thanks to the money that Kip had left with George. Her computer business wouldn't be able to start without the solar panels. Having attended six weeks of meetings, she was ready to ask for a loan.

She'd put together her business plan and costings with the help of Mrs. Wintonze. At the meeting that day, she was going to ask for the loan for the solar panels. She told her father as she packed her stuff up, ready to leave.

"I'm coming with you," Albert said.

Semmy didn't know what to say. Her father had never accompanied her to a meeting. He then did something even more out of character; he bent down and picked up Hope from the floor.

It was the smallest of things, but it meant so much to her. Semmy couldn't help but smile as they walked through the village. Albert carrying Hope for the first time, as if he'd finally accepted her as one of the family.

The savings and loan meeting were held on the outskirts of the village. When they arrived, there were already twenty people sitting under the shade of a large mango tree. It was already warm, and Semmy and Albert were grateful to get out of the sun.

A handful of people sat on white plastic garden chairs whilst most sat on the floor. At least 80% of the group were women. Most had their hair covered with scarfs. They fanned themselves with their savings books to keep cool.

Semmy was never sure why more women joined than men. Her assumption was that they were usually the ones who were responsible for running the home. It could also be that the women were more likely to trust a scheme like this.

Semmy was the youngest person there by a few years. They all smiled at her and seemed pleased that Albert had come with her for support. Mrs. Wintonze was sitting behind a wooden desk. The Chairperson was to her left, and the group secretary was to her right.

When everyone had arrived, the Chairperson, Mrs. Karungi, called the meeting to a start. She invited members to bring up their savings, which was how every meeting began. One by one, members said the amount they wished to save. They passed this to Mrs. Wintonze, the group treasurer. She would log the amount in her hardback exercise book. The savings were then put into a cash box. To keep the money safe, two different keys were kept at two different homes.

Next, the Chairperson announced that they'd take repayment of any loans with interest. Three outstanding loans needed to be repaid. This took a little time. One of the farmers, Irene Lutwama, had struggled to repay her loan. Armyworms infected her crops. There was a lengthy discussion about the best way to deal with this pest. Semmy enjoyed seeing her father so animated as he joined in the debate. The group resolved the issue. They agreed to extend her loan so she could buy an insecticide. Irene thanked the group and sat back down.

The last part of the meeting was for the approval of new loans. Semmy's neighbour, Samuel, a tall man in his early thirties, stood up. He wore a pressed white shirt, blue suit trousers, and leather flip-flops.

"I borrowed money to set up my bike repair business last year." He explained. "I used the loan to buy a tool kit and spare parts, which I paid back with interest. I would like to request a second loan. This will be to buy a bike. Several people in the village don't have the means or need for their own. They borrow from their neighbours, except it's difficult as this is not always convenient. I plan to buy a bike that I can rent out by the day. It will have a seat, so those who can't ride I will provide a bike taxi service for."

Samuel presented the numbers to the group. The money he'd saved, the amount he wished to borrow and what he'd make from his bike rental business. Mrs. Wintonze asked the group to vote on approving the loan. Every member raised their hand.

Semmy was next. She was nervous. If they didn't trust she could repay a loan, her hope of starting her computer business was over. She looked at her father and stood up.

"I've been saving with this group for eight weeks. I would like to borrow money to buy solar panels to run a computer at my home. I am going to start a computer business. School children will be able to use my computer for homework and they will pay what they can afford. Farmers can check the weather so they can plan when they are planting and harvesting their crops. My computer will also enable them to check the price of maize at the big markets. This will mean when traders come to buy maize from their small holdings, they'll know what a fair price is. It will stop farmers selling their maize for less than what it is worth. For those people that don't know how to use a computer. I will teach them."

Semmy told the group how much she planned to make from her business and how she'd repay the loan. Again, Mrs. Wintonze asked the group to vote, and everyone approved.

Walking away from the meeting, Semmy felt ten feet tall. She'd been grateful for the help from the charity, but it was nothing like the pride she'd had in securing money on her own.

SEVENTY-FOUR
ANNA

I'd hardly spoken to Kip since the funeral. He'd text a few times. Short messages inquiring how I was and updating me on news from Uganda. Semmy had begun her new computer business. Edna had been to see Margaret at her hotel, and there was still no sign of Richard.

I was still living with Helen and her family and hadn't yet got another job. Helen's administration assistant was on maternity leave, and so I was helping her most days.

June had been unusually hot. On the last Saturday of the month Helen and I decided to take the boys down to the local river for a wild swim. We'd packed a picnic, camping chairs, and an inflatable dinghy. I was wearing the thinnest summer dress I could find to stop me from melting. I'd forgotten my book. I ran inside to find it and had Helen screaming that we had to be quick, or we'd lose the best places on the riverbank.

It took me a few minutes to find my book and I knew Helen would be getting flustered. I finally emerged from the house and expected to see Helen glaring impatiently at me, but instead Kip was standing there. It was like he'd been teleported onto Helen's front lawn wearing his denim shorts, yellow t-shirt, and red ray bans. His scruffy black hair falling over his face.

"I need to speak to you." He said.

My mind was racing. What could be so urgent that he needed to show up unannounced at Helen's at 10 a.m. on a

Saturday morning.

"What is it?"

He removed his sunglasses and looked nervous. I'd seen Kip happy, excited, angry, and sad, but never nervous.

"I've got a problem."

"Okay."

"You see since I returned to France, I've been trying to get on with my old life. Mountain biking and climbing all day and working behind the bar and get pissed every night. My problem is this constant nagging feeling that something's wrong. I thought at first, it was everything that happened with Rose. The uncertainty about the day she died. The nagging regret I didn't do more to protect her from Richard."

I looked across to Helen who was now glaring impatiently at me from the car.

"Look, Kip, I really want to help you sort this out. It's just the boys have been excited about going to the river since 6 a.m. this morning. Would you mind if I come and see you later? I promise you'll have my full attention then, and I will gladly help you figure out why your life in the Alps sucks."

"I don't need you to help me figure it out Anna," Kip said, "That's not the problem."

"What is it then?"

"The reason I'm not happy in my old life is because I miss you."

I laughed. It was an instinctual reaction, to hide my embarrassment.

"I thought I knew where we stood with one another," he continued. "We were mates with benefits. Then at the funeral, you told me you liked me, and I didn't what to say"

"I seem to remember that you didn't say you liked me

too."

He looked at me with his big brown eyes. "I realise how crazy this sounds, but when you told me you had feelings for me, all I wanted to do was to go back to France and forget all about it. My problem is no matter how hard I try, I can't."

"Would it help if I told you that my feelings had changed?"

"And have they?"

I laughed, "annoyingly not."

He pulled me close to him and kissed me. Helen honked her horn, and I could hear my nephews laughing from their backseats.

"Does this mean I'm allowed to start liking you?" I asked and he kissed me again.

SEVENTY-FIVE
SEMMY

Two months later...

Semmy was sitting in her new computer hut with Mrs. Wintonze. It was a simple hut that Albert had built for her with mud, wattle, and sticks. He'd even built a desk for the computer and monitor to sit on and two stools.

Since starting her business, Mrs. Wintonze had been Semmy's most regular customer. Two or three times a week she'd pay to use the computer. Once Semmy had taught her how to search the web, she didn't need lessons. She'd just sit browsing for dress patterns or recipes whilst chatting to Semmy.

Semmy liked having Mrs. Wintonze to talk to. It reminded her of conversations she'd had with her mother. They'd talk about everything. Semmy had even told Mrs. Wintonze her hopes to return to school and to rekindle her friendship with Sydney.

It was her neighbour that had suggested Semmy take out a new loan for school fees. Her computer business was doing better than expected. She'd already paid off over half of her loan. Semmy said she'd think about it.

On this day, Mrs. Wintonze sat in the computer hut with Semmy. She was there to search the web for dress patterns. It was her daughter Masiko's 18th birthday. She'd insisted on a modern dress, not an African one. They were scrolling through hundreds of images. Semmy heard voices outside the hut. She recognized the familiar sound of George. He was speaking to her father. Then, she heard another male voice. Her stomach turned. Was she imagining it or was Sydney here? As she stood up to leave the hut, his face appeared in the doorway.

"I hear this is the place to come if I'm looking for computer lessons," Sydney said, smiling at her.

"What are you doing here?"

"My father brought me, is it okay that I came?"

Semmy looked behind Sydney, where she could see her father talking to George.

"Of course it is, it's so good to see you again." Semmy was aware that her smile was as big as her face, but she didn't care.

Mrs. Wintonze picked up her pad and pencil, in which she had been sketching dress ideas.

"I'll leave you to it." She said, smiling knowingly, as she left.

"You still haven't told me what you're doing here?" Semmy said.

"I wanted to know when you're coming back to school; my lunchtimes are not the same without you. My father told me about your new business. I thought if you could afford school fees that maybe you'd be back soon." Sydney was scratching his head and looked nervous.

"I was thinking about enrolling." She said. "I'll need to see if my father or Aunt Grace can take care of Hope. I will also need to juggle my studies with my new business, but I think I can make it work."

"That's great news. I knew you'd find a way to come back. Does this mean I can write you into a new play I'm working on?"

Semmy smiled and Syndey took two steps forward.

"Can I hug you?" He asked.

"Yes," she smiled as he wrapped his arms around her. It was, by far, the happiest moment of her entire life; she wanted to stay in his arms forever. Except her father had other ideas.

"Semmy, are you going to come out here and say hello to George?"

Semmy looked up at Sydney.

"Sorry, you know what my father's like."

Sydney bent down and kissed her. His lips lingering softly on her own.

"Do you think I could win him over in time?" Sydney asked.

Semmy laughed. "I think anything is possible now." She said.

SEVENTY-SIX
ANNA

Two months after Kip arrived on Helen's doorstep, we'd travelled back to Uganda together. We were staying at what was once Rose's Masindi house, but now belonged to Kip. It was a holiday and chance for us to catch up with Semmy and decide how best to spend the remaining money from WOMAID. Though it was modest a sum, it would be a fitting legacy for Rose.

We arrived at Entebbe airport, and it was a million times more relaxed than our last visit. Kip didn't get annoyed by young Americans hitting him with maps as we queued for our visas. The chaotic traffic made us laugh, and it all made more sense a second time around. I fell asleep again a few miles out of Kampala and didn't wake until we arrived in Masindi.

Edna greeted us when we arrived. She'd insisted on going to the house to get everything ready for us, like she'd done when Rose was visiting. It was like we were family. Edna fussed over Kip, and I could tell he secretly enjoyed it.

We sat out the back of the house, catching up on the local news. Edna had a new granddaughter, which kept her busy. Semmy's computer business was doing well. Margaret was enjoying the success of her new hotel.

For holiday activities we drove out to the stunning Murchinson falls. We went on safari, twice and even travelled down to Bwindi to trek with the gorillas.

George arranged for Kip and me to visit Semmy and

Hope. Albert was clearly nervous about our intentions. Kip reassured him that our visit was as friends. It was good to see Semmy so settled and happy in her life.

Kip told Semmy about the remaining charity money and his intention to spend it as a legacy to Rose.

"You must come and visit us often while you are living in Masindi. Only then can you see what we need and what will help."

Every visit was an education. We'd visit Semmy at her savings and loan group or meet families in the fields, seeing how they farmed their land. Groups of children from the village would run over to see us whenever we visited. Kip would pull funny faces and chase them to make them laugh.

One day we were leaving Semmy's homestead. An old woman, sitting outside her hut, mimicked eating. I shook my head. I'd assumed she was hungry and asking for food. It turned out she was offering to feed me.

"It's the African way to feed visitors; it's a sign that you are welcome," Semmy said.

I felt embarrassed. The more time I spent with Semmy, I realised the less I had understood about her life. It was during a visit to Semmy's that we'd first discussed the writing of this book. She agreed to tell me her side of the story about her time with the charity. We both wanted to show how WOMAID helped us and changed us.

Several weeks into our stay, we were sitting on the veranda of the Masindi house with Semmy and Hope. It was a warm day, and Edna had brought out plates of fresh fruit and glasses of cold lemonade. There was a knock at the front door. Edna was gone for several minutes, and when she appeared, Florence was by her side.

Semmy gasped with shock and threw her arms around her.

"I never thought I'd see you again." She cried with relief.

Florence looked transformed from the photos I'd see when she'd first arrived at the house. She was fuller in face and her eyes sparkled.

"I've missed you," Florence said, lifting Hope and hugging her tightly.

After the reunions and introductions, Florence talked about her life since she'd left. She was living in Kampala, where she was training to be a nurse at the main hospital. During the evenings, she worked in a bar to earn money and rented a house with three other girls from her course. She'd come back as she'd been desperate to see Semmy and Hope.

"Why did you leave?" Semmy asked.

"I had to; I was afraid of what Richard would do if I stayed."

"Why?"

Florence looked at Kip.

"I was standing in the doorway on the day Albert came. I saw him leaving, carrying Hope with Semmy by his side. Rose was shouting at Richard to put the gun down. He looked so angry I was sure he'd shoot.

Rose stood in front of Richard. Her body shielded Semmy and her family. I felt relieved, thinking he would give up, but instead he pulled the trigger. I screamed. Richard turned and I thought he'd kill me too. I ran out of the back gate and didn't stop running until I got to town. A man with a truck full of bananas was driving to Kampala. I asked him for a lift and was not able to return before now, I'm sorry."

"At least I know the truth," Kip said, "it doesn't make it easier, and I still want to kill him."

"Maybe he's already dead," Semmy said.

We looked at Semmy when she said this, and I couldn't help thinking there was something she hadn't told us. Six months on and Kip and I are still living in Masindi. We're using the rest of the charity money to help members of Mrs. Wintonze's savings and loan group. We're helping them to grow their businesses. The first person to take a loan was Semmy, so she could buy a second computer.

We accept that we don't have all the answers. What we provide is tiny against the magnitude of problems such as climate change, political corruption, and chronic hunger. Charity is difficult, but it's a force for good. It is a small beacon of hope and individuals like Richard are the exception.

As for my life now, I'm happier than I've ever been. I get to wake up every day with a man I love. I live in a country where the joy from the people I meet is infectious. I even have my sister Helen and my nephews coming to stay tomorrow; what more could I wish for!

THE END

Dedication
To Pod, Seb & Leo

Acknowledgements
To Nathan Stell for a wonderful cover design.

To Harry Harrold for my brilliant blurb.

To my early readers who read my novel and gave me incredibly useful feedback.

To my friends and family that have encouraged me to write and to take the step to self-publish.

To all the people that work for and support charities.

Thank you

Copyright © 2024 Sonja Lawrence
All rights reserved.
ISBN: 9798328240093

Printed in Great Britain
by Amazon